A 380 Degree View
A Real Estate Diva Mystery

Catharine Bramkamp

A 380 Degree View
First edition copyright 2011 Catharine Bramkamp

This is a work of fiction. Names, characters, some locations and incidents are products of the author's fevered imagination or are used fictiously and are not be construed as real. Any resemblances to actual events, local organization or person, living or dead, is entirely coincidental. It's not about you.

August 2011

Cover design by Stacey Meinzen

Acknowledgments

Thank you to photographer Deanne Fitzmaurice
who makes me look good.
Thank you to Stacey Meinzen for a killer book cover.
Richard Koelling, a sympathetic and helpful editor – the rest of
the mistakes are mine.
Andrew Hutchins who is unfailingly supportive
and to you, dear reader, for taking a chance on a new book.

Other Books by Catharine Bramkamp

Death Revokes the Offer (A Real Estate Diva Mystery)
Time is of the Essence (A Real Estate Diva Mystery)
In Good Faith (A Real Estate Diva Mystery)

Woman on the Verge of Wyoming
Being Miss Behaved
Don't Write Like You Talk: A Smart Girl's Guide to Practical Writing and Editing.
Ammonia Sunrise (Poetry Collection)
The Cheap Retreat Workbook

Anthologies
Chicken Soup for the Writer's Soul
Chicken Soup for the Woman's Soul
Vintage Voices Anthology 2008
Vintage Voices Anthology 2009
Vintage Voices Anthology 2011
Pen house Ink
California Women Poets

To Andrew

Chapter One

The only phrase slightly less obnoxious than *It's God will,* is *It was probably for the best.* Platitudes do not make a person feel better, then again, this person in question didn't know what else would.

Ben Stone, my boyfriend and owner of Rock Solid Service, a handyman sole proprietorship, stayed by my side at the hospital the whole time. Carrie, my best friend, held my hand and whispered that I could try again. Patrick, her fiancée, sent me an extravagant bouquet of roses.

A girl couldn't ask for more.

Or maybe a girl could. Perhaps a girl could ask for more sympathy from her favorite grandmother, Prue, who apparently was not as impressed by the whole experience as I was. She said a few nice things, but wasn't *really present*, in the parlance of our modern therapy-speak. Since she wouldn't call me, I manifested my own outcomes, and called her.

"I hear gunshots." I hoped she was watching TV, except my grandmother never watches TV.

"That's just the shooting range". My grandmother's voice wavered a bit. "You know how sound echoes up here. It sounds closer since the fire."

"That's not comforting." I pointed out. Could the guns be closer as well? No, that was ridiculous. The shooting range was only within walking distance if Prue cut through about a dozen privately owned back yards, but she would never cut through nor did she need to visit the gun club. No, she was safe.

"I don't really hear it honey. Inside the house it's not loud at all." She sighed.

"Grandma what's wrong?"

"Oh," she said airily, as if it was nothing at all. "I broke my foot. You know how inconvenient that is."

My stomach tightened and my own complaints died on my lips. "How did you break your foot?" When it came to my grandmother, Prue Singleton, there were too many options: she slipped in her greenhouse where she grew "medicinal" marijuana; she decided to repair the roof herself and slipped, falling two stories to the cement walkway below; she was shoveling her own sidewalk and twisted her ankle; she fell down two flights of stairs and had laid motionless for hours before one of her tenants wanted a martini and found her on the hardwood.

"Oh, it was silly, I just slipped. How are you feeling? All recovered?" She was actually interested in my answer, I could tell. Perhaps she hadn't expressed much sympathy at the time, because I'm unusual. All Sullivan women get pregnant early and completely, there are no half measures. This genetic propensities explains why I have an older brother and a relatively young mother (do not confront her with the math) and why my grandmother is "more youthful" than people think she should be. I'm thirty-six, well past any expectation by the family that I will ever reproduce and certainly past the "mistake" phase. But couldn't I get at least some sympathy?

I could, if anyone knew. Announcing my current challenge (we don't say the word *problem* in sales and marketing, we use words like challenge, opportunity and situation) wasn't really an option, or appropriate. Inez, my manager at New Century Realty, was not aware of my loss and thus was not cutting me any slack.

Inez had problems (challenges, opportunities, situations) of her own. The numbers for our office were not good, or even sustainable. It must be dire; I was forced to interrupt my Pirates of the Caribbean marathon to slouch down to the office for a special mandatory meeting with my manager.

"You're not working as hard as you should." Inez flicked her long red nails at me and then tapped on a stack of spreadsheets. I was one of her top producers, had been for a long time. I was not used to hearing that I was not working hard enough. My small hiatus in the last month or so was an exception, and as I stated before, I think I deserved it.

"Rosemary," Inez pushed back her heavily styled hair, "has three listings, and Katherine has four, not great, but at least they are out hustling." Inez patted her coif in place. She returned to the Excel spreadsheet on her desk. I shifted uncomfortably.

Rosemary and Katherine held the other two top producer monikers in our office; I'm usually a comfortable two or three escrows behind them. Was that now a problem?

"What have you been doing?" Inez pursed her lipsticked mouth and scanned the spreadsheet filled with escrows listed for this month. She didn't need to look; I could have just told her my name was conspicuously absent from the list.

"Looking for houses," For myself, not for clients. I didn't say that out loud.

"Yeah, like Goldilocks." Inez tugged at a heavy gold hoop and then took it off and tossed it into her IN box. "This one is too small, this one is too mid-century, this one is too much work. This one's in a flood zone."

"Not enough choices I suppose." It was a lame excuse, for a month I had looked for a house with one set of features: a study, a guest room for grandmothers, walk to restaurants. Then abruptly I was searching for good schools, an enclosed yard and a separate master bedroom suit.

Three weeks later I was back to looking for studies and views. It was a merry-go-round of emotions that made me sicker than I had felt during the whole month of January. Inez did not know all this; I did not hold her ignorance against her.

Instead she said, "You need to focus on your work. Mary at the head office is only focused on escrow's closed, not effort." She dragged out the word. "And I don't have to tell you, your name is not on this list," she rattled the spreadsheet. "We might have to stop carrying you."

"Carrying me? I'm one of your top sellers!" My confidence that my past history would do exactly that, carry me through the present, quickly eroded. "But I'm one of your stars! Carrying me?"

"And what are you doing right now?" her voice rose. "I'll tell you what you *should* be doing right now: contacting all your old clients for referrals, sending out direct mail pieces, renewing your directorship in the local MLS. You should be on the phone at least five hours a day."

She chanted it out like a mantra with magic properties: pick up the phone, sell a house, repeat. Dialing for dollars.

"I know." But I couldn't bear to pick up a phone. How exactly could I answer the question, "What have you been up to lately?"

"Allison, I just need to let you know. We can't afford to keep any agent who isn't contributing."

I must have looked pretty startled. Inez reached over her desk and grabbed my hand. Her manicure was freshly done, my nails looked ragged and pathetic in contrast. I couldn't pull my focus away from that trivial comparison.

"Please," her voice was low and pleading, as if the economy was in my control and I just chose to create the worst real estate market since the Great Depression. "You are one of my stars, but New Century National is on a rampage to cut out all un-producing agents, and they aren't looking that deeply into history. You need to do something."

I need to do something.

So when my grandmother, Prue Sullivan, told me about her injury, I wasn't in a particularly stable mood.

"Well, honey it's difficult right now." My grandmother unconsciously mimicked the very words I used in my conversation with Inez. It was hard to think I was only as good as my last escrow. Times were tough, it's just business, relationships don't matter.

"But how are you doing?" I asked. I grabbed the opportunity to distract myself from my own increasing spiral of doom, despair and misery.

I heard and could almost feel another heavy sigh over the phone.

"Oh, you know, friends drive me. The members of the Brotherhood leave food on the porch for me, I have to walk to get it, but," she countered quickly, "I have a walking cast and so it's not too hard, and the boys have been great. Pat and Mike are excellent but don't want to stay in the house. Brick and Raul are lovely but Brick is a disaster in the kitchen and I have to clean up the whole kitchen including the floor every time he warms up the soup that the ladies leave, and all Raul wants to do is film me and ask me questions about how I'm feeling." She paused giving me time to imagine some other issues she did not mention: help with bath, getting dressed in the morning, getting her coffee.

"I have a funeral tomorrow and no one can drive me, it's down in Auburn."

"You didn't mention one of your friends was sick."

"It was sudden," she said.

I heard another volley of gunshots in the background.

"I'll be right up."

I had to explain to Inez that I had an emergency and tried not to keep the relief out of my voice when I did.

"My grandmother needs me."

"Why doesn't she need your mother?"

It was a most reasonable question. My mother won't step foot in Claim Jump for her own personal and historical reasons. She also will most certainly not attract the kind of help and aid my poor, seventy-year-old grandmother requires.

Inez rattled the paper with our escrows.

"Don't take too much time, that doesn't look good either. I told you, Mary, the western vice president is calling every day for an update on our progress."

"As if a day makes a difference," I retorted.

Inez just looked at me.

"I'll be making calls while I'm up there," I promised.

"Good, at least get some listings down, that will work. And who's taking your floor?"

"I'll only be gone over the weekend," I was quite certain of my self-imposed time line.

My nascent plan was to drive up to Claim Jump that afternoon, comfort my grandmother, hire better help, chastise Raul and Brick for not doing a better job helping. They live on the property for heaven's sake, how hard can it be to help grandma? And yes, make a few phone calls and be back down in time for the Monday meeting.

"We'll be working on phone calls and role playing." Inez arched a thin eyebrow in my direction. "I think you all could use a refresher course. You know Rosemary claims she's never employed any of the techniques I mentioned."

"Well, maybe she's just good." I countered. Rosemary has a deep abiding faith in New Age solutions for every problem. Inez was right; it was highly probable that Rosemary never employed any suggestion made by either National or Inez. My guess is that Rosemary clutches her crystals, adjusts her magnets and watches a tidal wave of good energy engulf her problems and toss up a few new clients on the shore just when she needs the business.

"Maybe she's just lucky." Inez pointed to the paper. "See you Monday."

I nodded. But I wasn't as worried about Monday as I was about Prue. I didn't like the sound of guns; I didn't like the sound of her voice. I didn't like it at all.

What was going on up there?

Mine was not a clean escape. Just as I opened the door to the River's Bend New Century office, Rosemary and Katherine bustled out of their respective offices (at opposite ends of the building) and bore down on me like the Queen Mary and QEII.

"Listen," Rosemary huffed. Rosemary is a substantial woman who out weighed me by at least seventy-five pounds. She backed me up against the high counter in the front lobby. I did not try to get away, especially since Katherine was docked by the front door, her arms crossed, ready to steam into the fray should Rosemary require help. Patricia, our Goth inspired receptionist, just smirked and focused on her latest Internet search. She was no help at all.

"We all go through hard times," Rosemary lectured. "Look at the eighties, interest rates were up to 18 percent, you don't think that was difficult?"

"This is different." Neither Rosemary nor her doppelganger, Katherine, were aware of my most recent challenge, problem, opportunity. I did not want to indulge in full disclosure, nor did I wish to invite a chalk circle surrounding my hospital bed and crystals dangling from the ceiling coupled with five hours of motivational videos (and there would be a quiz to make sure I had watched each one). I had enough to cope with.

I focused on the argument at hand. Interest rates were one thing, cajoling banks and mortgage companies to accept Short Sales or offers on REOs was another thing entirely, and I said so.

"Ha! Just something else to negotiate," Rosemary snorted. "You have talent, stick it out, the market will pick up, it always does."

I didn't want to say I was tired of waiting for the market to pick up. I was tired of the stubborn banks, the idiot lending companies, the cranky buyers and tearful sellers. When did this business become more depressing than social work?

"You make your own life," Katherine intoned with all the solidity and confidence of a pagan priestess.

"We ride these markets out." Katherine stepped forward and stood shoulder to shoulder next to Rosemary. The one time they stood together in solidarity, it had to be against me. Great, my failure finally united them with a common platform.

"It will pick up, I promise, it always does," Katherine announced with complete confidence.

"People always need new houses," Rosemary agreed.

"They marry, they have children," Katherine continued. I felt I was watching a coordinated vaudeville act. Tweedle Dee and Tweedle Dum.

"And most important, they divorce," Rosemary pointed out with relish. "A lot of divorce."

"And die. REO and Short Sales, those are still available," Katherine offered. "You could be like the Christophers and just work with foreclosures."

"I like first-time home buyers," I ventured. I did not want to say that I really hated foreclosures. I did not want to specialize in pain and suffering. I already had dinner with my mother once a week that was enough pain for the month.

No, I take that back, they were not a vaudeville act; they were more like two thirds of Team Witch from Macbeth. For the first time in human memory, Katherine and Rosemary, who were always in competition for most escrows, best commissions and most listing, and sometimes in dire times, weight-loss competitions, were standing united again me, their sometimes protégé.

"There are lots of homes, what about that one on Shiloh?" Katherine switched tactics from the general to the specific. What they did know, what everyone knew, was that I was searching for a house Ben and I could purchase together. They also knew that nothing had satisfied me. Certainly not a single house had caught Ben's attention.

"I know that one, they're asking 2.4 million." I tried to forestall any more information. I wanted to leave right now, I was anxious to check on my grandmother, I was even more anxious to escape town.

"So you want something cheaper? Can't he afford it?"

"It's not what Ben can afford, it's what works for both of us," I pointed out patiently.

"Anything listed for 2.4 million will work," Rosemary said with confidence. "What are you waiting for?"

"CPS may have a pocket listing up on the avenues if you want to be more downtown." Katherine offered. "I think it's about a million, totally worth it."

"Okay, sure, ask, I'd love to see it. I'll call them Monday when I get back." They were right; money was not the problem.

"You're leaving?" They chorused together.

"You can't leave at a time like this. You can take one of my open houses this Sunday," Katherine generously offered.

But I didn't want to take anyone's open house, not even mine, even if I had one. I was tired of wasting a perfectly good Sunday afternoon trapped for four lonely hours in an empty house. I could practically hear Patricia roll her eyes behind me, but she cleverly did not get involved.

"I am scheduled to take floor on Monday. Just in case I don't make it back, can I call one of you?" I asked as sweetly as I could.

They both shrugged, again with the synchronized movements. It worried me. They were far too formidable as a united pair, better to divide and conquer, except I was not in the conquering mood.

"Great," I said brightly. "I'll be in touch."

Normally I'd explain about my grandmother's foot, how I was worried, how I took my inability to find the perfect house as an ominous sign, how I felt after the dressing down by Inez, but not today. Today I did not wish to discuss any of it.

"Thank you," I patted Rosemary's arm because she was the closest. "I'll be in touch."

"Better be," they chorused after me.

I arrived in good time that Thursday afternoon, I didn't feel like dealing with the commute traffic so I left right after my meeting with Inez (and Rosemary and Katherine). Inez made it sound like I was little better than this girl we hired last fall who was such an idiot she couldn't find her way to the office without a map. She was "carried" for three months before Inez booted her out. I closed two escrows in December, it was only March, and January is typically quite slow -- for everyone. What did they want from me?

I spent the three-hour drive to Claim Jump indulging in whiny, obnoxious thoughts, plus a milk shake at Carl's Junior, then a burrito at Jimmy's Tacos. I hadn't eaten much in January; I needed to make up for lost calories.

March in the Foothills was capricious; it often snowed, so I prepared. I carried chains in the back and cute boots in my suitcase. I was not sure if Prue was ready for anything. How was she managing the back stairs to the garage? Was she able to drive? Even if she was not able to drive, was she driving anyway? How many other times had she slipped and neglected to tell me?

We've all heard the stories of the sincere, yet befuddled, elderly driver who mistakes the gas pedal for the brake and pins a hapless pedestrian against a wall - mailbox - traffic cone. That would be Prue, and she hits the gas hard. It was only a matter of time and opportunity.

The back yard was dark when I arrived. I parked to the side of the drive behind the house and made my way to the kitchen door, tossing the remains of my cranky culinary indulgences into the garbage as I picked my way over the broken cement pavers.

The cement steps to the kitchen seemed narrower, the stair pitch more precarious than I remembered. I glanced at the greenhouse; a corner was just visible from the kitchen door. It glowed with the white grow lights. The greenhouse had *attractive nuisance* written all over it, I'm surprised there isn't a directional sign - trouble here. So my first guess was she tripped in the greenhouse.

"Have you been smoking your own product?" I greeted Prue as she opened the door to me. We are so careless with those we love the best.

"Things have been a little stressful around here," she widened her big blue eyes. Now, I'm not a mother (we went over that), but my friend Carrie pulls that kind of face when she wants something, and Carrie always gets what she wants.

Prue must have read my expression. I'm excellent at negotiations in business, but in my personal life, I just blurt out how I feel, or worse, my open expression completely and accurately reflects how I feel. Ben claims he can read me like a book, which is why some distance from Ben was important right now. I did not want him reading into my expressions, or making assumptions or suggestions. Oh, we're discussing my grandmother.

Prue pulled herself up to her full height, which used to be five foot six. "I can do what I want young lady."

"I'm not mom, it's okay," I reassured her.

"Right." She turned away and gave me room to negotiate my bags into the kitchen. She hobbled slowly to the kitchen table, a sturdy affair made by hand during my grandfather's craftsman furniture-making phase. He had mastered the techniques, created the table, then turned to other projects. This was his only piece of furniture. Probably for the best.

"Okay, you're right. Thank you for coming here so quickly. I need you to take me to the funeral tomorrow morning." I noticed she did not answer my question. I let it drop.

"Who died?" I suppressed the "this time." At Prue's age, attending a funeral was just as much as social event as Empire Club or the bi-weekly meeting of the Brotherhood of Cornish Men. Jolly occasions all.

"Elizabeth Stetton. You knew her; she's a member of the Brotherhood, a good one. She took over from the Sisleys as secretary. She kept really good notes through all this sale stuff."

"What sale stuff?"

"Oh, you know, the library is for sale." Prue moved some magazines aside, they were fashion magazines that she didn't read but saved for her friend Mary Beth who used them for collages for the children's hour at the new library. But if there was no more library, why were we saving five hundred pounds of magazines?

I would not bring that up right now. I noticed that not much had made it to the garage where I had set up bins for all her savables: Children's Festival, Brotherhood Christmas Bash, Empire Club, Fourth of July, parties, Children's Hour at the Library.

I calculated the geographic layers of junk. "How long have you been laid up?"

"A couple of weeks."

She was lying; there was more than a couple weeks worth of stuff-that-still-had-some-good-left-in-it lying in stacks up against the kitchen walls.

"Okay, a couple of weeks," I agreed, cooperating with the illusion. I leaned over and gathered up dozens of slippery periodicals and hefted the load into my arms.

"Those are for. . ." Prue took a breath ready to launch into a long dissertation on the library, the project, who was running the project and how they felt about it, how their children felt about it, how . . .

"The library," I stopped the flow of information hoping to get at least this stack to the barn before sun set. " I'll be back."

By the time I finished with clearing the kitchen. Prue had composed herself and created an adequate story for me concerning her current situation that was so innocuous and patently false that even my mother would believe it.

Friday morning I woke to the sound of gunshots. The sound was too distant to make me feel we were in immediate danger, but the staccato sound echoed around the street and through the house. I buried my head under the rumpled covers. Great, now my safe haven has the sound track from the Wild Wild West.

I pulled on my Chico State sweatshirt and sweat pants and padded barefoot downstairs, computer tucked under my arm.

The kitchen was a hive of activity. Raul, a small man who reminded me of Toulouse Lautrec, was hovering over the coffee maker. Prue was already up and dressed in one of her more eclectic black ensembles. I couldn't tell what was more disturbing, her huge black foot brace or her contrasting red rubber garden clog gracing her good foot. She had tossed a bright knitted scarf in yellow and red alternate stripes over the whole affair.

Often my grandmother is mistaken for a bag lady, and this would be one of those times. Need I mention that my mother, she of only-pressed-cashmere-twin–sets-are-appropriate –to-wear-to-the-club set finds my grandmother's lack of sartorial focus infuriating?

"You look, um, awake," I offered.

Raul jumped when the coffee maker beeped.

"All I Son!" He loved to draw out my name in his indistinguishable accent that he claims is Russian, but I'm not convinced.

"Allison, here is coffee for you too! Yes, so good to see you."

He gave me a big hug and nestled his face in my breasts.

"Ahh, you are so lovely." His voice was muffled.

"Thank you, you made the coffee." I disengaged him from my bosom and reached for the coffee mugs. "What else have you and Brick been doing to help Prue?"

Raul and Brick have been living, for free, in my grandmother's guesthouse since I was a teenager. I don't even remember exactly when they moved in and I'm sketchy about their reasons. I'm even less certain as to why they continue to stay-- probably because my grandmother's guest-house is a low cost housing solution for the two of them. Prue finds their company amusing and that's often enough for her to forego bringing up monthly payments.

Raul stepped back and put his hand to his heart, or the general area where his heart was likely to be.

"Allison. We have helped, have we not?" He glanced over at Prue, but she studied her cup and did not look up.

"I even installed a webcam in the bathroom so we could be sure Prue did not slip."

I dragged my hand over my face. I carefully set down the computer and opened the refrigerator for the milk. It was too old to use.

I took a deep draught of the black coffee and waited for the caffeine to take some effect. "Take it out,"

"But it is to help Prue!" Raul protested.

"Take it out now!" I wouldn't mind so much if it were Prue's best friends, Pat and Mike, but Raul? I am not sure on which side Raul stands, and I'm not good at detecting these things in the first place. But, just to be sure. I glared at him. He delivered a comical wiggle of his thick eyebrows. He is round and short but those realities did not stop him from being a tremendous flit.

"And you can take out the cam in my bathroom while you're at it."

"Oh, Allison I would never. . ."

I looked at him; he looked at me as guilelessly as possible and then caved. "I will take it down."

"Thank you." I took another sip of the mild coffee. I would need a Starbucks run before we headed down to a funeral.

Raul scrambled for the kitchen door.

"No," I grabbed his arm and easily hauled him back into the kitchen. "Now."

I did not shower and change until Raul removed the tiny cam from just above the shower head, all the while muttering about paid websites and the size of my breasts.

I don't blame him for making the attempt. But if someone makes money on my breasts, it better be me.

Chapter Two

I didn't realize it at the time, but this would be the first of a number of funerals I would attend in the weeks to come. I convinced myself through various methods of justification that I was only staying the weekend and only helping for this one funeral event. As as result, I was not attuned to dire portends of the future. Besides, in the grimmer (or realistic) portions of real estate training, funerals, wakes, memorial services, etc, are actually hotbeds of potential clients. I felt downright virtuous driving Prue down to Auburn for the nine o'clock funeral, I could claim that it was in the service of client solicitation, should Inez call and ask.

The members of the Brotherhood of Cornish Men a group that claims to be 150 years old with their clear ancedent in their title, filled the church basement. The ladies seemed to be the principal mourners as well. I recognized many of the members, most widowed, most active and most ready for any action that came their way, even though most of their activities seem to be limited to attending each other's funeral services.

Suzanne Chatterhill stalked over to us the minute I helped Prue clear the basement steps and the tricky threshhold.

"Allison, how nice to see you. Come up to take care of your grandmother?" Suzanne does not have an indoor voice, and her tone implied "it's about time", inspring many people turned to stare at us. I waved my hand to them in greeting and focused on Suzanne losing my grip on my grandmother in the process.

Mrs. Chatterhill is the president of the Brotherhood of Cornish Men and has been since her husband passed away. Suzanne was not especially big, but her bosom was. It overpowered every other body part and my eyes were reluctantly drawn to her chest and her single strand of swinging pearls. She carried herself with the aplomb of a prizefighter ready for his next round. I lumped Chatterhill in the same scary category as a local philanthropist in River's Bend, Martha Anderson. Both women were formidable and both women were intent on doing good no matter who gets hurt. Suzanne and Martha give me a creepy feeling that if I don't watch myself, I'll grow up to be just like them. I shuddered at the thought and greeted Suzanne as cordially as I could.

"Suzanne," Prue, the one I was so well taking care of, stumbled and clutched at my arm. "Did Louise have a stroke?"

I steadied her while keeping my eyes on Suzanne.

"No, they think she died of smoke inhalation. The fire took half the house with her in it." Suzanne shook her head; her tightly permed white curls bobbed with the effort, the pearls flapped back and forth. "I told her time and time again to stop smoking, and it happened just as I said."

"Then it really is tragic." Prue looked around the basement. "Is this a dry reception?" I took the cue and propped Prue against a bland beige wall and hustled off to retrieve, yes, non-alcohlic punch.

When I returned Prue and Suzanne were still discussing the situation. "I feel so badly about Elizabeth, where is her daughter?" Prue said.

Suzanne gestured to a woman who was about 46 years old. I consider that a very young age to lose your mother. Prue made a move and I grabbed her arm to help her negotiate through the three clusters of Brotherhood members.

"But you better catch her quick," Suzanne counseled as she followed in our wake. "She says she has to go back to work."

The comment caught me off guard. Work is good. Now a day's, work is everything.

I glanced at Suzanne, clearly puzzled. "Of course she has to work. What else is she suppose to do?"

"Investigate the accident, greet all her mother's friends. Honestly, she can't take one day off to devote to her mother's memory?" Suzanne put her hands on her ample hips and glared at me, daring me to defend working a mere job against this primitive set of social obligations that were written in stone and stored somewhere mysterious because I've never read the rules. Next she'll be instructing me on how long the poor woman will have to wear black.

Suzanne glanced back at Elizabeth's daughter, then abruptly dismissed the situation. "We're all going out," she said in a low voice, "to that new restaurant the Monkey Cat. You're welcome to bring Prue," she nodded to Prue. "Since she doesn't drive."

This was the kind of help that made a person feel more depressed than bolstered. It was the kind of intention that paved the road to hell. No wonder Prue called me in.

"I have to get back home and do some work of my own." I said quickly, before my grandmother had a chance to respond. "You know, we are a terrible generation, have no idea how to do the right thing, right?" I nodded to Elizabeth's wayward daughter, who, to her credit, looked exhausted. *Done-in* is a phrase my grandfather would have employed.

Suzanne reeled back at the word *work*. I smiled. "But I'll take good care of Prue. I'll be up here for a while." I lied.

"Of course."

I leaned over and touched Suzanne's arm. "I knew you'd understand."

I offered my arm to Grandma who got the hint and exaggerated her limp as we made our way over to the daughter to express out condolences, which, I believe, is the right thing to do, written in stone or not.

Prue sank into the leather seat of my car and I switched on the heat.

"Thank you for driving, I just didn't want any more of the Brotherhood today. Suzanne's been holding extra meetings to discuss the sale of the library and who will take the archives and all that, plus this accident with Elizabeth has put us all on edge, can you imagine dying in your bed?"

"I thought that was the goal." I couldn't resist.

"Peacefully Allison, peacefully in our own beds, not go up like a premature pyre."

"Okay, that is not a good way to go. It was an accident wasn't it?"

"It all just makes me tired. The pain medicine makes me tired." She gazed out the window at the green, waterlogged, view. "This whole thing is making me feel very old."

There is nothing to say when a seventy-year-old plays the age card. She wins. I shut up.

The phone buzzed. I glanced at Prue who was concentrating out the window and picked it up.

"Allison!"

It was Patrick, who never calls me except when he can't find his fiance and my best friend, Carrie. If she's not with him, she is usually with me.

"Is Carrie with you?" His voice sounded ragged.

"No, I'm up in Claim Jump. Carrie is with you."

"No, she's not. She's not picking up her phone, she not answering my voice mail, e-mail. She's not at her place, I just called there."

You may think this is a bit hysterical, even for the CEO of the largest milk production company in Sonoma County, but Carrie has a tendency to be in the wrong place at the wrong time. The last time Patrick and I couldn't get hold of her, she almost died. Patrick has some justification for panic.

"She may be in West County and out of cell range," I suggested.

He knows that, he contracts with dairies out in that part of the county.

"Oh."

"Look, it's early, as soon as I hear from her, I'll call."

He paused.

"And you call me," I added.

"Oh, yes, certainly I'll call you. Where could she be?"

"For once, I don't know."

I hung up the phone and passed a slow lumber truck.

"Carrie okay?" Prue asked.

"I'm pretty sure," I replied. "She's under some pressure from the engagement and the wedding of course, but it's everything she wanted in life."

I cleared the truck and scrolled down on my phone to find Carrie's number.

"Sometimes getting everything you want in life can be just as stressful as not getting everything you want," Prue commented.

"Did you read that on an embroidered pillow?" I asked. I hit call and listened to the ringing.

"Not everything I say is a platitude you know," she shot back. "Speaking of platitudes, you looked a little wane in the *Town and County* photos of Carrie's engagement party."

I was dumped into voice mail.

"You don't read *Town and Country*." I pointed out.

"Pat and Mike bring me their copy when they are finished. You looked a bit pale."

I left a quick message for Carrie to call because Patrick was annoying me and hung up.

"It was New Years," I countered, "my Christmas had not been that restful."

"Oh, you think?" She retorted.

While I keep a few things from my immediate family, I don't keep that much from my grandmother. She was conversant with the details of my last adventure that included a dismembered client, a turkey used as a blunt instrument and a face to face with a murderer. Not necessarily in that order. Christmas had been more difficult than usual and I wasn't sure I had recovered. I couldn't get over that I almost lost Carrie as well (between the dismemberment and the turkey), and clearly neither does her fiancé. He had convinced Carrie to quit her job at the Senior Center and now she was casting around for something meaningful to do with her time.

I knew how she felt.

But I worked hard to not burden her, she had the wedding to plan and issues of her own to scrupulously avoid. She didn't have the energy to help me avoid my own problems.

"And how is Ben?" Prue broke into my thoughts. She leaned her head against the window and closed her eyes, but she was listening. The gesture was worrisome. Had she always been this tired? I glanced at my dashboard; it was going on noon, hardly nap-time.

I sped up, anxious to get her home and more comfortable.

By the time I cleaned Prue's refrigerator, threw out the suspicious milk, flat soda water and liquefied lettuce and shopped for replacement milk, soda and tonic, ground two weeks of coffee and shoved in and extracted five loads of laundry, the afternoon was almost finished.

I felt good, despite the fact that I hadn't called a single old prospect; I hadn't even e-mailed old friends to shake them down for real estate prospects. I also had not indulged in doing anything for myself. I virtuously worked for my grandmother. It felt good and bad simultaneously. I knew I should be working, even if it was really just for show. Some of what is necessary for work, is just show, career theater. I knew Inez had not been kidding, I may be asked to leave and that did not bode well for my prospects at other offices in Sonoma County. I've never been out of work. But I just couldn't get motivated to do anything about it. So I did laundry.

I hefted up the last load of clean clothes to Prue's room and put away the thick sensible socks and heavy sensible cotton panties. I couldn't do this forever.

Damn, I was stuck.

I trailed down stairs where I had left Prue with her foot up and any stray marijuana out of reach. She could take Aleve and Advil like the rest of us.

"Thank you Allison, now we can go to the play." Prue announced as I rounded the door from the hallway.

"What play?" I knew it was a rather silly question. There was always a play or event in Claim Jump, not usually in the early, early spring. Or like today, at 40 degrees, what served for the dead of winter.

"Summer Theater is putting on the *Wizard of Oz* and we are all supporting Sarah Miller. We made her an honorary member of the Brotherhood, you know."

I nodded as if I knew Sarah Miller. I have found, over the years, it's easier to nod and simply allow the person in question to unfold before me like a well-written novel. I had little doubt that this Sarah Miller would be revealed to me in the course of the evening and it is easier to learn the players in order of appearance than to ask the question and thus submit to a full biography delivered in one breathless recitation.

"Good, I don't know how well Sarah is doing with the part. Summer seems to think she's just fine." Prue struggled with her walking cast cover. It was like watching a toddler. I helped her re-attach the Velcro straps.

Summer Johnson is the theater director and calls it, tongue in cheek, Summer Theater. The actors perform year round if they can. Since Summer is on the City Council and currently acting as mayor (the position rotates around council members; you are only mayor for one year), I supposed she could do what she pleased. Summer and I used to run into each other at the river. Summer dyes her hair, mine is naturally blond. We know this little detail about each other.

I closed my eyes. "So we're off to see the Wizard?"

"Don't look so disgusted," Prue chided me. "Besides, Brick, Raul, Pat and Mike are coming too."

All the boys. My grandmother is a card-carrying fag hag. I should find one (a card, she has enough gay men in her life) and laminate it for her, if she thought that would be funny. I think she would.

There really wasn't more discussion than that. I helped Prue clean up and change into fresh black slacks and a yellow tunic. She slipped on a yellow gardening clog that wasn't too disreputable, once I hosed it off outside.

At the appointed time (early, since parking is always a problem, according to Prue), we all bundled up in our warm (and unfashionable, it's difficult to dress simultaneously warmly and elegantly unless you wear fur and I was not going to do that with this group). After coats, gloves and scarves were found the theater-goers, now warm, piled into my Lexus SUV.

Brick and Raul attend all the performances of Summer Theater. Brick is a retired high school PE teacher and always seems to know at least half the cast. Raul is a wizard himself, of the web variety. He had rigged up a half dozen web cams in the theater with Summer's blessing. He runs the plays on his web site in real time. Wasn't Summer concerned about losing audience share to the web?

"Oh no, the theater is a live art form, we are just advertising the product. Do you not agree Allison?" Raul happily snuggled against Brick in the back of the car.

Mike and Pat greeted us at the theater door. They distributed the tickets and we turned and gave them up to the young man standing directly behind Mike. It seemed a redundant gesture, but maybe there were official theater rules.

"Allison darling," Mike and Pat kissed and hugged and kissed and hugged again. "Darling so what are you running away from now?" Mike asked.

"I'm not running away, Prue asked me to help her."

"Of course you are," Pat said.

"I understand you had a bad Christmas." Both men, forever friends of my grandmother, gazed at me in honest sympathy. Even if Prue had not told them everything, and I know she does, my Christmas activities were gruesome enough to be quite a sensation on the Internet. Patricia, the receptionist for New Century, had created a blog devoted to describing the serial murders, how the victims were cut into pieces, and my involvement with the whole situation. I refused her offer to link to my real estate website.

The men nodded. It was not my favorite subject, since I narrowly missed making the news myself as one of the victims. I was all done, no more murder for Allison.

"Allison and Ben are moving in together," Prue announced.

"Ah, that fabulous Ben Stone." Raul crooned. "He looks so lovely on camera, don't you think?"

"Yes," I frowned. Where had Raul seen Ben on camera? Was there a cam in my bedroom? Were there cameras placed around the guest apartment over the garage? Were there cameras in the guest bathroom? Shit, I'd have to do a sweep when I returned to Prue's.

The old theater in Claim Jump is marvelous. It was not the oldest theater in the state, it was the second oldest, but it did have the requisite leaky roof and bad plumbing to give the whole place historic credibility.

Summer was in the lobby to greet her audience.

Summer looked more like winter had blown in. Her solid blue-black hair was strident, cut into a perfect symmetrical bob. She favored dark eyeliner extended a half-inch from the corners of her gray eyes. She wore high-heeled boots, which helped make her taller than me. A fake fox stole was carefully "tossed" over her navy suit and gave her a contradictory air, garden club Goth. She could be the elder twin of Patricia, our Goth office manager. I always felt that after a certain age, a look as extreme as Goth was rather unsustainable. Apparently not. In Claim Jump, it does not matter what decade you choose to honor, no one cares, few actually acknowledge that fashion changes from one decade to the next.

"Dorothy better make it to Oz before 9:00 PM." Mike greeted Summer with an air kiss in the general direction of both her cheeks. She didn't look particularly happy but she put up with all four men. Donors, all of them.

"Don't worry, you know we always take the needs of our audience into consideration when we stage the plays." Summer worked with the neighboring restaurants. If she released her audience by 9:00, they agreed to take dinner orders until 9:30. Her voice was smooth and modulated, practiced. Summer had trod the boards in an earlier life. She looked like she could make a convincing Wicked Witch, but clearly, she was not playing that part tonight.

"Hello Summer, how are the permits going?" Prue took Summer's hand, but the other woman didn't really acknowledge Prue.

"Fine," she said absently, she focused on the front doors, eyeing the audience members, clearly disappointed with what she saw or didn't see.

"Looking for someone more important?" Prue asked caustically.

"Lucky was supposed to come tonight." Summer answered without rancor. "You know he told me he created a CRT with the theater as the recipient. Which is just wonderful!" she trailed off. "I just wanted to confirm . . . excuse me."

She left us standing in the center of the lobby, not feeling as important as when we entered.

"I suppose to get more attention I'll have to increase my donation level." Mike complained.

"I thought you were a symphony man," Prue pointed out. Need I say it? In the summer there is county-wide music festival.

"Symphony, theater, ballet so many arts, so little funding." Mike said with a wave of his hand. "I suppose to get attention now, I'll have to name the theater in my will like Lucky apparently did. Come on, I understand the beleaguered Sarah Miller is starring as Dorothy."

"She was terrible in *Music Man*," Prue commented.

Then why are we here? I did not say that out loud, but followed the crowd like a good girl.

"Where else can Summer find a bona fined ingénue in this town who isn't in school full time? And doesn't look," he paused searching for the word. "Shopworn?"

"True, and Sarah has been a trooper for years." Mike held Prue's arm as we filed into our designated seats.

"And an ingénue for longer than that."

"Any day now she'll have to take the part of the mother." Prue settled down on the aisle seat and gingerly extended her leg.

"Or the wicked witch," Raul wiggled his eye brows. "Excuse, I must check the cameras."

I love the Claim Jump Theater. When I was a kid, Prue signed me up for summer drama classes. I loved those classes, I loved showing off and I loved escaping my older brothers and parents. In my eyes, nostalgia and affection trumps any realistic depiction of the small theater house. The seats are very old; the original red velvet has worn to a threadbare pink. The house only seats about two hundred audience members, which contributes to Summer's claim that her performances sell out every night.

But a theater does not make the rent on ticket sales. There was a good reason Summer was searching for Lucky Masters.

I glanced up as a woman dressed in a costume straight from the summer of love galumphed down the aisle barely missing Prue's casted foot.

"That's Debbie Smith," Mike whispered.

"Local?" I asked.

Pat shook his head. "She's only been here a few years."

"Debbie needs to update her look," Mike, to my left, mused.

"I lost to her," Prue commented.

"Her? I thought you lost to a high powered attorney from the city."

Prue and Mike nodded simultaneously.

If Debbie Smith was a high-powered attorney, I was a runway model. Ms Smith was not built for speed, she was low to the ground, full figured and possibly quite buoyant in water. She was dressed in a long oversized blazer that was fashionable in the late '80s but not beyond. Under the blazer she sported a bright orange and yellow tie-dyed tee. The fashion magazines would say that the shirt "popped", as in a pop of color. But this pop was more of the illegal BB gun pop than a moment of true fashion savvy.

"She wants to do everything by the book." Prue complained.

"Has anyone in Claim Jump found the book?" I was accustomed to Claim Jump residents doing what they wanted, when they wanted, with small regard to permits, EPA, even water restrictions, and so were most of the older residents. I was surprised anyone cared about doing it by the book at this late date.

"She actually wants to prosecute Lucky for violating about 30 years of EPA restrictions. She even wants Hank to fix his sidewalk."

"Hank's sidewalk has always been like that," I commented. Hank's Roadhouse was a fixture on Main Street, as was the rather large bump in the sidewalk right in front of his entrance. Tourists hit the bump and it magically sends them careening through the doors of the roadhouse. At night, patrons staggered and hit the bump on the way out. If they fell down, the police chief Tom Marten was justified in asking for a sobriety test. Denizens of Hank's learned to be light on their feet.

"Even so, we all know to step over the hump, but she sees lawsuit everywhere she looks."

A hammer thinks every problem is a nail. Wow, I can come up with my own pillow worthy clichés. Prue must be rubbing off on me.

"So what's the solution?"

"The problem was almost solved when she first moved here, her rental house caught fire." Pat leaned over Mike to whisper, more or less, in my ear.

"What is it with you guys and fire?"

Prue shrugged. "Old houses, old wiring, we all know fire is a danger."

And don't smoke in bed. I kept that option to myself.

It probably was a pretty prevalent problem. For too many years remodels were executed without the help of any professionals whatsoever. Homeowners armed with their Time-Life series of do-it-yourself books, did the job themselves. No one bothered with codes and permits. Locals considered the lack of surety part of the price paid for independence. No one complained, but new homes not up to code could be a different matter entirely. It's one thing to hang the drywall in your own house; it's another to unintentionally buy substandard housing. How ironic for a lawyer from the City to be caught up in the problem.

I watched the apparently odious Debbie Smith pause and exchange a couple words with Summer who, for her part, was still looking for someone else. Debbie shook her head and Summer clutched her arm momentarily, and then quickly released it.

Could the exchange between Debbie and Summer be more than business? The councilwoman and the mayor? There were too many possibilities. Maybe it was as simple as love. Would they hyphenate and be Summer-Debbie? I suspected there was far more drama out in the lobby than would appear on the stage all evening.

My evil thoughts were interrupted by the recorded overture.

There is no need to describe the play, the plot or anything else. Sarah Miller was pretty, engaging and a terrible vocalist. I cringed when she reached vainly for the high notes in *Somewhere Over the Rainbow*.

The munchkins were played by local children who either enjoyed too little rehearsal time, or never listened to direction in the first place (I played a child in *Music Man*, so I know). The munchkins milled around on stage, looking like a crowd with no one to lynch. It worked fine, cute can still carry a scene. Dorothy was game and focused, but it seemed Sarah was losing her edge. She looked weary, as if she had already spent too much time on a farm in Kansas.

I snuck a peek at my phone in case Carrie had called back. No messages unless you count the four from the office. I ignored those.

As soon as the curtain fell on the first act, a young man, (young by Claim Jump standards) stood and applauded. The rest of the audience murmured and cautiously scooted to the lobby. *Goodbye Yellow Brick Road* played softly in the background as we all regrouped for a short intermission.

"That's him," Prue whispered.

"What's him?"

"That's the boy who just put in a bid to buy the Library."

"He can't do that," I said automatically. "It's state owned."

"No, no, the old library."

"My library!"

Prue rolled her eyes. "Yes, your library. Anyway there he is."

"Very cute," Raul observed. "Should we call on him?" He glanced at Brick who studiously looked through the advertising in the program; he showed great interest in a picture of lawn furniture.

"You could," Prue encouraged. "So far he only has met the members of the Brotherhood of Cornish Men."

"Mores the pity, that's a formidable group, I'm surprised they didn't frighten the poor boy away."

"They tried, no luck. They, I mean we, are not happy with having to put the building on sale, if that's what you mean. Lucky put in the competing bid, the state can't support it anymore."

I did not ask how my grandmother knew who put in a sealed bid for a former state-owned property. She herself was a member of the Brotherhood of Cornish Men, and they knew everything there was to know in Claim Jump.

The young man in question was attractive in a rakish, irresponsible way. He gave the impression he never really held a job. I automatically compared him to Mr. Ben Stone (Rock Solid Service), no comparison.

I did know Sarah Miller after all. Just as I thought, once I saw her, I remembered more about her. Sarah is a player in the long narrative that is Claim Jump. Sarah was born here and never left. Her mother left both Claim Jump and baby Sarah and moved to the Ridge in a haze of pot smoke and acromony. The grandparents, being most excellent Christians, took in the baby even while they disowned their own daughter.

Prue shook her head. " I don't know what will happen to her when her grandparents die. She has no job, fewer prospects."

That's Prue, always looking on the bright side.

Summer was back. She clutched a plastic glass of Charles Shaw red and stalked around the lobby. She periodically dashed out to the sidewalk, checked, then returned with a dejected expression on her face.

The theater lobby is small and hot. Winter or summer, the audience spills out the entrance doors to the sidewalk. Some patrons wander all the way down the sidewalk to the Mine Shaft bar and never return. One year, during a particularly painful interpretation of *Fiddler on the Roof*, a majority, enough to be noticeable, never returned for the second act. Summer actually walked down to the bar and rounded up a good dozen members of her audience and forced marched them back to the theater. We all knew then how the residents of Anatevka must have felt.

I usually don't dress to attend any event or program in Claim Jump; it's just not necessary. No one wears makeup around here, not even the women who own retail businesses and should know better. No one worries about the latest fashion because up until about five minutes ago, there weren't any stores that carried interesting, fashionable clothing. The stores now have upgraded their merchandise, but the women in town still ignore every opportunity to look better, fashionable and uncomfortable. Even I admit that comfort can be rather compelling. Debbie on the other hand, had elevated comfort to an extreme sport.

She slid up next to be and started to talk, no introduction, no hello, no "how are you" or "how do you like the play?"

"The theater needs to be retrofitted," she announced into my ear.

"Retrofitted?" I glanced around. Sure, one little 4.6 tremor and this place would crumble down to a pile of rubble. If we were cataloging the dangers of Summer Theater, it was also a fire trap, the chairs were so full of dust I sneezed for days after just one evening here, and there was a real risk of helplessly witnessing a truly painful performance of a Broadway show that used to be a favorite but now was forever ruined. And who knew if the water heater was secured? But that was part of the performance art: the disrepair of it, the bold embrace of the mediocre. It all served to enhance the veneer of old time charm.

"Yes," Debbie continued as if I had agreed with her. "We have a real problem in this town, so few of the buildings are up to code. I blame the past councils for letting things slide and I even thought we should sue some of business owners for not repairing and upgrading when they sold their buildings, but I couldn't find the minutes from the seventies."

"Oh," I said. I suspected the minutes went up in a forest fire - long story - but I wasn't going to share history with Debbie.

"Weren't they in the old library?" I asked instead, because that's where I once searched for the old council minutes, before I learned the meeting mintes of the seventies had been taken by a private citizen to "keep them safe." The private citizen had lived miles above my grandmother's place on the upper reaches of Red Dog Road in one of Lucky Masters' homes. And there had been that fire.

Debbie nodded. "They were moved to City Hall when the library was decommissioned. Easier to keep them safe."

I had no comment to make about the relative safety of paperwork and possible guilty parties. In the rather immediate past I had discovered that so much of what went on in Claim Jump was not recorded, at least not officially. Prue had access to a number of documents, but those were kept safe to keep her safe.

She may have some paperwork that revealed lax permitting, bribes, incidents of council members looking the other way so that developers could have their way with the forests surrounding the town. But she didn't flaunt it. We just kept it around for Prue's own benefit. But it had nothing to do with what Debbie searched for. What Debbie wanted had actually, legitimately, gone up in smoke.

"Are you enjoying your time on the council?" I asked brightly.

"Enjoying?" She barked. "I don't have time to enjoy, do you know how much has been left to chance in this town? Do you know how little regard these owners have for codes and regulations?"

It was odd to hear a woman draped in tie-dyed splendor speak of codes and regulations. I watched Mike elaborately sneak up behind Debbie making terrible faces and mock snarling. He and Pat, who owned a number of the buildings downtown, were probably the bane of her existence, codewise, and she theirs.

"Debbie, how lovely to see you and you are so, colorful tonight!" Mike swooped around her and issued a bear hug that took her breath away.

"Oh, uh, yes."

"Enjoying the play?" Mike twinkled at her.

"I was hoping to catch Lucky Masters. He needs to file his EPA before he starts building again and I heard he was starting to hire workers before all his paper work was cleared."

"No!" Mike placed his hand on his heart. "I am shocked, not file the right papers?"

Debbie apparently had little to no sense of humor, which is too bad. Mike is rather amusing if a person is relaxed enough to appreciate it.

"Yes," Debbie replied with a straight face. "And I wanted to stop him with an injunction." She patted her leather-tooled purse, hand made, straight from 1975. She wore it slung from one shoulder to the opposite hip. The strap cut across her chest, effectively isolating each breast so they looked like islands floating in a riot of orange swirls. Don't ever do that. Even if you are all about comfort, don't ever do that.

"You were going to serve papers during an amateur theater production?" I asked. I had to ask.

"Did you find him?" Debbie caught Summer on one of her return trips from the sidewalk. Summer shook her head.

"How is Penny Masters?" I asked Summer.

"Oh," The theater director finally focused on me. "Penny is marvelous. We're organizing a house tour for April first and that's taking up a lot of our time. Will you be in town?"

"Probably not," I reassured her.

"You should come back up for it, Penny is displaying her quilts at the house as well, that's one of them." She pointed to a large colorful quilt hanging behind the snack table in the lobby. Its bright colors just served to make the red carpet look more faded in contrast.

"She made that?"

"Yes, we're raffling that one off to raise money to upgrade the heating system. She's very generous, just like her father."

"Is it up to code?" I couldn't resist asking.

Summer gave me a puzzled look. Debbie harrumphed and stalked away, probably to cover the exits so Lucky couldn't sneak out the back doors. It would not be good evening for Lucky should either woman find him, which is probably why he was not anywhere in evidence.

I wandered over, bought some of the bad wine and knocked it back before intermission was over.

By the time we all reorganized into our seats and admired the placement of Raul's cameras, which were very hard to see, so I took it on faith and just nodded, I noticed that our young man - that's what Mike and Pat had dubbed him, our young man - had moved up to a front row seat.

Chapter Three

I wasn't really tired. The play didn't take up too much mental bandwidth and the fettuccini Alfredo at Cirinos after the play was a nice pick-me-up. But Prue looked exhausted, so we said good-bye to all the boys and I helped her get to bed.

I wandered around downstairs. The air had a suspicious nip in it and I wanted to make sure all the doors were firmly closed against the rain that could turn to snow overnight. I glanced at my computer, partially buried under the *Claim Jump Union*. I picked up the front page of the local paper. " Library under bid, two possible buyers. Bids due today at 5:00 PM."

I read further with interest. *Historic library under siege, Lucky Masters, local developer, is rumored to be purchasing the state historic site. He plans to tear down the historic building to build a live/work complex.*

"While we think that live/ work is the way of the future," commented mayor Summer Johnson, *"we don't think that sacrificing such a fabulous building is the answer."*

Ms. Johnson is also the director of the Summer Theater in the old theater building and admits, for the record, that much of her funding comes from Mr. Masters' company, Lucky in Love, and that she acknowledges conflict of interest. She had recused herself from both the planning commission vote as well as the final approval set to be put forward to the city council at the April meeting.

The odds were good Lucky will win the bid, which will give Prue as well as the Brotherhood an excellent reason to get not only terribly worked up about the fate of the library, but also terribly righteous about it. Summer was one of the few people disposed to think fondly of Lucky Masters. Maybe Penny, his daughter, loved him as well.

A lound pounding at from the front of the house startled me. I dropped the paper and hurried to the door before a second bang woke Prue.

I jerked it open without bothering to peek through the narrow side windows or even trill "who is it?" Stading on the porch looking much like one of her own rescue kittens just saved from drowning was the elusive, not answering her messages, Carrie Eliot. Her long, dark hair clung to her neck and shoulders in dripping strands. She hadn't bothered to belt her raincoat and the front of her sweater and jeans were soaked. You can get surprisingly wet just making the trek from the street to the front of the house.

"They came to my house," she breathed, without even a hello.

But of course she didn't need a hello. I'm her best friend and as such it is my job to be able to dispense with the formal greetings and go straight to what I knew was the heart of the matter.

She took a ragged breath and stepped onto the mat just inside the door. She shook off her raincoat and handed it to me, I took it gingerly and hung it over the newel post. It instantly created a pool on the floor.

She wrung out her hair. "God, it rains hard up here. And it's cold, you didn't say it was cold up here!" She looked at me accusingly as if I controlled the weather. I would love to control the weather; I'd make so much more money.

"Yes it does, when it rains in Sonoma County, it pours in Claim Jump." I stood and waited for her to start.

She didn't, so I started. "I assume when you say they showed up at your door, you are not talking about zombies."

"I wish."

"If not zombies, then your parents," I guessed.

"They came bearing the newspaper article on our engagement."

"Ah."

"And they want money."

"And offered forgiveness in exchange?" I said, although I knew perfectly well her parents thought nothing of what they inflicted upon their only daughter. In their world, girls were expendable and boys were valuable since boys worked for the family. Maybe Carrie's parents were zombies; they were certainly abusive and decidedly odd. The Eliots made my mother look like a saint. They even made Ben's mother look like a saint and that is saying something.

"And you said," I prompted my wet friend.

"I told them to go to hell. And then I drove straight up here."

"Welcome," I gingerly hugged her sopping wet body. "Don't slip on the puddle."

Carrie's parents are alcoholics and drug addicts. Her sister married an abusive alcoholic just to keep the family tradition going. Carrie's brother, the promising one, the one on whom all family attention was lavished, is currently a guest at Folsom prison. Twice a year, her parents shake themselves from their stupor and either contact Carrie for money, booze or bail. She has as little to do with them as possible. The really big question is, will her parents redeem themselves in the final hour, clean up, dress in long sleeves to cover the track marks and the tattoos, and engender a loving family reunion just in time for Carrie's fairy tale wedding?

Probably not, not even clean and sober families have that kind of capacity.

Before she could take another step into the sanctuary that is my grandmother's home, her phone buzzed. She answered without thinking.

"Oh, no mother," Carrie drawled the words. It was as close to sarcasm as my friend would venture.

I gestured to the kitchen, just in case she wanted to be alone.

She shook her head violently and gestured for me to stay.

"I'm out of town, so getting together won't work for this weekend. No I haven't picked my dress."

I gestured to the far eastern corner of the parlor. She followed me obediently.

"Your dress?"

I mouthed, "we're walking, we're walking." She followed and suddenly said, "Mom, you're cutting out, I can't hear, Oh, damn."

By then she had squeezed up against the far wall, getting as far out of range as she could.

"That damn was pretty sincere," I complimented her.

"I hope so, thank you, that was pretty smart." She flipped her phone, and frowned.

"Five messages from Patrick."

"You haven't called him back?"

She rubbed her eyes. I took her hand and led her to the warmer kitchen.

"How can I talk to him Allison? How can I explain these people to Patrick?"

"The truth?" I ventured. I know, for a saleswoman, the truth is not necessarily the best first line of defense, but I was becoming fonder of the truth over other methods of mendacity. Sometimes it's just easier, and as a bonus you don't have to remember what you said.

"He would never understand!" Carrie declared. She collapsed at the kitchen table and weakly accepted a glass of white wine.

"I love this table," she murmured running a hand over the scarred wood. "Patrick has everything in the world including not a single problem in his family, everyone is wonderful. How can I admit I have drug abusers as parents?"

I was reminded of something Ben said over Christmas. If everyone has a relative who is an alcoholic, then when do we stop saying it runs in the family and just admit it runs in the human race?

I repeated that to Carrie.

"Yeah, but Richard keeps it under control."

"My brother controls his drinking to the best of our knowledge," I said. "But no one knows for sure, maybe his wife, but I wouldn't bet on it." Debbie, my sister-in-law is blessed with the ability to only see what she wants to see. That includes my brother's drinking problem.

"I wouldn't bet on it." Prue emerged from the dark hall wrapped in a worn terry robe, limping on her casted foot.

"Hello, Carrie. Welcome, I thought I heard your voice."

Carried leapt up and threw her arms around Prue. "Thank you, I knew I could come here."

"Always," Prue said. "Stay as long as you want."

Carrie was more in tune to my grandmother than I was. She didn't linger but insisted she was tired so Prue could go back to bed. We all trooped up the stairs, Carrie leading the way, me bringing up the rear. If Prue fell backwards, she could land on me. I'm soft.

Carrie instinctively headed to the third floor rooms. I stayed in my usual room on the second floor, Prue's room was close by.

"Are you sure?" Carrie moved to her favorite bedroom with confidence born of many visits.

"Of course, if I can escape, so can you."

"I'm not escaping."

I thrust an armload of sheets and towels into her arms. "And neither am I."

Scott Lewis woke early, well before noon. The early hour did nothing for him; there was little to do in his hotel room and he was too anxious to watch TV or listen to music or surf the net or any number of activities that in the past, could consume the better part of an afternoon.

It was different here, in this little town. He had made the biggest single bid in his life, the largest, most adult gesture he had ever made in the course of his whole existence, and today he would learn if he won. If "won" is the right word to describe the priveledge to spend a large boatload of money on something he wasn't entirely sure he wanted. He dressed and decided to walk through the cold misty morning to the library. He already had a key, the president of the Brotherhood of Cornish Men offered it -- a key to something he did not even own yet. Apparently it was a normal gesture in Claim Jump.

"Don't take any records." Scott recalled her name was Suzanne. To him, she had no distinguishing features, she was round, full breasted, wore bifocal glasses and stomped around the main floor of the library in sensible, squeak free shoes.

The rubber soles of Scott's own Nike running shoes made a terrible squeaking sound as he crept around the worn linoleum flooring. Maybe he'd replace all the flooring with hardwood. He could so that as soon as he owned the place and as soon as he figured out a plan.

He didn't really have a plan locked down.

Scott hustled up the main street. Few shops were open yet. He felt virtuous by being up and out before even regular people. The library's gray granite facade loomed up out of the mist. Scott climbed the four wide steps and was about to insert the key into the deadbolt when her heard a voice behind him.

"Have you seen Lucky Masters?" It was the woman who couldn't stand still during intermission last night - bouncing in and out of the lobby.

"Who is Lucky Masters?" Scott asked.

"Only the most influential man in town. He put in the other bid for this place. Didn't you know?"

Scott shrugged. "I didn't, the bids were sealed; the decision was made yesterday." He pulled out his phone, frowned and slipped it back in his pocket.

"Nice phone."

"Oh, yeah, a gift from my Dad's boss."

"And you're sure you haven't seen Lucky?" She eyed Scott suspiciously as if he personally had something to do with this Masters' disappearance.

"I really don't know. What does he look like?"

The mayor put her hands on her hips and chewed her bottom lip. "I haven't heard from him in over 24 hours. Suzanne said she called and called but there was no answer at Lucky's home or his office. Debbie has calls into him as well, but of course he's not going to return her calls."

Scott slipped the key in the new deadbolt lock.

"Doesn't he have people?" Scott's father had people. For years those people were the closest Scott could get to his father.

"His daughter, Penny, used to work for him, but she's busy with the Home Tour and hasn't been over to the office for over a month, I don't think they're speaking right now," she trailed off and continued to chew at her lip. Each time she caught her lip, the dark red lipstick stuck to her teeth and the naturally light color of her mouth seeped through.

"What do you plan to do with the place?" she finally asked. Not an idle question. The editor of the paper had called yesterday and asked the same question.

"I don't quite know yet," Scott admitted. The front door finally gave. A burst of cold air, colder than the outdoor temperature, smacked him in the face. Okay, not very cozy. But maybe he could find some place that was. He gazed up at the building facade and made his decision. It was the second most adult decision he had made in his life.

"Do you know someone who could help me find a house?"

Her face brightened either from a desire to perform honest help or from calculation, he wasn't sure. He didn't read people very well, not like his father could.

"I do. Allison Little is up visiting her grandmother. I just saw her last night. You saw her too. She was sitting with a bunch of guys. She can help you."

He had to admit he hadn't really focused on anyone else but the girl playing Dorothy.

"But if she's visiting."

"Allison is like a local, and she'll know where to place you. Here." Summer pulled out her phone and found the number. He entered the number into his phone.

"How soon does this Allison start her day?" he asked. The prefix was from the Bay Area.

"Santa Claus," Summer turned away to head back down to Main Street.

"What?"

"Lucky Masters looks like Santa Claus."

Sarah Miller was restless. She felt that her Friday night performance wasn't her best. Those high notes were killing her. She knew she'd hear about it Monday, either in line at Safeway, or at the Brotherhood meeting, or from a casual comment dropped by Melissa who worked full time for Hospice and called every day to see if she could help now.

Hospice could not help. Her grandparents were just fine.

Sarah was determined to do better tonight.

Chapter Four

Where was Ben Stone? He had performed well over the last month, he held my hand, whispered he loved me, reiterated that we needed to find a house to move in together. He sent flowers, and then more flowers. He was doing as much as he could because I was the one who kept him at arm's length. I'm the one who is not coping.

"You're still grieving," Carrie observed Saturday morning.

"Am not. It's no big deal, right? Happens all the time, right?"

Prue finished her first cup of coffee. "I lost one early, but got pregnant the next month, with your uncle." Prue had a bad night, I heard her rise more than once and knock around her bedroom as though she wanted to make as much noise as she could. So we all knew she had been up and uncomfortable, thank you for sharing.

Carrie, on the other hand, looked rested and pretty.

She patted Prue's hand and poured her another cup of coffee.

Prue took a sip and set the mug carefully on the bare table. "Sorry, that's not a solution for you, is it?"

"Can you be totally numb?" I ventured. I sipped my coffee - good, I could feel the heat, taste the coffee. I wasn't quite dead and numb to the world.

"Did you call Patrick?" I asked Carrie.

"Did you call Ben?" Carrie asked me.

Touché. "Okay, I'll go first." I slowly dragged my phone towards me and lifted it as if it weighed nineteen pounds.

He answered immediately. My heart fluttered and my stomach dropped. Which indicates that I still cared very much for this man. The thrill was there, obvious and happy. I'm using all the wrong words. Perhaps I've never really been in love? I don't seem to access the vocabulary that women who are in love seem to find so easily and declare so loudly. So I went for the simple.

"I was thinking of you," I said.

"Ran away to your grandmother's again didn't you?" he guessed immediately.

"Maybe."

I looked around the kitchen. Prue was up again. She and Carrie stood together at the far counter and loaded the automatic drip machine. Brick was outside wielding a broom against the wet leaves on the path between the garage and the house. It was about time. Raul wasn't working at all; he was filming the kitchen scene for his blog and You Tube postings.

"Prue needs me." I did not say she needed help in general. Her imagined helpers would take offense and I still needed that walkway cleared off. I kept it personal.

"I understand."

"If you're not doing anything," I paused. "Come up and join us."

"Really? You're ready for that?"

"Oh sure, why not?" I kept my voice light and breezy. *It happens all the time; it was a blessing.*

"I'll take that in spirit rather than tone. Okay, I will come up and you'll have to talk to me and explain why one of the best Realtors in the county can't find us a decent house to share."

I had that coming. "I've been distracted," I offered as my only defense.

"I know," his tone softened. "I haven't forgotten. I'll be up by afternoon."

"Drive safe."

My phone beeped. "Gotta go." I hung up before he could say goodbye, but he knew what I meant.

" Is Ben coming up?"

"Yes."

"Good, I have a leak in the upstairs bath," Prue said with some satisfaction.

I readily agreed to meet Mr. Scott Lewis at the library, my favorite building in Claim Jump. Any excuse, and now, with the possibility of Lucky getting his hands on it, it became that much more precious.

The library wasn't tall or imposing, not like the Methodist church that dominated Main Street and possessed all the charm and character that made it the most photographed building in town. The library sits a block uphill from the church, at the crest of the Main Street hill, which aids its imposing features, since it's edifice is not as high as the church steeple.

I think the library building lends the town a bit of gravitas. The miners and owners in this town were surprisingly literate, establishing reading rooms long before the actual library was built in 1907. I appreciated how the library carried the weight of secular intellectualism to counter the soaring wood steeple of the church. The old theater was down one more block from the church. So we have it all: art, religion and science on a single street. Science and intellect teeters at the top of the hill, which always pleased me.

"So you're Allison Little." Scott Lewis was a slight man, handsome in an immature way, his features not really formed, which seemed odd for someone in his thirties. Then again, maybe he hadn't had much life thrust upon him. I made my way up the familiar steps of the library. I felt a bit of nostalgic twinge with each step. What would Lucky do? Would he really tear down the place in favor of condos?

"Hello." I took his hand; his grip was strong. Good, not a wimpy man. If I'm lucky, a buyer who knows what he wants. Wait until Inez hears about this, I'll be the golden girl again in no time.

"If you get the bid here, will you turn it into a bed and breakfast?" I asked casually. He could name each small room after a famous author, or local author, it's been done before, but tourists love it.

"Turn myself into an innkeeper? No I don't have the personality or the patience. We once stayed in a bed and breakfast, here as a matter of fact, but dad couldn't stand it, he said he didn't want to make friends at 9:00 in the morning, and we moved over to the Northern Queen."

"Where are you staying now?"

"The Northern Queen, of course."

"Is your dad with you?"

A raw, pained expression clouded his features. I backed off and changed the subject.

"If you don't know if you'll get bid, why a house?"

He sighed, taking in the brightly colored quilts hanging over half-filled shelves, the special section reserved for Cornish genealogy. Tall wood columns carved in the Corinthian style still held up the ceiling. I glanced up at the same time he did.

"You're a local? You can help me?" he asked instead.

"I'm enough of a local," I straightened my shoulders.

"Your grandmother is a member of the Brotherhood of Cornish Men, isn't she?"

"Yes she is." I didn't comment on what I thought about the members of the purported brotherhood. The ladies, it turned out, were too embroiled in the sale of the building, meeting, protesting among themselves, composing letters to the editor, meeting again, to pay much attention to my grandmother's needs. I was not impressed at all.

"That's good enough for me."

I nodded. "What are you interested in?"

Scott and I agreed to meet in a few hours to view houses. I was impressed with his focus and drive. It was refreshing. I had a number of things to do before taking Scott out to view homes this afternoon. The first was to check in at Prue's. I walked into Carrie describing her complex wedding arrangements; Prue was a new and rapt audience.

"We have an A list, a B list, a C list and a D list."

"Who's on the D list?" Prue dutifully asked.

"Everyone else."

Carrie rubbed her eyes. For a woman whose dream just came true, she was ill at ease. Her gigantic diamond engagement ring sparkled even in the dim March sunlight.

"Who is on the A list?" Prue asked. She patted the table to indicate I should sit down.

"Three hundred people," Carrie's voice was close to despair as if she was creating the guest list for a memorial service instead of a wedding.

"You only invited one hundred guests to the engagement party," I pointed out. I know; I was there. I didn't sit, I moved over to the coffee to see if there was any left.

I wondered if that put me in the A Plus list, but she didn't look like she'd appreciate a joke or light tone. Who knew getting married was so damn serious?

"That's as many as the French Laundry could hold," she pointed out.

"Ah, of course."

"Did your family make the A list?" I asked tentatively.

"They would be on the D list if I had my way." She rubbed her face vigorously; I held my breath, waiting for layers of make-up to be inevitably smeared off. But not even a dramatic gesture such as that would mar her lovely, natural, skin.

"Or the F list," she finished.

Carrie has been my best friend for many years, she proved her worth when she stepped in during one of my own complete disasters. She barely knew me, but knew enough to whisk me off to my grandmother's to save me from suicide, or at least a long string of ill advised choices. I couldn't get in as much trouble in Claim Jump as I could in Marin and she knew it. At maybe 100 pounds, Carrie is stronger than she looks. I just hoped her fiancé appreciated it.

He probably did.

"Patrick says he wants to meet my family," she finally blurted out.

"Before you're married?" I poured out the last of the coffee and moved to the opposite end of the table.

"The wedding is in September, he wants to meet them like, this spring, or something," she trailed off.

"It's already spring, it's March, I think that counts as spring," I flipped open my laptop. As Carrie continued to speak to both Prue and me, I began searching around for listings. I had already called Inez to arrange to pick up a lock box key from the New Century office here, on Main Street. Inez was mildly pleased I had a new client. I had hoped for more enthusiasm.

Carrie had two months left of spring to produce parents. Patrick was often quite precise.

"And the C list?" Prue prompted.

"Those are just the media and hangers on, all the worker at the plant." Cooper Milk, an odd fore-shortened name for the original idea of a milk co-op, continued to play to the audience in this case, the community. The marriage of their current CEO, and third generation Sullivan to run the place, would be shared. Thus the outdoor wedding, the winery location, the volume of guests.

"Wait, you're getting married during Crush?" I lifted my head like a prairie dog.

"Right before, we want to get married in the fall, it's so beautiful. We just don't know where yet, you'd think Patrick would be able to easily secure some place beautiful like Gloria Ferrer or that Castle D'ambrosia something in Napa."

"Please don't marry in Napa." I begged.

She grinned. "Got you."

I smiled back but concentrated on the shared MLS system. It was quirky, but usable. I found five houses in the 700 range and printed them from Prue's color printer.

Carrie regarded my grandmother. "I could use you. You could be my grandmother; I can walk myself down the aisle. We could explain that the rest of my family perished in a fiery car accident, the bodies burned beyond recognition, something like that."

"Happens all the time, it was really for the best," I muttered.

"Didn't you already admit you had family?" Prue's tone effectively categorized Carrie's family in the same classification as, say herpes. She wasn't that far off.

"Yes, he does know I have a family, but the accident could be recent - today." Her expression brightened. "They could have a terrible accident today and the bodies burned beyond recognition. A closed casket service, of course, no, just the memorial service, I could say they requested closed casket in their will!"

She was quite cheered by the scenario.

This may sound harsh; we all love our parents, especially if they live in another state. Carrie grew up on the other side of the tracks of Rivers Bend. If the Ridge existed in Sonoma County, that's where her parents would live, that's where all refugees from responsibility and legal drugs hide. Carrie only let her background slip once. From what I can guess, both from allusions and late night conversations including one when she let it rip that if I thought my situation was stressful, try abuse, try a mother who turned her back. She begged me never to mention that slip up again, and I haven't. Carrie left home too young, but she looked at it as escape and survival. Friends do not insist that you relive the worst parts of your life.

That's part of our own pirate code.

I picked up the supra key from the New Century Office on my way to the Library to pick up Scott.

The New Century office in Claim Jump was located on Main Street and had a perfect view of Hank's Roadhouse. Three desks were illuminated by the watery afternoon sunlight but not one was occupied. A woman perched at the front desk as if her presence there was temporary. She greeted me as I entered.

"Hi, you must be Allison, your office just called, your manager was pretty enthusiastic."

"I'm sure she was. Thank you for loaning me a key." I rummaged around my purse for my wallet and ID.

This local New Century agent was tall, taller than me, and was dressed in formal Claim Jump business attire: jeans and matching jean jacket with New Century embroidered over the left pocket.

"No problem, we've lost enough agents so we had a few keys just floating around." She pulled out a manual key, a chunky piece of equipment the size of an ancient cell phone and handed it to me. The four-digit code allowing me to enter any house in Nevada County was written in ink on masking tape and stuck to the back.

"Do you need a deposit? Want me to sign anything?" I flipped open my wallet to my ID and dug out my DRE card. I glanced around for a form to fill out; I was prepared to write a check for the privilege of the loan.

"Oh no, just return it before you go back to the Bay Area. I know your grandmother."

"Well, thanks!"

I dropped the key into my purse and headed up to the parking lot to meet Scott. My phone (much smaller than the key) buzzed.

"I'm running late. Dinner?"

"Works for me, Carrie's here."

"Did she call Patrick?" Ben asked.

I paused by my car. Scott saw me and headed down from the library doors, locking it behind him.

"I still haven't heard about the sale outcome," Scott complained as he approached my car. Are people around here always slow to get back to you?"

"Why, did Patrick call you?" I asked Ben.

"We'll talk, can you tell Patrick she's here?"

"I'm with a client, can you call, tell him she's fine. I don't want him freaking out." It started to rain again; I unlocked the passenger door for Scott and hurried around to my side.

"Sure, how are you doing?" Ben asked conversationally. It sounded on the surface as conversation, but there was far more loaded into that sentence.

"I told you, I'm with a client." I wrestled with the door and hopped in.

"I'll call him." He understood my sitation immediately. "See you tonight."

"What if your bid is accepted for the library? Didn't that require an all cash offer?"

"Yes, that's why they agreed to let me make a bid," Scott confirmed.

"And you have more?" I meant money; cash would be lovely, even in a foreclosure, cash can move the process along quite quickly. I love cash, but I hardly ever work with it.

"Yes." He shook himself like a large goofy Labrador and rained inside the car, leaving me feeling damp and a bit cranky. " I do have more. Do you think I could turn it into a bar?"

"No."

"What do you know about Sarah Miller?" He quickly changed the subject.

"She doesn't sing very well," One of the few verifiable facts I knew about Sarah.

"No kidding. Uh, don't tell her I said that out loud."

"Your secret is safe." I drove to the first house, only a few blocks from the library.

I did know something about Sarah, all courtesy of Prue, who heard it through Suzanne Chatterhill, who heard it through various members of the Brotherhood. Sarah Miller was like a ward of the town, many of the women from the Brotherhood doted on Sarah and found it shocking that her grandparents were so narrow minded and inflicted their world view on the girl. Never mind that many in Claim Jump were perfectly aligned with the far right of the world. Narrow minded was categorized differently depending on the situation and the person doing the categorization.

Mind you, no one actually came out and blamed Sarah's mother for hiding out at the Ridge, either. Anyone who knew the Millers knew they were on the right side of rigid and judgmental. Sarah did graduate from the local public high school but never made it to classes at Sierra College, the local community college. Girls, according to Sarah's grandparents, were not worth educating.

"Now there's a girl who has every right to run amok with an ax and hack her grandparents into tiny pieces," Prue said last night at dinner.

"Please, grandma."

"Sorry," she forked up her chicken, "but you know it happens."

"Just not in Claim Jump," Mike said. "Nothing ever happens in Claim Jump."

To Scott I said, "Sarah was born here, when her mother left her as a baby, her grandparents raised her. And now Sarah is returning the favor." I skipped all the really interesting details of her story. Let the girl tell him herself, that way they would have something to discuss on their first date.

"She must be pretty innocent," he mused.

"I haven't met a single millennial who is," I countered, thinking of my nieces and nephews. They are too wired to the whole world. I consider myself part of the cranky X generation. The only thing I can't complain about is that my mother never worked. I would have loved being a latchkey kid, think of the privacy, think of the freedom, think of all the books I could have read!

But this is not about me.

I dismissed the Sarah question. Did I wonder why Scott asked? I did not. I know how slim the pickings are in Claim Jump; I've had my own moments. Now I import Ben.

Where did Scott want to live? He did not know. Did he want to walk to the old part of town (the cute part, rather than the practical part across the freeway that in turn spawned a couple of large midcentury developments, which were fine for what they were, considering Lucky built them in the fifties, but you can live anywhere and have a tract home. This was Claim Jump, go for Victorian, I prayed Scott wanted character, it would make our time together much more interesting.)

"I thought I'd go for character."

"That's what I like to hear."

I will not bore you, but what I loved, Scott didn't and what he loved, I saw problems, because that's my job. But by the fifth house - he had impressive home viewing stamina - we converged on an adorable house just around the corner from the elementary school. He could walk to work and get winter exercise by shoveling his car out of the driveway because there was no garage. He liked it.

"What do you think?" he asked politely.

I liked all five of the houses we investigated, and all for selfish reasons. I liked the large ones because I could use the extra bedrooms for home office space. I liked the house that backed into the creek for a low maintenance water feature. I liked the huge new house on Gold Mountain. So much for complete professionalism. If only I could take two of the houses I liked in Nevada County and situate them between Geyserville and River's Bend; I'd have the perfect home. It seemed a fantasy house was the only kind Ben and I could share.

"I like this one." I agreed. "Get an estimate of the work once escrow closes. I know the local contractors."

"Do I do that now?"

"No," I counseled.

I called the listing agent to see what kind of offer we could make. I know Scott was willing to pay asking price, but I also know you never really have to.

"Hi, this is Allison Little from New Century Realty,." I began.

"Are you there with Scott Lewis?" the agent, or receptionist responded; he was probably an agent on floor. My, this is a small town.

"Yes," I confirmed, a bit tentatively.

"He just won the bid for the library. Ask him what he's going to do with it."

"I'll get back to you."

"You just got the library," I announced to my client.

He clapped his hands. "Good, Great! Now what do I do?"

"Wonder how the hell you managed to beat Lucky Masters at his own game," I responded.

Chapter Five

Sarah's mother may have viewed her parents as simultaneously evil and indestructible, but Sarah knew better.

"I sort of thought," she addressed her grandparents, "that you'd be around forever, you know?"

Her grandfather grunted; her grandmother snored.

"I'm going to call Hospice," she informed them. "The Hospice ladies are very nice. They promised to send Melissa; she is good with this kind of thing. She will help get you out of the chairs, and other stuff, because I can't."

It had been so messy, these last three days. She couldn't leave them alone; they weren't moving from their chairs or moving much even in their chairs. It was torture to leave them just for the few hours she performed. The bathroom was a very big issue and the cans of Ensure she set out on their TV trays went untouched.

"You'll be fine, on your feet in no time." She left the TV on for company and wiped the drool from her grandfather's lips.

"Tell them Lucky knew all the time," he mumbled.

"I'll tell them Grandpa." She didn't really listen to the old man, not anymore, maybe not ever. He was harshly opinionated when she was little. He told her what to do, told her to follow Jesus and that Jesus was always right, as if Jesus could choose winning stocks. But Sarah could never figure out if Jesus was heading in a direction Sarah was interested in taking. She learned, over the years, to just say yes and ignore her grandparent's grim, narrow view of the world.

Tell them Lucky knew. Her grandfather worshiped Lucky Masters. The best job grandfather ever had was with Lucky Masters. Lucky Masters knew how to raise a house in no time. Lucky Masters, blah, blah, blah. Sarah knew who Mr. Masters was of course. She saw him in the theater. But who would *them* be? Didn't Lucky Masters know everyone?

Sarah climbed the narrow stairs to her own little apartment. She wanted to change clothes before she walked down to the theater to become Dorothy, who got to leave her house behind and head for a more magical place filled with possibilities and adventure.

She pulled down jeans and her comfortable boots from a sparsely filled closet. She could hear the TV, but it wasn't too loud, and she could definitely hear if one of them moved or tried to move: the chairs creaked loudly; the thump of their heavy landing would reverberate throughout the walls of the old house.

The old place really needed insulation. Her grandpa could have used some leftover insulation from a job he did for Lucky back in the '80s but he hadn't, and never explained why. They had been good grandparents in their own way. They did let her go to high school and if she said nothing, she could take part in as many after school activities as she liked, as long as it didn't inconvenience them.

They used to be busy people: Bible study, church, more Bible study, Brotherhood meetings, and at night, the news. All the terrors of the world brought to you directly to your living room, in livid color.

Maybe she could get a computer when they passed, maybe there would be some money. Her mother would need some of course. But Sarah would not count her chickens before they hatched, she knew better than that.

Her thoughts wandered to that cute guy at the theater, the one who sat in front.

I dropped off Scott at the front of the library, his library now. I was on the verge of escape, but a woman hailed me. I was conditioned to be polite and waited for her to catch up to the car. The rain had abated but the air was still cold. I hoped the chilly air would encourage a quick conversation.

"I heard you were in town," she panted. "Nice car, four wheel drive?"

"Of course." I squinted, working hard to remember her. Had we met during one of my many summers here? If she were one of the many people I met at the river, odds were good I would never recognize her with her clothes on.

"I'm sorry," I gave up. It was too cold to play guessing games. "Do I know you?"

"No you don't. I'm Mattie Timmons, Danny's ex-wife. You dated him this summer." Mattie looked like she used to belong to the Future Farmers of America and had never changed her look after sophomore year. Her hair was scorched by years of perms and stood out from her head in kinked blond strands. Her thick stomach strained against her tight low riding Lee jeans. I couldn't see, but I guessed she wore cowboy boots.

"I didn't date him," I corrected. "We connected again and had few drinks."

"You know what happened to Danny? Lucky thinks I don't know, but I do."

I nodded; Danny had shared his suspicions about how Lucky cut corners on his buildings, which included pumping cheap, and flammable insulation into the walls of every house he constructed. But Danny decided to prove his theory by immolating himself in a conflagration of his own creation. Don't drink and start fires. He started the fire to prove how flammable the homes were, and of course all the evidence burned along with the homes. Apparently Danny hadn't really thought that part through.

I did not share my insight with Danny's divorced widow.

Mattie dropped her voice, although there wasn't a soul on the street, not in this weather. "Lucky was pumping bad insulation into those homes, but Danny couldn't really prove it, he had no backup information or expert witness, that kind of thing."

"That makes it kind of awkward, don't you think?' Taking on Lucky Masters was not for the faint of heart, or for the unprepared. Lucky was very powerful, well hated and must have dozens of attorneys on retainer. In the I Hate Lucky Masters Club, Mattie Timmons would have to take a number.

"I can prove it," Mattie insisted. "I have Danny's old notes back when he worked on those first houses. He used to tell me how the guys on the crew used to squirt some insulation onto a bunch of wood and light a fire, it worked better than gas."

Lovely.

"And I told Lucky. He owes me, he owes the kids." She folded her arms across her puffy ski parka and glared at me as if I was defending Lucky's actions.

I knew I should have been more impressed, by both her revelations and her take-charge attitude, but I get tired of people like Mattie who possess a huge vainglorious sense of themselves. They threaten to hire lawyers when their coffee is too hot. They call the police if a dog shits in their yard. They want to look at million-dollar homes because a deal with their cousin is about to go through and they will make enough to pay cash, tomorrow.

I drop these potential "clients" as quickly as I can at the first sign of litigious propensities; they are not worth it, and I certainly didn't intend to volunteer to hang around such a person.

"Lucky can have the notes, if he's willing to pay for them." Mattie declared.

"Why are you telling me this?" it finally occurred to me to ask.

"Danny trusted you, and he didn't trust many people. If this thing with Lucky doesn't go through, I wanted someone else to know."

Now she was just being dramatic. Lucky cut corners, sure, but the man wasn't dangerous.

"I was jealous of you, you know," she switched to a more conversational tone, just girl talk, out here in front of the library. In the cold. "He talked about you all the time when we was first married."

Oh great.

"That was a long time ago," I pointed out hopefully.

"Yeah, he liked women, especially pretty women." She acknowledged me in that category which was nice, not accurate, but nice.

"Danny was a sweet man," I offered. Danny and I had been an items a very, very long time ago, and recently we had intereacted as just friends, my term, not his, he wanted to be much more than friends.

"Not too bright though," Mattie sighed. "He couldn't keep a steady job and with the children I needed someone more stable. It was only after our divorce that he found work with Lucky."

"And do you have someone more stable?" Please say yes, I thought, a steady boyfriend would do wonders for her.

She looked me in the eye. "Have you tried dating in this town?"

"Yes, once, and it didn't end well," I admitted.

"Welcome to my world. The last guy I dated ended up in jail for beating his wife. No, it's just me and the kids."

I hate the phrase *you owe me*. I wanted to tell her to get an education and get a better job and care for your own children yourself. It's the Republican in me that rears up during encounters like this.

"You probably should leave this alone." It was the best I could offer in lieu of delivering the lecture in my head. "Lucky doesn't lose, ever."

She pouted, but her expression told me she already knew as much. I was not going to help her; there was nothing either of us could do against Lucky.

I thought it would be the end of it. I said good-bye with, I hoped, some finality and drove back to Prue's. I had faith in my abilities to talk people out of things, out of painting the house orange, out of installing Italian marble in a $250,000 tract house, out of buying in a flood zone, out of taking on Lucky Masters. I was good. I was all that.

I swaggered as I stepped out of the Lexus and marched to the kitchen door.

Chapter Six

Summer and Mattie were not the only people gunning and/or searching for the infamous Lucky Masters. Tom Marten bounced up to the front door seconds after I let myself into the kitchen.

I answered. Since my job is to be the door answerer for the disabled and eventually infirm, I thought I might as well practice.

Tom Marten is the chief of police for Claim Jump and commands a staff of four. As a result he does most of his own stunts. As a second result, he has retained his tall, dark and handsome looks. He still worked out, his broad chest filled out his modest uniform quite nicely. I knew a lot about that chest as well as other things. Tom and I go back in much the same way poor Danny and I had gone back. But un-like Danny, Tom could be considered a temptation. But he has a family and I have Ben, so we only nod when we see each other on the street and don't say anything more.

But here he was. "Hi Allison, here to take care of your grandmother?"

"Yes I am."

"When did you come in to town?"

"Thursday night."

He nodded. He didn't take any notes, but I knew him, he had an excellent memory, which was good and bad news for me. I probably should keep he and Ben apart. If that was possible.

"Why do you ask?"

He pulled his light jacket around him against the cold.

"Sorry, come in. We're all in the kitchen, I don't want Prue to move more than she needs to."

He nodded. "That's right, she broke her foot. Tripped in the greenhouse."

"Er, yes." He probably knew about the greenhouse, but since it was county property and not city property, it was not his concern.

He strode down the hall. "Hey, Prue."

"Well hello Tommy, here for a social visit? How is your mother, is she back from that cruise?"

He shook his head. Another hazard of small town life is the ever-circulating information system. Everyone knows everything there is to know about everybody. My grandmother thinks Facebook is superfluous.

"No, business. Summer filed a missing persons report on Lucky Masters," he gestured helplessly. "I'm here to ask if you've seen him in the last 48 hours."

"Why would I have seen Lucky Masters?" Prue inquired mildly.

"I don't know, but you threatened him at the council meeting last week. So it was strongly suggested that I pay you a visit."

"Oh, for God's sake Tom, that was about re-building up the road and the EPA and land rights! It wasn't a fight."

"You were pretty mad, there were a lot of witnesses," he frowned.

"I should hope so," Prue declared hotly. "There should be as many witnesses as possible to hear that Lucky Masters is a thief and intent on destroying this community. He needs to have another EPA report, that's the law. His claim that since he didn't need an EPA report when he first built and so doesn't need one now is bullshit and you know it."

"Not destroying," Tom argued. "He donates a lot to Claim Jump."

"At any rate," Prue studiously brushed invisible crumbs from the table. "I would be happy if I never see Lucky again."

Did I mention my grandmother can be rather improvident? One does not make threats when one is under investigation.

"Is Prue under investigation?" I blurted out, in my own improvident way. Must run in the family.

"There's no crime. Summer is just freaked out. Lucky was suppose to show up at the theater last night, and he missed a meeting this morning."

"He lost the bid for the library," I said.

Tom gave me a sharp look. "That's right, that was the news that pushed Summer over the edge. Lucky has never missed a bid, courthouse steps auction, or any opportunity to acquire more Claim Jump property. She's right, it's worth checking out."

"What about Penny, his daughter?"

"She's not picking up. We left messages all day. We may have to send a car out to her place and check up on her."

"Meaning you?"

He nodded. "And get back in time for tonight's performance."

"Your daughter is a Munchkin," Prue nodded.

"I know the Ding Dong the Witch is Dead song backwards and forwards." He rubbed his head as if the memory brought about a headache.

"What about you Allison? Kids?" He turned to me with his a very reasonable question.

I blinked, then composed myself more quickly than I would have even been able to do just last week. "No, no I don't think kids are for me."

He nodded. "Lots of work." He stood and regarded me for about a second too long. "Thanks you two, if you hear anything about Lucky, give me a call?"

We nodded and I escorted Tom out the kitchen door.

His real estate agent dropped him off at the library - his library, his real estate agent. He felt even more adult now that he had people. The lights from inside the building illuminated the wet sidewalk in the dim afternoon, welcoming him, warning him.

"Can we look again tomorrow?" he leaned through the window of his real estate agent's car.

"Certainly."

"Not too early, I'm going to the play tonight."

She smiled. She had enormous hair and, other things. "Of course you are."

He glanced up at the building, squared his shoulders and walked up to meet the current, past and President Elect of the Brotherhood of Cornish Men.

"Congratulations." Suzanne Chatterhill fingered her long necklace and immediately graded him as unworthy of his new position.

"Thank you." He gazed around the main room, seeing it in a completely different light. What does a person do with a decommissioned library? He hadn't really given it much thought aside from tossing out random phrases, because it hadn't really been a reality, just an idea, a whim. Now it was his. His and Dad's.

Suzanne cleared her throat. He glanced over at her. If he thought the final sale of the library would magically alter their relationship. If he thought he would suddenly be transformed into the man in charge, the man to whom Mrs. Chatterhill would have to ask, or plead to use the library for her work, he was greviously mistaken. He'd have to drop a house on her.

"We feel, and I speak for all the Brotherhood," Suzanne cleared her throat and spoke loudly as if he was an audience of thousands. "That that as long as our meeting place stays intact, and the genealogy records stay unmolested, and we have full use of the facilities twice a year, once for the annual event and now for the Christmas party, we will be fine." She eyed him with a rather severe look, which made him think that perhaps she had been a junior high teacher in one of her previous incarnations. Or a witch from the East.

"What if I turn it into a spa?" He tried to keep a straight face.

"Don't be ridiculous, the city will never give you a permit for that."

What if he changed the locks? Now that was a possibility, one that gave him a tiny riff of pleasure.

"The Cornish were excellent hard rock miners." Suzanne walked around the main room as if, she was inspecting the library for the first time. Her sensible shoes made no sound on the ancient tile floor. "Have you ever had a pasty?"

Scott admitted that no, he had not, but he quickly promised he would, as soon as he could.

That seemed to satisfy Mrs. Chatterhill.

"What about the quilts?" He asked.

"Lucky donated the quilts to the library and we can keep them as long as they stay in the library. We hung them to hide the empty book cases, most of the books were moved to the new library of course."

"I see. And who made the quilts?"

"Penny Masters. Lucky's daughter?"

"Is she a member of the Brotherhood?" He gazed at the quilts; they were loosely based on traditional patterns. He recognized some of the basics: wedding ring, log cabin and of course crazy quilt. But the artist didn't adhere to tradition; the quilts were masterworks of modern interpretation. Patterns flowed with movement, colors shaded from one bright primary to the next on the rainbow line up. Pieces snaked and writhed, unlike any work he'd ever seen. He thought they were lovely, and even he could see they were valuable works of art. Maybe he could buy one and take it home or to whatever his new home would be.

"Oh good heaven's no," Mrs. Chatterhill protested vehemently. "Not with Lucky Masters as a father."

"We can't choose our parents," he offered mildly.

"Maybe you can't, but we can." Mrs. Chatterhill gathered up her purse, key and a half dozen documents and exited on her silent shoes.

That must be the beauty of being part of a genealogical organization. They probably did change the past.

Worked for him.

Ben arrived just as Tom Marten disappeared down the hill.

Prue was delighted at his arrival, as were all the boys. Another cute man in town, what the hell, right? I had to burst their bubble by explaining that Ben belonged to me, and their new boy was interested in Sarah.

"He's even attending the play again tonight," I delivered the coup de grace.

"There's a play?" Ben walked into the kitchen as if he lived there. I accidentally knocked over a chair as I turned to greet him. He was so much larger than I remembered.

"Hi," he wrapped his arms around me and held me tightly.

I sighed and for one minute forgot the kitchen was packed with consummate, professional gossips.

"The fabulous Ben Stone!" Raul saluted Ben and scurried to the one open spot at the kitchen table to set up his laptop.

Ben released me and greeted Prue; he gingerly hugged her as if her whole body, not just her foot was damaged.

"Did you bring your tools?"

"Grandma!"

"I always have my tools with me," Ben replied.

Pat, Mike and Raul sighed noisily. Ben just grinned. "Missed you guys."

Pat shook up the first round of martinis for the group. I'm no nurse and don't even pretend to act like one, so I cheerfully offered Prue her pain medication with one hand and gave her a martini with the other. That which does not kill us, makes us stronger.

"Carrie," Ben turned this attention to my friend as soon as he released my grandmother.

"I called him," Carried said grumpily. "He's not happy with me. He doesn't understand."

I accepted a martini from Pat. Carrie took hers and knocked it back in one gulp. Pat raised an eyebrow and looked at me. I toasted him silently and gestured to the bottle of Skye vodka on the counter. It was just as well that Carrie drink then pass out, she needed the rest. I think that's part of the pirate code as well; get drunk in your own house.

Carrie twirled her empty glass. I know I retreated to Prue's to heal, but once here, I had little to say about it. Talking doesn't help. Carrie's problems were more refreshing, and the solutions more interesting in a grim, black humor way.

"I just don't know what to do." She gazed with considerable dismay at her vibrating phone, it was one of those lovely newer kinds that do everything except wash the dishes and screen calls from destitute but persistent relatives.

"Tell them to get lost," Ben suggested.

"They can't be that bad," Prue offered at the same time.

"Yes they can," I defended my friend's position.

Mike circled back around and created another batch of drinks.

"What if they contact Patrick directly? What then?"

"Well," piped up Pat, "I know from experience it's better to deliver really awful news directly to the people involved. Waiting will not help, you don't want your parents to be a surprise."

Carrie twisted around to look directly at Mike. "You would know that wouldn't you?"

"Honey, we've all stood up to our relatives and delivered bad news of one kind or another."

"Sometimes we have even delivered it to loved ones," Raul said absently as he trolled the Internet.

"Sometimes, it's not as bad as you think it will be," Mike offered. He stopped Carrie from twirling her glass and filled it again from the silver shaker.

"I think this will be bad," Carrie confirmed.

"Parents can be difficult." Ben sipped his drink.

We were at a conversational impasse with that pithy comment. I broke it up by offering to get pizzas and bring them back. Prue was in no condition to climb back in and out of my car, and I knew that once settled in, Pat and Mike were here for the duration and of course, Raul and. . .

"Where's Brick?"

"He is dining with friends." Raul said. "Saturday night, a few old teachers from the high school. He is going to get more information on this Sarah."

"Why?"

Raul shrugged. "I have much footage of her yesterday. I want to write up more information in the blog."

"I can tell you," Prue held out her empty glass.

Sarah lingered in the doorway of her grandparent's apartment. The small television played at full volume, a talking head, an angry talking head, was ranting about immigration.

"I'm walking to the theater now, I have to be there early for make up." She yelled over the noise.

"Okay," her grandfather coughed. He coughed as often as he spoke; Sarah knew that soon the coughing would overtake the talking. Already Grandmother more often than not spoke for both of them, when she wasn't coughing herself.

"We would like tuna today for lunch. We need more milk in the house, your grandfather is cold."

Sarah made the sandwiches, brought hand-crocheted afghans to their chairs and offered her grandfather more cough drops.

Grandfather was fond of saying he acquired his cough in the seventies. "Breathing in all that airborne insulation." He bragged, as if that was a badge of honor.

That was back in the day when it was not only okay, but important, to kill yourself for a job. Sarah thought that kind of attitude was ridiculous. She only expressed that once and had the opposition beat out of her by this very same oxygen-impaired grandparent. The beating did not change her mind. She knew that a mere job, any job, was never worth dying for.

"I will come home right after the play at eleven o'clock." She automatically padded her arrival time, that way she was always home early. She once heard her grandmother bragging to Mrs. Chatterhill about how Sarah was always early, particularly when she was caring for her grandparents. She had been caring for them forever.

Her grandmother waved her hand, engrossed in the talking heads: the heads were yelling at each other. Sarah gazed at the scene in dismay. Her grandparents seemed to be slowly sinking into their matching Barcaloungers: hers a harvest gold, his avocado green. Sarah knew that at some point they would become one with the chairs and be lost forever. She had no plan for when that day came. Hers was not a planning generation. There didn't seem to be much point.

She closed the apartment door and walked down the narrow hall to the front door. She locked it after herself. You can't be too careful, with tourists and out of town people milling around on a Saturday night. Oh, and what was on the news just now? Terrorists. She was careful to secure the house against potential terrorist threats.

Sarah paused outside and finally dared take a deep breath. She had done as much as she could. Sarah walked to the theater; it was easier than driving. She didn't like wrestling her grandparent's Cutlass into the narrow parking spaces of the Claim Jump city lots.

She shoved her hands in her jacket pockets and trudged downhill. Sarah Miller knew what the good citizens of Claim Jump thought of her, it was difficult to ignore the looks and comments. The members of the Cornish Brotherhood of Men were not retiring women. Once the Millers joined, Sarah became an honorary member and a pet project for the group, for better or worse.

Sarah possessed a troubled past, what was euphemistically referred to as an unhappy childhood. She would argue that her years in the Claim Jump Elementary School were pretty satisfactory, and her grandparents always fed her, they even let her stay in the upstairs apartment. It was like living in her own place. Despite all these advantages, any child with a mother living on the Ridge was an object of some pity.

And now at twenty-two, she cared for her grandparents the same way they cared for her. Not exactly the same.

Her grandparents had been old for a very long time. Grandfather retired from construction at age 55, which was a thousand in child years. He was only 75 now, but looked and acted ninety. How was that possible? Prue Singleton was the same age as the Millers, but she was lively and active. She got around even after breaking her foot in her greenhouse.

A black SUV passed Sarah at the corner and headed up the street. See? Another tourist, Sarah didn't recognize the car.

I headed up the street, the car filled with pizzas. I love pizza. I made sure to order enough so I could load up on as much as I wanted without worrying about shorting the others. Rosemary would tell me to focus on my own abundance, but when it comes to pepperoni and sausage, I like to hedge my bets and purchase the abundance ahead of time.

"Never left town," Prue was winding up the Sarah Saga as I came in with boxes of dinner. "She has always been here."

"Like the poor?" Ben asked archly.

"Why?" Carrie asked.

Mike and Pat relieved me of the pizza boxes and began to serve. People didn't bother to move to the table, they took an offered plate, a piece of pizza and ate where they were standing. My mother would have gone nuts. Good thing she's not here. Raul searched for his theater webcam with one hand, the other clutched a wedge of the vegetarian pizza.

"Why," I wandered over to Raul, "are you watching the *Wizard of Oz* again?"

"Checking on the webcams," Raul muttered around his crust.

Ben listened with rapt attention to a story I already knew by heart, so Prue had a new audience for one of her favorites topics, the perils of Sarah Miller.

"Her mother was a drug abuser. It's a wonder Sarah wasn't born with one arm or an inflated head."

Carrie gasped. Pat rolled his eyes. Prue was on a role. Ben chewed and swallowed, his eyes never leaving his hostess. "The Millers are strict Baptists, holier than God. He used to work for Lucky in the seventies." Prue waved her hand in the direction of all the tract homes (some recently burned to the ground) north of the house.

"God used to work for Lucky Masters?" Ben asked.

"Lucky is very influential," I explained.

"But he didn't get the library," Pat smacked his lips in satisfaction.

"This Scott could be gay and not know it," Mike mused.

"Happens all the time," Raul squinted and angled his screen.

"At least they took in their granddaughter," Carrie retorted.

"And now she is their sole caregiver, " Prue said. "Won't have anyone else. I don't know what that girl is going to do when they really need help. They won't even allow a house cleaner. Melissa with Hospice told me she tried to come in last week and was practically thrown out."

"That's pretty harsh," I said. "The girl needs some help, I'm sure."

Prue sighed. "They are pretty harsh people."

"And you don't really blame the daughter for escaping to the Ridge."

"There are two sides to every story." Ben finished his first piece and opened every box looking for inspiration for his second piece.

"No," Carrie bit into a slice of pepperoni and swallowed. "No, sometimes there's not."

"Shhhh," Raul waved his hands, "the overture."

"As if we didn't already know all the words, remember the *Wizard of Oz* sing-a-long?" Pat turned to Mike, gesturing with his wedge of chicken/pesto pizza.

"That was marvelous, those were fun years."

Mike nodded, "Everyone was there, it was the place to be."

Raul grunted and focused on the computer screen. I suppose this is his art, which means I don't have to participate.

"Does Summer know you broadcast this all over the net?" I asked.

"Certainly, it's good for business, makes a person want to see the real thing."

Pat snorted.

We went on like that, watching poor Sarah hold up her end of the vocals as best she could. The little dog playing Toto was pretty cute. Ben pulled up a chair and raptly watched the drama unfold on the screen. The tornado scene wasn't as dramatic as in the movie, but what could Summer to do on a budget? The tornado was mostly just Sarah spinning around and around in the middle of the stage accompanied by whistling and howling.

The cardboard house dropped, color was restored to the stage and about a dozen Claim Jump third graders dressed in period costumes descended on our heroine.

A second bang, louder than the sound of the house hitting the hallowed ground of Oz, reverberated through the theater. Sarah stumbled on her line about not being any kind of witch.

A howl came up from the front of the theater, just out of cam range, but Summer quickly appeared in view. Her black eyeliner was smudged into semicircles under her eyes, her black hair was no longer sleek and she looked to be on the verge of rending her black jacket and throwing ashes into the air. She looked worse than the flattened dummy under the house.

"Noooo," Summer howled. "He can't be dead!" She jumped up on the stage and elbowed Dorothy/Sarah away. "He's dead!"

Sarah backed away from Summer so fast she almost tripped over a Munchkin.

"I thought the Wicked Witch was dead," piped up a Munchkin. Without my program, I did not know their real names. The Munchkins were just listed as Munchkin number two, etc.

Another Munchkin began to cry. "You said it was pretend, that she really wasn't dead!" The child pointed to the stuffed legs sticking from the fake house and raised her wail another pitch.

"Honey, it's okay," a parental voice from the audience valiantly tried to reassure the child.

"Ladies and gentlemen, I'm so sorry," Summer her harsh voice projected past the back of the theater and out to the street. It was difficult to tell if she was really sorry or just relishing the spotlight again. She paused dramatically and took a deep breath.

"It is my painful duty to inform you, that our patron, our friend of the theater, yes, a friend of all of Claim Jump. . ."

"It better be God," Prue muttered.

"Lucky Masters was found dead."

Three more Munchkins began to howl in sympathy sensing that this was not make-believe, and their boss, the fabulous Summer, was not only truly upset, but was also not making this up.

A general murmur rose from the audience. Two parents rushed the stage and scooped up a Munchkin or two.

"In light of such a shocking event," Summer continued, ignoring the exodus, "It is my sad duty to cancel the rest of the performance. I know you all share my grief and I hope you understand."

"Can we go for ice cream now?" a high little voice asked in the silence.

"What happened to the show must go on?" Raul asked reaching for another slice of the vegetarian.

I opened a bottle of wine while Raul immediately pulled up more information about the death. *Hacked* is the word, but he prefers the term necessary immediate discovery.

"I would have thought a jealous wife." Raul mumbled as he surfed through information options.

"Wife?"

"Husband, man of course," Raul backtracked. Pat and Mike rolled their eyes and moved back a step so we all could crowd around Raul's computer screen.

We did not find out much, but what we did learn seemed more than enough.

"They found him this afternoon out at the shooting range," Raul reported.

"The shooting range?" Prue frowned. "He had a heart attack? I didn't think shooting was that stressful."

"Quite the contrary," Ben put in. "Firing off rounds seems to be quite relaxing." He glanced at Carrie. Her eyes were huge. "For some people," Ben amended quickly.

"He's a founding member of the range. Was a founding member," Prue said for the benefit of those in the room who were not local.

"Of course, Lucky would found something like a shooting range within the City Limits."

"The manager of the range didn't find the body until five o'clock at closing time. They must do a sweep of the shooting area at the end of the week," Raul read and editorialized at the same time.

I remember visiting the firing range once with my grandfather. It had been in use, unofficially, since the Gold Rush. The area was stripped clean by hydraulic mining. It was a nice try, but the weight of the tons of topsoil sluiced onto the farmland of the Sacramento Valley was far out of proportion to the amount of gold found. The area was quickly closed and the hydraulic nozzles moved up the hill to Malakoff. All that was accomplished was destruction; on the other hand it was a great place to shoot your gun, who would care? Bored miners, some of them Cornish, I'm sure, claimed the land as their own and formed a gun club to justify the land grab. Even after 150 years, the area is still devoid of any real vegetation or life. I remember seeing some plucky low scrub brush growing in the crevices of the bare hills, and of course, Poison Oak but that's it.

By creating a shooting club, Lucky was merely following the order of the universe.

"How far away is it?" Ben asked.

"Less than a mile, but you can't take a shortcut any more, so it's about five miles around the back of the mountain. And there's a fence now. Lucky put that up when they incorporated the range into a club."

"Short cut?" Ben asked faintly. Since he is a former boy, I imagine he can visualize how to best exploit an attractive nuisance better than I can. And indeed, taking the short cut to and through a firing range would be difficult to resist. It would make an appealing dare to any number of boys.

"We used to walk from here to the range." Prue explained. "Your grandfather and I tried it out a couple of times."

"You know how to shoot a gun?" Great. I didn't ask if she owned a gun because I didn't want to hear that it was registered because she always meant to get around to it, but never had.

"Well honey, what with the pot and all, it seemed like a good skill to have."

"Is there a short cut now?" Ben tried to keep the conversation on track.

"No, you'd have to travel through too many properties," Prue waved a hand to dismiss the idea, "and Fred Majors just got a dog."

"No one would be foolish enough to walk onto a firing range."

Prue hesitated.

"What?" I girded for a story, there was always a story.

"It almost closed once," Prue hedged. "Do you remember the Feinster boys?

"Now, why would I remember the Feinster boys?" I countered.

"I forget you didn't grow up here. Seems like you did. Anyway, they and a group of friends dared each other to dash across the shooting range using garbage can lids as shields."

All the men in the room nodded, as if that was an excellent idea. Garbage can lids should deflect bullets, why not?

I recalled the truly idiotic dares I witnessed out at the river where copious amounts of jug wine and weed made some of my male companions superhuman and thus impervious to freezing water, strong unpredictable currents and submerged rocks. If you don't know the depth of a swimming hole, don't dive head first into it. Make a note of that. I stopped counting the close calls; there wasn't enough wine to stop me from panicking every time a boy was too long underwater after a dive. Made me crazy. But not crazy enough to stop going to the river.

"The club members were shooting at the time," Prue cleared her throat. "One of the brothers was shot in the head, killed instantly, the others escaped with only a few wounds in their legs and arms."

I closed my eyes, thinking not of the child, but of the parents. What an incredibly stupid thing to do. How tragic for the mother to hear the news. The brother trying desperately to figure out whose idea it really was, then trying to explain. Can you lay blame? They probably tried. Like Mattie Timmons after Danny was caught in the fire last fall. Who do you blame? Who takes responsibility? We always think it is "Them". Who are them?

Raul lifted a hand to silence the audience. The pizza was gone. I started breaking down the boxes.

"Not a heart attack," he announced with relish.

We all waited dutifully, Raul liked his drama, much like Summer. "They found him out on the range."

"Yes, you just said that."

"No, no, on the range a foot past the shooting targets."

"On the range? What was he doing out there?"

"They don't know." Raul wiggled his thick eyebrows for effect. "He was shot more than twenty times."

How could anyone shoot Santa Claus? Repeatedly?

Chapter Seven

Lucky or not, my own show had to go on. I promised to meet Scott Lewis on Sunday no later than ten o'clock.

"I won't be that long," I announced to Ben as I pulled on the same outfit I wore driving up on Thursday. I had a limited wardrobe for showing houses. I had not planned on finding a client up here, which was great, I was happy to have the client, but I had floor Monday. I wasn't concerned about my lack of wardrobe options. Yet.

"I have floor Monday," I said, as I finished explaining my whole, reasonable plan to Ben.

"Get someone else. You have a hot client with cash, doesn't that trump answering phone calls that, in your words, are more often than not, wrong numbers?"

I glanced at my watch. 9:30. I had to hurry if I wanted to drink enough coffee to sustain me for a morning of house viewing.

"I really do appreciate you driving up here, but now we'll have to drive down tonight, are you okay with that?"

Ben lounged in the narrow lumpy bed looking perfectly relaxed. I discovered that I could take Ben anywhere and he would not only be appropriate, but also, for the most part, comfortable. Was that the result of a more upper class education? Or was that just Ben?

"You look better than when you left on Thursday," he observed.

"Death will do that for me. Perk me right up. As long as it isn't me."

He grinned. "There is no way you're getting out of here tonight and you know it. Call."

He picked up his phone and offered it to me.

"You don't have the office number."

"Yes I do," he scrolled down with his thumb. "I have all the numbers pertaining to you and some that I may need in the future that pertain to you."

"Like who?" I accepted his phone and pressed the office number.

"Like my attorney, flower shop, minister, clothing shops. I had the hospital . . ." He trailed off.

I caught my breath but the call to the office was picked up on the first ring.

"New Century Realty, your vision is our reality."

"That's not our tag line."

Ben waved at me to leave the room while I talked. I turned and walked downstairs.

Katherine had floor. So she was first to answer the main office line. I wasn't all that excited about talking to her because I knew she'd do exactly what she launched into doing: lecturing me on productivity.

"Are you still in the foothills?" she asked suspiciously.

"Yeah," I admitted. "That's why I'm calling."

Prue and Carrie were already up and in the kitchen. Carrie must have helped her dress because Prue's pale blue sweater complimented her tan slacks and her hair was brushed.

I nodded to both; they raised their hands in greeting, but did not move. They were each embroiled in sections of the Sunday paper.

"Running away again," Katherine pronounced.

"I am not running away!"

Prue and Carrie looked up, I waved my hand to indicate that no I was not running away and not again. Jeez.

"You know, you could become an expert in REO and Short Sales, those are still available," Katherine offered. "You could be like the Christopher's and just work with foreclosures."

"That's a consideration," I already heard this from Rosemary. Honestly I thought they were working together, they needed to compare notes before harassing me. I poured some coffee and leaned against the counter.

"Katherine, I need," I started.

"It's not that hard, if Rosemary and the Christophers can do it, then you certainly can do it."

I did not point out that I really hated foreclosures. I did not want to specialize in pain and suffering. I did not say that Christophers, a husband and wife team, seemed to thrive on the misfortune of others and that was not the kind of karma I was interested in acquiring. Rosemary would understand, I was not sure Katherine did.

"Thanks for the vote of confidence. Katherine, can you . . ."

"There's a seminar on Wednesday. I can sign you up. Just give me your credit card, it's only five hundred dollars. Includes lunch."

"That won't be necessary." By this time, Carrie was smirking and my grandmother was grinning like a maniac. I'm so glad I could bring some levity and joy to their Sunday morning.

Ben shuffled in and pushed me to one side to get to the coffee.

I thought you were leaving, he mouthed.

I have your phone, I mouthed back at him.

He kissed me and joined the peanut gallery at the kitchen table.

"Katherine, I just need to find someone to take floor," I said it all in a rush to get the words in.

"Oh, is that all? Rosemary can take it."

"Thanks." I knew perfectly well that Katherine just crossed off my name on the schedule and inserted Rosemary's, and that Rosemary will be quite surprised to find her name on the schedule, but I didn't care. I ended the call and handed the phone back to Ben while I took a swallow of coffee.

"Now I'm taking off. I'll see you all later."

They all waved the royal good-bye wave. For a moment I paused, thinking how cozy they all looked, my favorite people, busy with the paper and coffee, the morning stretching ahead empty of specific plans, ready for spontaneous pleasure. No, I had a job and I was grateful for the work.

I stomped outside to my car and drove downtown.

There was no movement at the library. I parked and figured I had just enough time for a hazelnut mocha latte before tackling Scott's needs.

Tom stood in line in front of me. Dressed in his uniform he must have been grabbing a drink before work, just like me.

"Buy you a drink?" I offered.

He nodded gratefully. "I suppose I'm persona non grata at your house."

"Prue doesn't hold it against you," I assured him. I neglected to mention me.

We took our drinks to the far corner of the shop, neither of us wanted to sit in the window.

"My kids were pretty upset last night," he started.

"Your daughter was a Munchkin."

"Munchkin number four, and my son was a flying monkey." He grinned, "pretty much to type."

I smiled and sipped my coffee drink.

"Anyway, as you probably heard, Summer cancelled the play last night. My son was devastated. He was the monkey who picked up Toto. It was a big part."

"What is she going to do? I noticed she has a summer repertory program scheduled."

"I don't' know, Lucky was a big supporter. He was a big supporter for lots of events and programs around here."

"Did that help him circumvent the permit process?" I just went to the heart of the matter; might as well, I wasn't going to be up here for long.

"You haven't met Debbie have you? She is one by-the-book woman, she brings a little of the big city into our small sleepy town, as she calls it. She wouldn't let Lucky get away with doing anything that wasn't signed, sealed and officially stamped."

"Do you suspect Debbie along with Prue?" I asked.

"Oh hell, Allison, I have to talk to everyone. Prue didn't kill Lucky."

"I'm glad to hear it."

He twirled his coffee cup. "I don't know why we even thought of the shooting range. You know those guys just shoot at anything unlucky enough to wander into the field. The manager calls us every other week to pick up dead rabbits, possum, sometimes quail. This was, of course, different."

He took a long drink of his coffee. He knew I was going to ask, and I knew I shouldn't ask, and he shouldn't tell me, but as this Debbie pointed out, we were a sleepy little town and didn't know any better.

I waited.

"There were too many bullets in his body to even begin to figure which bullet did him in." Tom finally admitted.

"Good God," I swallowed my coffee and surreptitiously glanced at my watch.

"He was out in the rain for at least a day, maybe longer. He was missing all Friday. Penny said she spoke to him on Wednesday."

I made a face and Tom answered with a sympathetic expression of his own.

"Yeah, it was pretty gross. We recognized him of course, the beard and the white hair, but Christ, it was like stuffing St. Nick back into his own pack."

I placed my hand on his arm. "Did Penny identify the body?"

"We couldn't get her to come in, she was in hysterics so we sent up her doctor instead. You remember Sam Chesney? He used to come out to the river with us. He's back in town, that's who Penny sees now." He sipped his coffee "We all seem to be back in town."

"It's a nice town," I confirmed vaguely. "Then who could ID the body?"

"The mayor came down, she's as official as anything we have."

"Poor Summer." She loved Lucky, he was her savior and probably father figure, but that's just conjecture on my part.

"Yes, poor Summer, now she doesn't know what will happen to the theater."

"Well, after this last production of *Wizard of Oz*," I trailed off.

"Yeah, pretty bad wasn't it? There's a saying that having a live theater in a community shows that the community has culture and is appreciative of the arts, but couldn't we do that with a nice sculpture in the park?"

"What? And move the hydraulic mining nozzles?" I said in mock protest.

"Yeah, that would be a problem."

"Do you have any suspects?"

He sighed and downed the rest of his coffee. "You mean, besides the whole town? I have to talk to everyone who hated Lucky Masters enough to kill him."

"That will keep you busy until the 4th of July."

"No shit." His expression was one of pure misery.

I did not envy Tom Marten. Who would talk with him? Who would admit their real feelings about Lucky? And why should anyone care? Lucky's death would make life very difficult for Summer, but for others, like Debbie, it was a blessing. Now the homes above Prue's house would be built with permits and home inspections and possibly less dangerous insulation. Many people would benefit.

It was like a late Agatha Christie novel; the whole town could be guilty.

Scott arrived early. This was a rather astonishing new habit of his, this rising early in the morning business, this moving around before noon stuff. He unlocked the library door at 9:00 AM and turned on the heat. Hands on his hips he regarded the empty lobby and decided he needed more coffee from that little place two doors down before he could seriously consider his purchase. What would he do with this?

He almost ran into Sarah as he sprinted out of the library main doors. The front steps leading to the main floor were worn with age and slippery. He shot down the stairs, lost his balance, fell through the front door that did not slow his progress but rather launched him like a fun house entrance down the second set of outdoor steps and directly into a girl. She dropped one grocery bag and almost dropped the second bag, just barely catching it before it hit the cracked sidewalk.

"Sorry, sorry!" He reached for the bag that landed on the street. It broke open at his touch, cans of Ensure tumbled out of the ripped opening and rolled down to the gutter. He clutched what was left in the paper bag - Depends - and gathered up the cans as quickly as he could.

He bundled together the items and handed them back to her with another sorry. She looked a bit young for such purchases. But he was learning not to ask anything about anything when it came to the eccentricities of Claim Jump residents.

Despite years of tutelage at the hands of sincere fashion and lifestyle magazines: *Always look good, you never know when you'll run into the man of your dreams.* Here she was, standing before the man of her dreams with no make-up and a bag full of adult diapers.

Sarah knew he wasn't considered the stuff of dreams. She listened to all the rumors circulating around town. Scott Lewis hadn't earned his money, he had inherited money from his father. Scott Lewis had no prospects. Scott Lewis did not grow up in Claim Jump. Every one of Scott's major personality features were a strike against him in the vast and bottomless opinion of the Brotherhood members and everyone she met in the check-out line at Safeway.

"Are you hurt? Did I hurt you?" He brushed ineffectually at her coat. She gathered up the bag with the cans and held them awkwardly under her arm.

"There are grocery bags inside." He gestured to the library doors. "Under the main desk, to the right. I'll get them for you." He left her on the chilly sidewalk and bounded back up the stairs, almost lost his balance, recovered and dashed inside. He returned with two paper bags and thrust them at her.

"You're the guy who bought the library aren't you?" She didn't really say it as a question but to be polite she made her voice inflect.

"Yeah," he reached up and scratched his neck, then scratched his head. "You probably heard about me."

Sarah waited for him to continue. She wanted to know what he thought she thought. She hadn't really made up her mind about him. Her grandparents taught her that all men are just after one thing, which contradicted every magazine article she ever read; look perfect to attract the right man, yes they want one thing, and so do you. The members of the Brotherhood specifically told her that Scott was probably bad news which prompted her to walk the long way home right past the library.

"I heard about you, I saw you at the theater Friday night and last night," she started the conversation.

"I guess I was, you know there isn't much to do in Claim Jump over the weekend." He looked sheepish.

"Just the wine-tasting extravaganza, the Cornish Brotherhood Spaghetti Feed, the Methodist church raffle and the little league silent auction and crab dinner," she automatically rattled off. Then wanted to kick herself, she wasn't suppose to be too aggressive and sound like she was too smart. Or was it she wasn't suppose to sound too needy or stupid? He was watching her with interest.

"What are you, the Chamber of Commerce?"

She felt heat rise to her cheeks. "No, that's a day job, I'm busy during the day."

"What do you do?" his voice was kind, maybe she hadn't blown it after all.

"I care for my grandparents."

"Can I help you carry all this?" he offered. He didn't know what the time was, but he was sure his real estate agent would wait for him. " Where do you live?"

"Grove Street, it's only a few blocks from here."

"Isn't this a little out of your way from the grocery store?"

She thought quickly. "I got a ride from a friend but she got a call from her boyfriend, so this was as far she she'd take me into town. He lives out in Lake of the Pines."

Scott hadn't heard of a local lake of that name, but he didn't want to distract her with an irrelevant geography inquiry. Her eyes were brilliant blue and her hair was fine and naturally blond. He itched to touch it, but that would be too forward. She was just as beautiful close up as she had been on stage.

"I'm so sorry," he meant that she had to walk all the way home and her friend couldn't even drop her off before rushing to her boyfriend.

"Oh, don't, they've been good to me, it's my turn," she said enigmatically.

"Is that good or bad?" It was a reasonable question.

"They told me I'll inherit the house when they go, to make sure I have something to bring to a relationship, you know like a dowry."

"That was far thinking of them."

Sarah juggled the bag of cans. She wasn't sure if he was being sarcastic or not. "They want me to be taken care of, and to them, that means finding a good man. But not too soon, you understand, only after I'm finished caring for them." She looked at Scott a bit sharply as if daring him to laugh.

He nodded. "I can understand, just do one thing at a time." He took a breath, and plunged in, risking doing it wrong, but not caring. "But maybe we could have dinner together anyway?"

She grinned and tightened her grip on her embarrassing purchases. He hadn't made fun of her; he had said nothing about the Ensure, the diapers, nothing at all. Now there was something the Brotherhood did not know about Scott Lewis. She made up her mind.

"Can you do a late dinner? 9:00? Cirinos is still open."

"I can do that," he assured her, wondering if Cirinos was in town or located in the mythical Lake of the Pines. He'd ask around. Mrs. Chatterhill would be more than happy to lecture him on the restaurants in Claim Jump both current and past.

"How about tonight? Is the show over?"

He knew perfectly well it was, but he wanted to be polite. Was that how it was done? This polite back and forth? He hadn't dated much, what he usually indulged in wasn't really dating per se.

"Yeah, the show is over. Before I get all dressed up, is there anything I should know about you?"

"That Suzanne Chatterhill hasn't already circulated?"

She gathered up the fresh bags into each arm to balance the load.

"I'm Holden Caulfield, only old." He was succinct.

She smiled. "I loved that book. He needed to join more clubs at school."

Scott watched her swing down the slope of the sidewalk with the same walk she used in the play. Follow the Yellow Brick Road. Follow, follow.

I arrived at the library at exactly 10:00. Scott was already outside on the front steps gazing down the street. I looked too; we automatically follow a stranger's gaze. You never know if your just missed an interesting sight, but I did not see anything of note.

"Come in," he invited.

I walked up the two sets of narrow stairs, wider and deeper when I climbed them as a child, and paused in the main library room. Huge color saturated quilts were festooned over the empty book shelves. Their color and number was breath taking. "How beautiful!" I know nothing of the domestic arts, but I could see that these were unusual patterns pieced together with beautiful colors. One quilt featured a single tree, sinuous and stunning as it climbed up the quilted surface of the blanket to a blue patterned sky.

"Oh, those belong to the members of the Brotherhood. They bought them, but Lucky insisted the quilts stay in the library."

"How can he dictate what they do with their own property?"

"I think it was the condition of the sale. Apparently Penny Masters makes them. You must know her, Lucky's daughter?"

I nodded. I knew of her of course, but not that well. She was much older than me and didn't run in the same circles as my grandmother, after all, Prue hated Lucky Masters with a passion.

"I can't imagine Suzanne taking suggestions from Lucky." I commented.

"Neither can I, but they did," Scott agreed. He sounded like a local.

"What happen to the one over there?" I pointed to a forlorn empty shelf, naked compared to the brilliantly covered neighbors.

"I don't know, it was gone when I," he paused. "I think a woman named Elizabeth took it."

I waved my hand. It didn't matter who, often the members of the Brotherhood act in a collective manner, they are like the

Borg in that way, the large conglomerate enemy on *Star Trek* that just assimilates people with no discussion or protest. And like the Borg, woe to anyone who resisted assimilation by the Brotherhood.

"Anyway, she took it, but the rest stay. I suppose now they will finally go to the owners."

"No Lucky to monitor the situation." I observed. "It will look pretty empty here without them. "

He nodded. "I'll think of something. How about a Laundromat?"

I glanced at him, disbelieving, and he gave me a wicked grin in return.

"That was good," I conceded. "Suggest a bordello next and see where that gets you."

"Why not, I have the quilts, plenty of room in the back." He regarded me with mock seriousness. "It's a tradition in the Gold Country."

I shook my head and grabbed his arm. There were only three more houses for sale in town. I wanted to get back to Ben and my grandmother. Who knows what they would be up to?

We opened the door to a blast of frigid air.

I managed to finish with Scott in record time. He displayed all the typical traits of a buyer, for which I'm prepared.

"Let me think about them." He climbed out of my car in front of the library. Could he just turn that place into a residence?

As if reading my mind, I'm a bit transparent when I'm not paying much attention, he replied out loud, "you know that Debbie Smith from the council? She informed me the library was commercial zoned only."

"Just a thought."

My phone buzzed, I automatically picked it up.

"I'm at an open house because that's what you do. You work every Sunday at every open house you can manage to get leads." Rosemary's voice was firm and a bit echoey, the open house in question must not be furnished.

I was working on Sunday. "And you take floor every chance you have, like tomorrow." I said, not without some satisfaction. "That ought to get you more leads."

"Who approved that?" She immediately dropped the motivational coach persona as I knew she would.

"Katherine, of course." With so much in common, these two should get along. But their sense of competition usually trumps their need for camaraderie. The only problem with their animosity is that I am so often in the middle, sometimes making peace, but mostly just stirring them up more, even when it's not my intent. Their last competition was to see who could lose fifteen pounds first. They both cheated, and they both gained the weight all back. See? They have lots in common.

Inez, our manager, works hard to channel their competitiveness into real estate transactions. She is mostly successful, except for that one awards banquet when Rosemary slipped Katherine some kind of herbal diuretic and Katherine missed her opportunity to walk on stage for her award. Rosemary accepted on Katherine's behalf. It was very sweet of her. I can't remember if Rosemary mentioned Katherine at all during the acceptance speech.

"Of course," Rosemary echoed. She must be in one of her REOs, empty, cleared out. For her sake, I hoped the appliances hadn't been ripped out by the disgruntled previous owner. When owners walk away from their over-leveraged homes, they sometimes feel quite justified taking a few mementos: the toilet, the water heater, chunks of cement from the driveway, just a few more reasons why I don't like the foreclosure category.

"Well for YOU, I'll take it. Listen," her voice was low and more urgent. "You cannot quit, you are too good to quit."

"I'm not quitting, it's corporate who has my head on the block."

"You make your own life." Rosemary repeated her favorite mantra. "And we ride these markets out. It will pick up, I promise, it always does."

She managed to stuff a whole bundle of empty platitudes into one sentence. I was impressed.

"I have a client." I guided the Lexus up through the lower half of Prue's street and crested the hill right before her house.

"Well that's good."

"A buyer," I delivered the bad news.

She paused. "Well, a buyer is at least something. See you Tuesday."

Tuesday. Maybe. I clicked off the phone and marched into the kitchen, ready for lunch.

What greeted me was pandemonium.

Chapter Eight

Carrie wailed like a mother cat mourning a bag of drowned kittens. Ben clutched his phone, he had not changed out of his sweats and tee. He was pacing up and down with the mien of a caged bear. Raul had inserted himself off to one side crouched over his laptop like an intelligent chimp. Prue was attempting to sooth Carrie, tentatively pawing at the howling woman.

It was like feeding time at the zoo.

I stood in the doorway for a full minute before anyone noticed me.

"We have a little challenge," Ben paused, and kissed me. "I'm on the phone with Patrick."

"She," I pointed to Carrie. "Should be the one on the phone with Patrick."

Ben whispered "not now," and and hurriedly spoke into the phone to the disembodied Patrick.

"They threatened to come up here." Carrie cried. "I was worried they find me here and they did."

"Where are they now?" I already knew the answer, based on the tableau I walked into.

"Apparently," Prue patted Carrie's arm rhythmically. "They descended on Patrick's office."

"With no appointment." Carrie shrieked.

"They burst into Patrick's office," Prue amended. "And loudly introduced themselves."

"Is it too late for the fiery car crash?" Carrie hiccupped. At least she was a bit quieter. Ben moved down the hall, I waved my arms to stop him. If he wandered too far into the front parlor, he'd lose reception.

"I think it's too late." I confirmed.

"Damn!" Ben's voice echoed down the hall. He had wandered too far into the parlor.

"This place is like a black hole." He growled, still acting the grouchy bear.

"Only for cell coverage." I soothed.

"What did he say?" Carrie looked up at Ben; her blue eyes were enormous and shiny with tears.

Ben touched her hair. "He's coming up."

"It's over then." She slumped down in her chair. "He'll call it off." She glanced down at her ring. "What a beautiful dream it was."

"It's not over." I soothed, but I didn't have much else to say. "Tell him the truth. You can explain that you didn't invite them to the engagement party because you were embarrassed. Now that he's met them, he'll certainly understand that part."

Her phone rang and she picked it up. Really, I had to talk with her about voice mail, very handy when you need to screen your calls.

"Hello?" She listened for about a second then hit the speaker button, too exhausted to repeat the story.

"And boy, he sure is handsome." Her mother's voice, gravely from a lifetime of smoking, floated up from the phone (like the wicked witch of the west). "Dad and me are just so proud that you made something of yourself."

"Marrying is what makes me something? Is that all? Leaving and making it on my own, that counts for nothing?" Carrie burst out, glaring at her pretty phone. It was just the messenger, I wanted to remind her, don't blame the cell.

Her mother ignored her daughter. "He's something, invited us direct to the wedding. We are pretty sure we can make it."

"Your schedule is so impacted." Carrie rolled her eyes.

"You know honey, if it doesn't work out you can always live back with us."

"What else did you say to him mother?" Carrie demanded.

"That you were a lucky girl rising out of poverty like you did, of course we're much better off, we have a double-wide now, the biggest place in the park. We have room, you sure you don't want to come home?"

How completely delusional was this woman? Even I knew Carrie would never, under any circumstance, come within ten feet of her abusive father. Unless he was dead. Then she'd approach cautiously, but only up to five feet.

I never asked for more details aboiut her past. The last thing Carrie needed was to relive her crappy childhood, but Patrick may ask. Patrick may insist. Frankly I recommended a while back that she spill her guts and tell him everything. I myself have told Ben everything about my own past, is it my fault that he happened to fall asleep just before I could reveal to the really good parts?

"I will never come home." Carrie said firmly. Tears streaked down her cheeks. Ben handed her a tissue. She clicked off and checked the number.

"How do you block numbers on your phone?"

"Now you're talking. Let me do it."

"If only they would just die." Carrie clapped her hands over her mouth and looked over her fingers in horror.

"I didn't mean to say that, of course I didn't mean to say that, they are my parents. I'm supposed to love them."

"Sure, from a long distance with a restraining order." I said briskly, but her expression was haunted. She was more upset about her own reaction that the rude abusive behavior of her parents. Typical Carrie.

I finished with the phone and looked at her. "You're going to have to tell him the truth."

"Not the whole truth, Oh God," she moaned, "I never intended to bring it up."

"He loves you, he'll understand." I tried to smile and appear encouraging. As if I knew Patrick. I did not really know Patrick, I only know about him through Carrie. I had no knowledge of his background; I imagined it was packed with private schools, private lessons and private summer homes.

"Will Patrick stay here?" Prue asked.

"I don't know." Carrie touched the phone, then pushed it away. "It depends on how our conversation goes."

I didn't know about Patrick, but I couldn't stand aside and let her father ruin her life again. He had already, irreparably, done it once and she escaped, all by herself. This time she was not alone, and that monster was not going to ruin my best friend's life. I had no plan to back up that bold assertion; I had a better chance figuring out who murdered Lucky.

"It's going to get crowded here." Ben observed. He was looking at Raul. Raul was ignoring Ben and everyone else. I figured it must be warmer in the kitchen than the guesthouse.

"Yes," said Prue. "But the days when students were willing to sleep under the dining room table are gone."

"We'll move." Ben suggested.

"Where?" I asked. Was this another replay of why I was up here in the first place? Our inability to share quarters?

"Is the apartment over the garage still empty?" Ben asked Prue.

She nodded. "Excellent idea. You two move there, Carrie and Patrick will have the third floor to themselves. Check the toilet while you're there. I think it's running."

"Thank you," Carrie said quietly.

"Come on, let's do this now." Ben rose and headed towards the hallway.

"We have time." I protested. I was hungry. I wanted my lunch.

"Patrick is flying up, we have half an hour."

The apartment above the garage was built in the seventies - no permits because you can't really see it from the street. It overlooked three neglected weed-choked lots that backed into our property. From the second floor we could see the rooftops of new homes that had been built after my senior year, when I stopped spending so much time up here. Prue usually allowed people to stay in the apartment for as long as they needed, which in Claim Jump time can be years. The most recent occupant stayed over Christmas, but Prue assured me she now had her own place.

Ben motioned me in and we climbed the narrow stairs to the second floor apartment. Last fall we tried to find privacy up here, but did not meet with success. This time I hoped for better.

As I climbed, I pulled out my phone.

"Checking for reception?" He pushed me up the last step and looked around. I wandered from corner to corner finally ending up in the tiny bathroom. "Here, four bars right here in the shower stall."

"That will keep the conversation short," he said genially, even cheerfully.

"Don't you have something else to do other than hang around here?" I finally asked.

"Nope, besides, you have another great Claim Jump murder, another mystery to cope with, and it's my job to keep you safe." He removed the toilet lid and peered inside.

"The last time we hung out together in Claim Jump, I almost got you killed."

He shrugged. "You are interesting that way. But I can't leave you, I certainly don't intend to strand Carrie." His expression darkened. "Are her parents that bad? Patrick said they were uncouth and clearly lower class, but not monsters."

"Monsters come in many disguises."

He raised one eyebrow. "Really."

"Really." I asserted.

We moved into the tiny apartment as if it were the real thing. We replaced the apartment mattress with one we found in an empty guest room in the main house. I filched towels and soap from my own upstairs bath and I grilled Raul until I was certain there were no web cams posted around the apartment.

"I took them all down in January," he admitted. "But All-Is-Son they were very helpful, really."

"I do not want to hear about it." But I looked around for the telltale camera eyes just in case.

Our privacy assured, even cozy, we left our new nest to hunt for a coffee maker, but were distracted by Patrick's arrival in the only cab in town. The Claim Jump airport is mostly reserved for the borate bombers, but occasionally private planes do zoom in and out. There is no baggage center. There is no TSA, no car rentals. No services.

Ben and I followed Patrick into the kitchen.

Prue hung up the phone. "The funeral is tomorrow, you are all to come."

Patrick paused in mid-step.

"Sorry, I'm Prue Singleton. Welcome."

Ben clapped Patrick on the back. "See what happens when you're spontaneous? Welcome to Allison's insanely bizarre home town."

Chapter Nine

"It's not my home town." I protested, giving Patrick a perfunctory hug.

"May as well be." Carrie and Prue chorused.

Patrick strode over to Carrie and picked her up off her chair. Carrie is a fairly small person, about five foot even, 100 pounds, maybe. Patrick is a foot taller and considerably broader, but not as big as Ben. Patrick is slighter, with dark Irish looks and a CEO build. He is a man who works from a desk. Ben works with his hands and likes to shatter big heavy objects using large unweidly sledgehammers; his version of the gym. The difference is obvious in their style and carriage. All the same, Patrick can be very commanding when he needs to be.

And this afternoon, he needed to be.

"Come with me," he said simply.

"Go to the parlor." I recommended. Carrie nodded as Patrick carried her out of the kitchen.

"That was certainly romantic." Prue stepped to the hallway opening and watched them turn to the parlor.

"Looked more like a kidnapping," Ben commented. "Where would we find a coffee maker?"

"Just use this one," Prue said, "Allison says you won't be here that long."

Ben sighed. He really did know me better than that. "Prue."

"Okay, Builder's and Consumers, across the freeway."

I glanced at the now empty hall. "I'll come with you."

"Allison Little." Summer's voice floated across the hardware store with the lilt of a feedback scream.

I paused knowing I had little choice. I couldn't ignore her, not here in public. Ben held the coffee maker box to his chest like a shield, as if that would protect him from a distraught theater director.

"You heard of course!" Summer descended on us like a seasonal cold.

"Of course," we both echoed.

If anything, Summer was slipping further and further into the winter of her discontent. Her hair was a wild nest in the back, her pale eyes looked lost in paler skin. The makeup-free look was not for her. It wasn't for me either, but I wasn't mourning the loss of my livelihood, so I looked just slightly better than poor Summer.

"We're waiting to hear from Lucky's lawyers, apparently his estate is very complicated." Summer cut right to the chase.

"Of course it is," I said automatically.

"And you are coming to the funeral tomorrow? I can't believe how quickly Penny put this thing together, money helps I'm sure."

She finally noticed Ben, which means that she really was in a complete state. Women usually notice Ben before even acknowledging me, and I'm difficult to miss.

"And who are you?" Summer's harsh tone quickly switched from distraught to sexy purr.

"Ben Stone." Ben reached around his protective Mr. Coffee and shook hands with Summer.

"So you are." Temporally distracted she eyed Ben with disturbing enthusiasm.

"My fiancé," I was compelled to clarify.

Ben raised both eyebrows. He had asked, right in the hospital. He even dropped to one knee. I was touched, but so distracted by a future I hadn't once considered, that was just as quickly obliterated and irretrievably lost, that I did not deliver a very good answer.

Once out of my mouth, I realized I may have delivered an answer right here in Builders and Consumers. How romantic, the answer to a proposal of marriage in asile 5, nuts and bolts.

"Nice to meet you." Summer dismissed the delectable Ben as Display Only and turned to me.

"Most of the town will be there," she said.

"To support Penny."

"Oh, hell no. You know no one in this town has ever supported that poor woman, not her mother, either."

A live mother often thwarts any adventure a person wants to embark on. Look at Disney Films, where are the mothers? Gone. Would Ariel have sold her voice if Mom had been on the scene? I think not. Would Nemo have been snatched by a dentist if Mom had survived? Nope. Cinderella? Snow White? Shrek? Absent mother equals excellent adventure. I wondered then what was Penny's excellent adventure? What could she do now that her father too, was gone? I resisted expressing any of this outloud.

"What happened to her mother?" Ben was only mildly interested, but since we weren't moving, he may as well learn more Claim Jump gossip.

"Suicide," Summer and I said together.

"It was years ago, I was still spending summers up here," I explained.

She nodded. "There were rumors about infidelity, but no one ever proved anything and Lucky wasn't saying. Penny sort of took over in her mother's place. She even worked for Lucky for a while, but she never entertained."

"That explains her exclusion from the Brotherhood."

"And Empire Club, Lucky dropped that group after his wife was gone, Penny didn't take her place."

The club Summer mentioned only allowed 100 members at any time. In order for one couple to join, another has to retire or die, to put it bluntly. I was surprised Lucky didn't hold on to that group, it was packed with lawyers, judges and retired generals.

"Are people helping Penny with the reception tomorrow?"

"I am." Summer laid her hand on her heart. Her nail polish was chipped and flaking. That woman needed a week at the spa.

"She hired caterers from Sacramento. Come. You too." She batted her lashes at Ben.

He inclined his head, the same gesture he uses when he capitulates to his mother.

We paid for the coffee machine, hurried across the parking lot and jumped into the car.

"Is it always this cold in spring?" He complained.

I started the car so the heated seats could warm us. "Sometimes we have lovely weather in March, but this isn't one of those times."

"Snow?"

"Sometimes through Easter."

"Great. And since you all can't go outside, rumor and gossip have evolved into contact sports."

"Everywhere. Looks like we are definitely attending a funeral tomorrow."

He nodded. I would not be surprised if he had packed a suit - just in case. He's that kind of prepared guy. I turned left out of the parking lot and headed towards Main Street.

"Where are you going?"

"I need a new outfit."

Never underestimate the tenacity created by the focus purpose generated by a group of determined septuagenarians. I thought it was quite reasonable to suspect the whole damn lot of the Brotherhood of Cornish Men in the death of Lucky Masters. Not a single member liked Lucky, but like so many citizens of Claim Jump, they were beholden to Lucky Masters in various and complicated ways. You don't spend a lifetime in a small town and not develop complicated and constantly changing relationships with your fellow community members. My theory was that the Brotherhood, acting as one body, killed Lucky Masters. It was easy. One member of the Brotherhood could have cleverly drugged Lucky's tea. He would get sleepy and another member would bop him on the head with her cane. All seven of them could easily drag the body to the shooting range because at least one member still held her husband's membership, and then they all shot at him, thus diluting the guilt.

It was a great idea and one I was determined to pursue because it made so much sense in the Claim Jump universe. The residents of Claim Jump have operated exclusively in the moral gray area since the town was founded. Gold will do that. Think of the town name, it's based on stealing another man's land. Claim Jump, for all its color, is one big morally gray area. This situation with Lucky was just the most recent manifestation.

I wondered how I would go about getting them all to admit culpability.

"I want to attend a Cornish Brotherhood of Men meeting." I announced to my grandmother.

"We aren't meeting. What with all the funerals lately, we've seen each other enough. We've seen enough of each other, at least I have."

I tried to visualize Suzanne drugging Lucky and dragging him to the center of a deserted shooting range. She didn't seem the type, but I've been wrong before.

"We didn't shoot Lucky." Prue rolled her eyes, if that's what you're thinking. "None of us are members of the shooting range club, no key."

"You could have broken in," I protested immediately, wanting to defend my nascent idea.

"No sign of breaking in." Prue countered triumphantly.

"How do you know that?"

"Tom Marten told me."

"And when did he talk to you?"

She nodded to the parlor, "they're still in there you know."

"You are avoiding the question."

"He asked about that council meeting."

Just then, like the dependable court jester he was, Raul banged though the kitchen door.

I turned to my grandmother. "Lucky is dead and Tom Marten knows you threatened Lucky. What exactly did you say at the last council meeting?"

"Before or after I banged my shoe on the table and yelled that I would bury him?" She asked sweetly.

"Oh God." I groaned.

Ben touched me on the shoulder and offered me a kitchen chair. I didn't even want to look at him, he was probably grinning like an idiot, he loves my grandmother as much as he loves the still rough and tumble local politics.

No one bangs the table at a council meeting.

"I have video!" Raul said happily.

"Of course you do." I rubbed my forehead. My job sucked, my family was crazy. A nice island in Hawaii sounded good, maybe the one that use to house leapers. No one would visit. "You know, one of these days that hobby will get you in trouble."

"Already, many times," he said absently. He cruised through YouTube and found what he was looking for. He was fast; I give him that.

"See?" Raul logged on to You Tube and pointed to the grainy video. "There is Lucky, all lovely and alive, nice cane, that's his second best, the silver one. Prue, you film so well, there is your grandmother, Allison."

Yes, there was my grandmother dressed in a faded to pink Stanford sweatshirt and smacking her rubber clog smartly on the podium. The rubber garden clog didn't make that much noise on the speaker's podium, but bits of dirt flew from the sole for added effect.

"And what were we protesting?" Ben asked.

"Building with no permits. See? That's what Debbie Smith is bringing up, she was also arguing for restitution for the owners who lost their homes in the fire. But there is no evidence, so it's been difficult for them to make a case."

"For what?" I was trying to figure out how Lucky could build with no permits. Ah, he wanted to use the old permits since he was replacing the homes, which, in Lucky's world is different, that building new. Clever.

"The fire honey, there was no evidence that Lucky was in any way responsible."

"They say Danny Timmons was responsible." Raul said.

"He did it to make his point," I said quietly, certain.

All three stopped and regarded me suspiciously.

"You may want to keep that to yourself," Prue advised.

"And you say I jump into things." Raul shook his head.

"Can Lucky's estate even make restitution?" Ben asked.

"Oh probably, it would bankrupt the estate, but people like Debbie don't really care about that."

I looked at the video again. "Who is that? The woman?"

Raul squinted at the screen. "That? She is the famous Penny Masters, how could you not know that?"

"Allison runs in different circles," Prue remarked.

"Like the Brotherhood of Cornish Men." I countered.

"She's attractive," Ben squinted at the screen and then angled it for a better look. I elbowed him.

"Yes," said Raul sadly, "she is, but does not have the lovely personality."

Chapter Ten

Carrie and Patrick kept to themselves for the rest of the evening. I did not ask who flew Patrick over, I did not ask why Patrick didn't pick up Carrie and carry her back to his family compound in Sonoma. I did not ask anything. The two of them pow-wowed in the parlor until Prue gave up waiting around for resolution and asked me to help her to bed.

I escaped to our own pied a terre, other wise known as our apartment over the garage, to cuddle with my fiancée.

"In a pinch you do come with the oddest confirmation of our relationship."

"It was an emergency."

"Apparently."

We behaved like a happily married couple the rest of the night. Or at least what I think a happily married couple acts like; I don't have many role models.

Ben insisted on escorting Prue and me to the funeral. Patrick had to leave first thing in the morning, leaving Carrie behind.

"I'm coming with you." Carrie looked wan and pale as if she too was mourning a death.

"Are you sure you're up for it?"

"What am I going to do? Mope around the house?" she demanded.

"What did you and Patrick agree on?"

"Nothing," she teared up. "We have agreed on nothing. And he had to go. Business," she said bitterly.

"He does run a large corporation," I dug through the hall table and found a more suitable shoe for Prue to wear. I was tired of the garden clogs masquerading as formal wear.

"Yes he does, but aren't I more important?"

"Don't ask that," I recommended quickly. "Don't make him choose."

The funeral was not a boisterous affair, but it was large. Neither the Methodist nor the Catholic churches, as picturesque as they were, could accommodate the anticipated crowd. Penny was forced to hold the event at the county fairgrounds. Not to attend the funeral was a public admission that you did not approve of Lucky Masters and we all know Lucky did SO MUCH for the community, so everyone attended. The fairground was not such a bizarre choice; Lucky had pumped a great deal of cash into the fairgrounds in the late 80s. Resistance is futile.

The four of us drove to the fairgrounds that sprawled along the border of town. It was slow going with Prue's limp, we slid into the last row of folding chairs just in time for a sonorous and complimentary sermon delivered by a preacher I did not recognize.

I amused myself by looking around at the assembled. The hall was normally used to show off prize winning plants and baked goods. Today it was packed with Claim Jump residents, some of whom cared about Lucky, and some of whom just cared that he was dead and wanted confirmation. I recognized quite a few people, and I'm sure I was recognized in turn.

The reception, I read on a printed program, would take place in the Lucky Masters Building, just to the right of the Hall of Flowers. That building was designed to display sewing, photography and ceramics.

The service began well enough. Lucky was apparently in no shape to make a personal appearance. Penny had the body quickly cremated and interred. The police, Pat and Mike informed us, did not have any objections because the body was so damaged there wasn't much that could be discovered.

"Couldn't they find a hair or something and analyze it?" I asked Pat, who seemed to know about these things. "You know, do those magical forensics stuff where the blood stain pattern is counterclockwise indicating that the murderer was left handed and holding a butter knife with the edge pointed out?"

Pat gave me a pitying look, then quickly relented. "I asked that. Could they find bullets and match the gun to the bullet? That kind of thing. Tom just rolled his eyes and made a couple of nasty comments on the CSI TV series and told me people now think the police force can find anyone and do anything armed with only a microscope and tweezers. He told me that last week a woman called dispatch and said a bottle was thrown on her lawn and could the police come out and get a fingerprint and match it up to find out who threw the bottle?"

"They said no?"

"No, they can't do it at all, and judging from Tom's expression, they don't want to either."

The generic sermon finished, the preacher invited Penny up to say a few words. Penny spoke well of her father, choking back tears after each sentence. I felt, at that moment, very sorry for Penny. She had no siblings to argue with, no one to stand next to her. She really was all alone in the world.

I wonder who was named in the will. Would Summer get her Charitable Remainder Trust after all? I knew the content of a will was not for public consumption, but this was Claim Jump, word would get out.

I thought of Prue's performance at the most recent City Council meeting. She should have popped a vessel right there and this could have been her funeral instead of Lukcy's. But my grandmother was made of sterner stuff.

Summer approached the make-shift altar. A wood podium rested on two tiers of temporary risers set up across at the far back of the building. Four enormous wreaths on easels marched across the back of the risers. Summer stepped up to the risers but waited until Penny wound down. She laid a hand on Penny's shoulder as Penny slumped away from the podium. Tears sprang to my eyes, it didn't matter what the Brotherhood or my grandmother thought, losing your father -- the poor woman.

Summer exchewed the microphone and overtook the stage with gestures and dramatic voice inflection. She spoke eloquently about a man she clearly worshiped. Summer had not married, so again, no support system. But she looked better than she had at the hardware store. I was happy for her.

As Summer broke into the climax of her speech, Prue leaned into me and whispered, "my God, that's Danny Timmons widow."

Mattie Timmons hovered in one of the double-door side entrances. She looked exactly like what she was, a divorced mother of two who had taken one too many night shifts at the

Humpty Dumpty (oh, sorry, it's a diner, open 24 hours, one of the few things in town that is). Mattie was dressed in a polyester pants suit and very high heels. Her puffy down ski jacket was so wet the padding lay flat and looked crushed. In fact, everything about poor Mattie was beginning to look a little flat in the padding.

There was only one reason Mattie was here, to make a scene. Summer wound down, bowed and relinquished the stage reluctantly to the preacher. He retrieved the microphone and scanned the guests expectantly, ready to give another bereaved guest their fifteen minutes of fame.

"I need to say something." Mattie Timmons strode to the platform.

Had the minister been a local boy, he would have recognized Mattie, and known she was no friend of either Lucky or Penny. But he was from out of town, and allowed Mattie to snatch the microphone without protest.

Mattie took a deep breath and the mike squealed with feedback.

This whole free speech thing has gotten way out of hand. Can we have some ground rules? Like don't let the beleaguered divorced widow of the man Lucky cheerfully blamed for an huge forest fire that engulfed miles and miles of national forest as well as a thousand homes and at least three lives and whom, according to Mattie herself, would not turn any of the insurance money over to this particular widow, speak at his funeral.

The feedback receded. Mattie stood solidly on her high heels and gripped the microphone in both hands.

"He was a crook," she croaked into the mike. She pushed back her permed hair, bright yellow glowing under the overhead lights of the hall.

"He was a crook and a murderer and I demand someone do something about it!"

Her vocabulary was not up for this kind of denouncement. Neither was anyone else's. The room remained ominously silent, probably because this was exactly the kind of scene people hoped for when they dressed this morning and ventured out in the cold.

"He killed my husband!" She cried, squeezing out one tear.

Her ex-husband, really, why are the ex-husbands suddenly so precious after they die? Oh that's right, Danny was paying a crushing amount of child support each month, I remember now. She probably missed her ex-husband very much indeed.

"And Lucky did it. Those houses weren't safe, Danny tried to tell all of you, but you wouldn't listen! They weren't safe and Lucky got away with it and now Danny is dead and so is Lucky and he deserved it!"

I was pretty sure she meant Lucky deserved it.

Finally the preacher, minister, I really don't know, it was one of those non-denominational ceremonies appropriate for a fairground venue, roused himself from his stupor and plucked the microphone from Mattie's hand. He then led her off the stage into the waiting arms of Tom Marten

"He should be punished!" she sobbed. "He hurt so many people!"

There was a rumble of agreement in the crowd but no one ventured to speak up. Tom led Mattie gingerly out of the Hall of Flowers and into the rain.

The Lucky Masters building wasn't any more cheerful than the Hall of Flowers. Cool and inviting in the heat of the August County Fair, the cement floor and high-windowed halls were depressingly dim in the rainy March afternoon. Rainy days and Mondays. . . The ambiance was just marginally more uplifting than sitting at the New Century reception area and listening to Patricia, our receptionist, announce the catalogue of current murders in the Sonoma County area. Marginally.

Prue was noticeably limping in her walking cast by the time we entered the reception hall fray. I watched her efforts, she was our excuse to leave early, so I was determined to watch her carefully for the first sign of fatigue so we could make our exit.

Penny had indeed hired enough help to create as festive an atmosphere as appropriate. A number of her colorful quilts decorated the walls and brightened the place with splashes of emerald green, turquoise and hot red. Long tables covered by bolts of fabric in purple and orange complimented the colors in the quilts. It wasn't morning black, but the day and overbuilding size was quite gloomy enough. A half dozen hurricane lamps protecting fat white candles illuminated faces of guests as they bent to pick up a cracker or chip.

Prue headed to the drinks table. The rest of us, Carrie, Ben and me, followed her like so many members of her entourage.

Prue nodded to many people as she passed. I saw Tom Marten standing at attention in an opposite corner by of the doors. I nodded. He nodded back.

"Where is our hostess?" Ben asked.

Suzanne Chatterhill marched up to us and took Prue's arm. "We have a problem," she hissed in Prue's ear so loudly that I could hear.

"What?" Prue allowed herself to be led away, but not before gesturing to where she last saw Penny Masters.

The grainy City Council video did not do her justice. Penny Masters was a magnificent woman. She is taller than me, and thinner, which gave her the edge in the elegance department. She was dressed in a black pants suit with a brilliantly colored silk scarf in orange and turquoise dramatically draped over her broad shoulders.

Summer sidled up to us and glanced over to where I was staring.

"Does she find those scarves on her travels?" Carrie asked Summer.

"No she finds them at estate sales. She deals in antiques."

"But she doesn't travel?" I somehow thought she did. "Oh, sorry. Summer, Carrie, Carrie, Summer."

The two women shook hands. Carrie nudged closer to Ben and took his arm. "And you must have already met Ben, Allison's fiancé."

I deserved that. After all, I made her talk to Patrick. Carrie also thinks I should marry before she does because I'm older so she pushes her agenda at every opportunity.

"Can I get you some wine?" I knew his offer was less a coutesy and more an excuse to escape the three of us. Summer agreed, pleased. Ben disappeared, relieved.

"Did you see Mattie? I can't believe they let her in!" Summer pushed away her damp hair and glared at us as if we had something to do with Mattie's sudden and unwelcome appearance

"Is she still here?"

"Eating their food, not too holy to pass that up." Summer said with disgust.

"It doesn't look like the outburst was too upsetting to Penny." I was impressed with how composed Penny seemed. I barely made it through Grandpa's funeral in one piece, I was scattered to the wind, to the four corners of the earth, to the Milkly Way. I don't even remember feeling my body. For weeks I forgot to eat. Grief does odd things to people. I felt we should all cut Penny Masters some slack. From the looks of it though, maybe she didn't need any slack, or help.

"I take it you don't agree with Mattie Timmons?" I distracted myself from my own morbid thoughts and addressed Summer.

"She's just trying to extort money from Penny and Penny will have none of it. Just like her dad, in that respect."

I nodded and turned towards the wine table expecting to find Ben, but he was missing. I poured a couple of glasses of what looked like Merlot; one for me, one for Ben and scanned the crowd for Ben. Summer had wandered off to greet future donors. I sipped my wine, light and unimpressive. Ah, there he was. He had wandered too close to our hostess. Crap.

I was fully prepared to overlook any behavior on the part of the bereaved, but I drew the line at flirting with my boy friend, now fiancé and current roommate. I casually strolled over to where Penny was chatting up Ben. I tried my best not to appear obvious but I don't think it worked, because Ben greeted me with a huge, triumphant grin as I approached.

Damn, I'm so obvious.

"Well," Ben drawled right after flashing his shit-eating grin (colorful metaphor courtesy of my grandfather, who was top of mind)."Sure little lady, but don't you have people around Claim Jump who do that kind of thing?"

I arrived just in time to hear her say, "yes, of course." Penny hesitated, then placed her hand protectively on his arm, giving his bicep a little squeeze. "But you understand that around here, a handyman comes to work when he feels like it, or when the moon enters the right house, or the Age of Aquarius is in full bloom. Or," she took a deep breath and gave him a winsome look, "indisposed. It's hard to get things done on time."

"Ah, and you think I'll be more prompt?" The grin chased across his features again. I felt like popping him, but that would destroy my disguise of fabulous, calm, confident fiancée. Instead I offered him the plastic glass of Merlot. He absently took it, his eyes still trained on Penny.

Penny in turn, eyed Ben up and down. "I'm sure of it."

Ben loves to help, I know because he helps me, he helps Prue, he helps his grandmother, he helps old friends, some of whom I'm not all that thrilled about, but I am even less thrilled about him helping new friends: especially new friends who are taller, thinner, and richer than me. And who are wounded. Ben is a sucker for wounded.

I wiggled up and placed a protective hand on Ben's other arm. I hoped it wouldn't come to a tug of war, we were both sturdy women; Ben may not survive. But to my great relief she dropped her hand from his arm.

"Ah, here she is, Penny, have you met Allison Little. She's in real estate down in the Bay Area."

"Penny Masters," she responded, her handshake was on the flaccid side, which made me quite happy, I squeezed hard and gave her hand a tug.

"Nice to meet you and I'm so sorry about your father."

Penny nodded but didn't seem all that upset. Maybe she and Dad weren't all that close after all, I had assumed they were. And now she was an heiress, which is a wonderful thing to be, lovely parting gifts and all that. She could move away from being Poor Penny to Lucky Penny.

"Penny was just explaining she and Summer have an open house next Saturday and. . . "

"I'm worried about a leak in the plumbing and your," she continued.

"Fiancé," I supplied for the third time in less than a week. The word was fitting better in my mouth. Ben gave me a glance but didn't interrupt, and thank God, didn't grin at me.

"Fiancé," Penny repeated smoothly. "Offered to take a look."

"He's very generous that way," I said, "always willing to look into things that are broken."

Ben raised his eyebrows but did not comment.

We were scheduled to leave tomorrow, but with this new invitation, apparently not. I glanced back at Prue. She was balancing her wine and a plate of cheese. A piece of hard cheese slipped off the plate and Prue was forced to ignore it.

Okay, maybe I wouldn't be leaving tomorrow for a number of reasons, some of them valid.

"Is this the fundraiser for the theater?" I asked.

"Yes," Penny confirmed. "Summer and I didn't think it was right to cancel. Dad would have wanted us to move forward. You must come," she invited, a bit insincerely, but I ignored that.

I grinned again because sometimes I'm my mother's daughter and I can be polite, even if I don't want to. "We wouldn't miss it."

With that happy comment I led the fabulous, resourceful and helpful Ben Stone back towards Prue and the cheese.

"You aren't pleased?" He tried to look innocent but was completely unsuccessful.

"No," I snapped back. "I'm not pleased. She's a predator and you know it. *Check my leaking*, please."

"I thought I was suppose to make friends."

"Not that fast!"

He just chuckled, it was almost as if he wanted me to react, just to make sure I was still interested. Couldn't he just send a quick text? Interested? Yes. See how easy that is?

Prue's cheeks were colorless, her cheese selection remainded untouched. She had enough. I was not sorry to leave the scene. Ben didn't need prompting. He took one look at my grandmother and exited for the car. Carrie materialized by my side and together we protected Prue from the oblivious crowd as she made her way slowly to the side exit. The three of us huddled under the inadequate eaves as we waited for Ben to bring the car around. The rain had increased and was feeling suspiciously solid and chunky, but there was no snow on the ground. Nothing was sticking, that was good news for driving.

I didn't see her until it was too late and we couldn't retreat back inside because that would just make more of a scene. Mattie Timmons must have been waiting in the rain ever since Tom escorted her out.

"There you are!" Her hair was plastered to her face; her foundation was loosening its grip on her skin, unable to withstand the onslaught of all the cold water pouring from the sky. She approached us with what could only be described as a menacing walk.

"We're waiting for our ride." I said, hoping that would deter her from any more conversation, but I was thwarted by one of the members of my own team.

"You seem very upset." Carrie said in her best here, kitty, kitty tone. She may have given up volunteering for Forgotten Felines but she still had the rescuing skills.

"Well, wouldn't you be upset?" Mattie demanded. "He's dead and now he won't pay what Danny is owed, and no one is doing anything about it. Except her. She's gonna pay." Mattie jabbed a finger over our head in the direction of the building.

"I didn't know Danny was owed anything," I said. But after making her statement to people whom, frankly, couldn't do anything about her situation, Mattie had disappeared into the thick pines lining the parking lot.

"What was that about?" Carrie asked.

Prue placed a hand on my arm to steady herself. "There's an issue about insurance. Debbie is behind it as well. Mattie is her key witness. I heard that without Mattie there was no way to file a class action suit."

"Why make a scene at the funeral?"

Ben pulled up with a splash of tires and I struggled to help Prue negotiate over the muddy puddles and into the front seat of my Lexus.

"Why not?" Prue shrugged.

Chapter Eleven

Prue collapsed against the comfortable seats of my car. I sat in the back with Carrie who suddenly was embroiled in a furious bout of texting.

"Better reception here," she muttered.

"It comes and goes," I assured her.

"You know, Allison, Mattie Timmons is wrong." Prue's voice wavered from fatigue, but she carried on. "Tom Marten actually started to look into Danny's claims that the houses Lucky Masters built on Red Dog Road were substandard. He even went as far as to look into the foam insulation. He even called for samples but the company had gone out of business, so he didn't get very far."

"There are other ways to get information." I thought of all the work-arounds I had to employ to get answers from loan companies, banks and even from the clients. It was exhausting, but if you persist, you can always get what you want.

"It didn't matter after all, Tom stopped his investigation."

"Why?"

"Lucky paid for a new computer system for the department."

"That will do it," I acknowledged. "And now poor Tom has to investigate Lucky's murder."

"Everyone is calling for it, everyone is concerned."

"What do the members of the Brotherhood of Cornish Men think?" I closed my eyes; funerals make me tired.

"Well," Prue drawled out. "They aren't exactly happy."

"What do you mean? They have their quilts, the library is the hands of a compliant owner, what could be wrong?"

"Lucky recently promised to help us purchase more first editions and original documents for our research library. Now with Penny in charge. . ."

"You may have to invite her to join." I finished. Or kiss your first editions good bye

"That's why Suzanne was so concerned."

I'd say Suzanne was more than concerned; she was foaming at the mouth. "That makes this rather complicated."

"That makes it typical for Claim Jump," Prue pointed out archly.

Ben and I dropped off Prue at her house and Carrie volunteered to stay with her. I felt like we dropped off the kids so we could have an afternoon alone. I almost offered Carrie cash so she could buy a pizza for their dinner.

"There's a reception after the reception?" I asked.

"Penny said she was just inviting a few special friends to the house for a late lunch."

I knew perfectly well I was not the special friend. Prue make her feelings about Lucky quite clear, and poor Penny had always been caught in that deadly silence that washed behind her father as he plowed ahead to do whatever he wanted, no matter the cost. It was too bad Lucky was born too late to be a robber baron, that role would have suited him.

"And you are now a special friend?"

He shrugged, "guess so."

I should have been upset but I wasn't. How many times had I passed Lucky's house on my way out to the river? How many times had I admired the huge elm tree in the front yard on my way to the library? Yet I had never been inside. If I had to sacrifice Ben on the altar of the bereaved Penny Masters to get inside and check out this infamous house, then so be it. If we can't exploit our loved ones, who can we exploit?

Reception number two was a more intimate and elaborate affair. We were treated to a catered lunch and much better quality wine. The atmosphere, however, was not any more festive which can't be helped: it was a funeral.

Ben and I didn't put that much effort into mingling, I knew some people, and a few knew me, we nodded or said hello and that was the extent of it. I did chat with Leonard the owner of the local Coldwell Banker franchise. He was a short man dressed in a blazer and jeans. He told me he had handled the sale and purchase of most of Lucky's properties. He was sincerely sorry Lucky was gone.

"It's terrible, and the police have no clues."

"But how can that be?" I opened my eyes as wide as they would go.

"It rained Friday, I heard the body was outdoors for at least 24 hours." He shuddered, not because he was trying to impress me with his tender sensitivities, but because the thought of what poor Tom Marten discovered on the shooting range was gross and disgusting.

"I preferr to think of Lucky as alive, with his cane and his booming voice and attitude." Leonard drained his beer and glanced around searching for a place to abandon the empty bottle.

"But didn't he build substandard housing? I asked innocently. "I mean that fire was pretty unusual."

He gave me a less sympathetic look. "Nothing was amiss, it was a hot fire but that was attributed to the Manzanita bushes. Plus so many of those homes were illegal, no permits at all so there's no record of them. We can't make an assumption on the whole based on the few." He settled on the window sill and left his bottle there.

He had clearly crafted this point often enough so it sounded like the truth. I wondered what the home owners thought. Were they re-building? Was the rebuild part of the problem? Were the former owners and residents of the now admitted illegal housing rebuilding as well? I visualized shacks covered with blue tarps bought in bulk from Builders and Consumers. I could travel up the hill to check all this out, but rejected the idea as soon as it formed. The last time I had been at the top of the mountain, I had been fleeing for my life. Bad memories.

"Look, I know that that sounds harsh, but," Leonard paused, "are you from around here?"

"Mostly," I assured him. "I spent my childhood summers here."

He nodded, "then you know how many people moved up to the ridge or even just up Red Dog and Gold Mountain so they could build their own huts from reclaimed wood and reclaimed aluminum siding. It's crazy trying to sell up there. I don't blame buyers for avoiding any home with an upper Red Dog Road address. Who wants to drive by a scene from Deliverance on the way home every day?"

I nodded; my expression of encouragement was enough to keep him going.

"But there is little we can do about it. If we bust one illegal squatter we'd have to bust them all. And sometimes the homes are just barely in the acceptable code range, so it would a colossal waste of time. The squatters would be found compliant and we would have made an enemy."

"Just plant a fast growing laurel hedge." I heard that advice from Pat and Mike. Plant a hedge, so your own yard is surround by greenery and you can almost forget about the hillbilly encampment next door, except for the banjo music.

It was part of the charm of Claim Jump. Not the fast growing Laurel hedges, but the odd semi-homeless camps that proliferate throughout the hilly regions and mountains of the county. Don't mess with their dogs or their "organic garden" and you will be fine.

Leonard gazed at the coffered ceiling. A Venetian glass chandelier in red and purple glass dangled tantalizingly from the center. "Penny asked me to do a CMA"

"But there is nothing to compare the place to," I automatically protested. An estimate of market price was based on the sale of comparable homes within a certain radius. Lucky's house was located a block below the Methodist Church and the Library. His was the first in a series of homes, all dating back to the Gold Rush, that graced this side of Main Street and contributed considerably to the charm of the town but not one was anything like its neighbor.

Lucky had also over improved. The house was built to be imposing and he encouraged the delusion of grandeur. The building was crowned by a superfulous widow's walk and buldged on one end with a Queen Anne turret slapped onto the northwest corner. Yet, because it was old and located in downtown Claim Jump, tourists considered it charming and quaint rather than guady and overwrought. There were no other homes to compare it to. Not a problem if you are the owner, but a considerable problem if you are charged with pricing and selling the property.

"How many square feet?"

"About 3,000."

Prue told me this house was one of Lucky's first purchases, back when an astute buyer could snap up ramshackle leftover Victorian mansions for a song. My grandparents bought at the same time and for the same reason.

"How much does Penny think it's worth?"

"Two million," he admitted morosely. He clenched and unclenched his hands as if he didn't know what to do with them. I thought maybe he needed another beer.

"How much work needs to be done?" I loved the antique chandelier, but there was probably a lot of corresponding antique dry rot.

"A lot," he acknowledged. "The Pest One inspection is pretty extensive."

"So how much are you going to list it for?" Often the margin between the owner's idea of value and the market reality is vast and wide as a redwood tree.

He rubbed his neck as if to ease future tension. "She hasn't exactly asked me to list it yet. And I didn't want to push her, not today."

"Furniture?"

"Penny doesn't want it. We'll keep it for showing, the open houses, then see. I'll call Pat and Mike, they'll do an appraisal on the whole houseful."

"I thought that's what Penny does."

"Not like them," he shook his head. "They are the best in the county."

I nodded. The house with it's high ceilings, elaborate molding, and rosettes in the ceilings would show fine empty, but it would show even better if the authentic antiques that littered the floor were allowed to stay.

I hate antique furniture - very uncomfortable. Prue loved antiques and what she didn't love; Pat and Mike talked her into buying anyway. Which is why, when I visit her house, I sit on the floor.

I released Leanord with Coldwell Banker and poured another glass of Amador County Zinfandel from the generously stocked bar. I shook hands with Lucky's lawyer, Buster Porter because he was blocking my escape from the bar. Mr. Porter looked the part of a prosperous small town lawyer; someone who takes on the case of proving to small children there is no tooth fairy. We did not linger in each other's company.

The typical Victorian home in Claim Jump is a warren of small parlors and sitting rooms surrounded by tiny bedrooms and miniature closets that are pressed into service as efficiency bathrooms all encased by wood siding that seems to need painting every other week. While I may not agree with Lucky's exterior improvements, I liked what he did with the interior. The miniscule front parlors had been joined to create one gracious room. The back of the house had been extended to accommodate a more modern great room that flowed into a modern kitchen, perfect for entertaining, or in my case, perfect for the caterers.

I did not know if Lucky entertained or not. Prue never mentioned attending a party hosted by Lucky or even Penny, and this is a town famous for holiday parties and open houses. Maybe he always drove up to Penny's house and they kept the holidays quiet.

I sipped the peppery wine and gazed through French doors that led to the damp back yard. The property was about one third of an acre, small if you live in the country or up the forested hills, but huge for a downtown location. The yard was terraced and planted with things not yet green even in the early spring. The whole area was fringed by yes, the ubiquitous laurel hedge.

"Does it have a garage?" Ben pulled in behind me and blew on my neck.

I peered out the back window. "I think so, Lucky always drove high end cars, BMWs I think, he wouldn't want to leave those to the elements."

After taking Scott Lewis around, I noticed garages were a premium around here. For instance, the homes on lower Marsh Avenue that lined the elevated sidewalk not only lack garages, there was no room to park on the street. I hadn't paid much attention to details like that before.

"Sometimes life here can be a challenge," I admitted.

"There's a stairs to the widow's walk, do you want to explore?"

"I don't think that would be appropriate." I dying to climb to the top of the house, but what if we got caught?

As soon as we said our goodbyes (resisting the lure of the widow's walk), I called the office.

"I have a client," I began.

"Good," Patricia said. "Because if all you're doing up there is just licking your wounds and pouting, Inez will have your scalp."

"On the war path?" Thank God Patricia picked up the phone, at least she wouldn't lecture me.

"Has been ever since National's been coming down on her. Lucky for me there's not a national rubric or stretch goals for secretaries."

"Since when did you become a secretary?" She used to hate the term.

"Since it was safer," she said equably.

"I need to cancel all my floor for this month." I just blurted it out; kind of like ripping off the SpongeBob band-aid in one quick flourish.

"You were scheduled for four this month," she unnecessarily pointed out.

"Tell Inez that I'm working up here and can't come down."

"You only have one buyer."

"An escrow is an escrow." I repeated the chant we uttered every staff meeting.

"True," Patricia conceded.

"Thanks." I clicked off before she could protest.

"Okay," I said to Ben. "I'm here for the rest of the week."

"Good, I need to go to Penny's house first thing tomorrow."

Was that supposed to make me feel better?

My phone vibrated on cue. "I don't want that place after all, I want to look some more, and I don't want to just settle on the first place I see." Scott Lewis, just your average first time home buyer

"Of course not," I soothed. "How about tomorrow morning?" If Ben could be busy, so could I.

"That will work great, thanks!"

The tall library shelves towered over me, empty, but the ladder I remembered as a kid was still propped up against one of the bookcases. A person could, if she wanted, re-enact the scene in *The Mummy* where the girl knocks over a whole room of bookshelves like dominoes. I'd like to try that. I was eyeing the ladder wondering if it would hold my weight, when Scott startled me.

"Hah," he exclaimed, "I didn't squeak that time!"

"You'd make a great librarian." The song, Marian, Madam Librarian from *Music Man* flitted through my head. I think I played a small child in the opening crowd scene. Or I just watched it with Prue, I couldn't remember.

"No," he said. "I'd have to finish school to do that."

"You never finished school? "

He puffed out his cheeks and exhaled. "I haven't finished much of anything."

"Why did you buy this then?"

"Honestly? To create focus. Dad loved this town and it seemed like the right thing to do, to put down roots, or a stake in the ground. For the first time, the right thing to do," he trailed off.

"Then let's find a house so you can stay the course, shall we?" I sounded like a Victorian schoolmarm. Or better, a Victorian Egyptologist; my favorite literary character. "There are a few more homes left in your price range."

"Then let's spend more," he offered suddenly. "Can we look for houses just under a million?" Out of habit and reflex, I did the math. I'm up to almost two percent of a sale, unless headquarters rescinds that, so it was well worth squiring Mr. Scott around in the pouring March rain. Without question, worth spending the week at Prue's. Once Scott was in escrow, I could work from Sonoma County.

"There are about a half dozen homes in that price range, many in town."

"In town," he repeated seriously. "I don't want those big homes in Lake of the Pines or in that other area you showed me, Oak Glen."

"Oak Glen is nice," I started. In fact Penny's house was at the top of that "exclusive" development and there was a house for sale across from her property. But I had dismissed it as too expensive for Scott. Apparently my instincts were very two days ago. The criteria had changed. I was happy it changed for the better.

"Are you sure?"

"I'm not that fancy or elegant a guy, can you see me wandering around Oak Glen? I'd need a little dog and plaid slacks."

I grinned, that was pretty good. He was showing some spunk, and I always like spunk.

"No one in Claim Jump is that fancy or elegant," I assured him. "But we'll stay in town."

We ventured out again in the everlasting rain. I liked a house on Nevada Street, it had a deep porch, rolling lawn that was terribly impractical, but lovely to look at, and the kitchen looked like it could handle at least two caterers and their staff.

"Nope," Scott dismissed it, "too big."

I bent the corner on the sales flyer and shoved it into my purse.

The next house was too small; the next one was too dark. Two houses, despite their location and price, lacked the necessary garage. I trailed him as he walked through the empty homes. When the client knows, they know. My job is to watch for that moment and point it out.

"I'm sorry," he apologized after three hours. "I know I'm looking for something but I can't figure out exactly what it is. Does that make sense? That I don't know what I'm looking for?"

"We often don't know what we're looking for until we found it." I soothed. How was that? I could embroider that on a pillow myself.

"Where did your grandmother live?" I shooed him back into my car.

"What?" He held onto the door and gazed at me, water dripping into his eyes.

"Where did you stay when you came here with your dad?" I repeated.

"Gold Way," he said immediately.

Gold Way was a small street tucked up behind the elementary school. There were probably nor more than a total of five houses on the street.

"But there aren't any for sale up there." He looked at me with those big puppy eyes guys are expert at producing during serious clutch moments.

"Let me make some calls."

Chapter Twelve

Before we launched ourselves into the merriment that characterized Prue's kitchen, Ben and I shared moring coffee in the apartment. The rain drummed on the roof a cozy, rather than depressing ambiance. I liked puttering around the small space with Ben.

He eased his big frame into the vintage chrome kitchen chair and ran his hands through his hair.

"Penny has quite a place." He steadied the fragile table and leaned away from it completely. "The open house is next Saturday, we should go. You should see this house; it's as huge as Summer claims. It overlooks a deep canyon filled with pine and fir trees. Penny told me she watches birds fly under the porch that's off the study, it's that high up. There's a lot right next to her house that she said she'd sell it to me for cheap."

"I bet she did," I said coolly.

"I could build something like Penny's house, views, big rooms, we could each have our own study," he offered.

Over the course of my years selling homes, I have found there are two upgrades that actually improve a marriage: double sinks in the bathroom and two separate studies, so both partners have a room of their own, so to speak. Katherine admitted that she and her husband have separate bedrooms too, but that didn't sound romantic to me.

She said, just wait.

"Did Penny offer to help you plan the house as well?" It wasn't difficult to picture the two of them, circling around each other in Penny's spacious house, leaning over blueprints, laughing and drinking wine.

"She has great taste," he said unabashedly.

"Oh fine, we can be neighbors, that's a lovely idea. We can have a potluck every Friday," I said sarcastically.

Ben grinned. "You are jealous. That is such a compliment. I wouldn't worry about it, Penny was fine, a little scattered and the problems she needed fixing weren't that serious. I think she's nervous about the event. She was fussing over every detail. She swept and scrubbed the fireplace twice while I was there. I heard her order the flowers, then she remembered she needed vases so she hunted all over the house and only found two she liked, you know that kind of thing. She's a little brittle."

"Okay." I said grudgingly.

"I love you, you know."

"I know," I pouted.

"I'm your fiancé, you know."

I glanced at my left hand; he didn't miss the gesture, but didn't comment either.

"I'm going back right before the event just to make sure everything works." He admitted.

I took a breath and worked on being an adult. It took all my concentration. We headed out of the apartment sharing an umbrella for the quick walk to the kitchen.

"Okay, be nice to her," I finally conceeded. "She probably needs a friend. But why is she doing this at all? Summer cancelled a show right in the middle of the production. Why don't they just cancel this as well? Her father just died for heaven's sake, people will understand."

"I asked that question myself. They sold too many tickets to out of towners, with no way to get hold of them to pass along the news. Plus, they don't want to return the ticket sale cash. Summer and Penny are adamant that Lucky would want the tour to go on as planned." He pulled out a flyer from his jacket pocket and handed to me as we entered the warm kitchen.

Beautiful home custom built by Lucky Masters himself. I read. *Designed by famous local artists. 380-degree views of the valley and mountains. State of the art kitchen, seven bedrooms, nine bathrooms, pool and waterfall. Gardens were featured in May 2008 issue of Sunset magazine.*

"Impressive." Tickets sold for $50 each and included a champagne reception hosted by the Penny herself.

"Especially the view." Ben pointed out.

"What? Oh yes, I remember when Lucky built on the side of the hill. He denuded a couple of acres of forest to do it, people were not happy. My grandfather was part of the protest group."

Prue looked up at the mention of grandpa's name.

"No, not that. Look at the flyer again."

I looked again. *380-degree view.*

"That's very good," I said happily.

"Isn't her office like in a loft surrounded by windows?" Prue asked.

"I don't know; I was under the house looking at pipes."

"We must go on the tour."

"It's for a good cause," Prue said.

"Everything done in Claim Jump is for a good cause," I intoned.

Ben glanced at his phone. "I'll get this in the front room." He disappeared from the table.

Carrie gave me a quizzical look; I shrugged my shoulders. I do not monitor Ben's business.

"I need to go back up to Penny's this morning." Ben returned to the kitchen. "She's having trouble with her pressure."

"I bet she is," Prue reached out for the flyer.

"She has no one else to call?" I asked archly.

"Apparently she doesn't have many friends."

Prue snorted, "she doesn't have many friends because she's a bitch."

"If you kept bitches out of the Brotherhood, there'd be no one to attend the meetings." Far from aggravating her, she laughed.

"Point well taken. She's an odd duck that girl, rarely leaves that huge house except to drop off quilts to Summer who dutifully auctions them off, then Lucky ends up buying them and keeps them at the theater."

"Or library."

"Or library," Prue agreed, she rubbed her eyes.

I should be upset with Ben for leaving again to take care of another woman, especially when I should be the one who was nurtured and cosseted, oh, hell, that's not me at all. I encouraged Prue to take a nap, I instructed Carrie to call Patrick and just start apologizing for everything and when she was done with the real stuff, apologize for imaginary stuff. I waved Ben off to help yet another damsel in distress. It would be idiotic to try to change him now.

"I love you." He kissed the top of my head.

"I love you too. Bundle up, it's getting colder."

"Will do. I'll buy tickets for Saturday while I'm up there."

"Four." Carried snapped her phone shut. "I left a message for Patrick to come up for the weekend."

"Good."

Carrie twisted her ring. "I hope so."

"You should marry him." Carrie said after Ben slammed the door behind him.

"Eventually. I don't know; will I be the second wife? Or even the third wife? His first wife didn't meet a very good end."

"That had nothing to do with Ben," Carrie protested.

"You're right, it's just, I don't know how many marriages he's had, or how many relationships. Or how many women he's helped. He's very closed mouth about it."

Carrie rolled her eyes. Being the better friend, I ignored the implicit sarcasm.

"And now he's busy with another woman's pipes." I rubbed at a sticky spot on the table. "It's going to get complicated, you can picture it - his people, my people, pre nups, my mother, his mother . . . "

Carrie furrowed her brow and focused on the ceiling.

My inch of the table clean, I looked up. "Oh lord, you signed a pre-nup didn't you? I told you I'd hire a lawyer, why didn't you take me up on it?"

"I don't want to be that way." Carrie insisted. "I don't want to be the woman who married Patrick for his money and his lifestyle."

"But you ARE marrying him for his money and his lifestyle." I protested. Did she not remember her plan? Had she forgotten how focused she had been? How she had cut Patrick out of the herd as if he was a wounded calf? Was she unaware that her plan completely and utterly worked? It had worked, except she honestly fell in love with the boy, which oddly, meant all previous bets were off.

The good news? Patrick was so in love with Carrie he can't even think straight when she's around. I know; I saw it myself. He flew up here didn't he?

"What are the terms?"

"If we ever divorce, all I'll get is ten million."

"You are one of the few women I know who could actually get by on ten million."

"It's not even a real number. I keep the ring too," she added. "I know you don't approve, but it was worth it to see the sheer relief on the Furies's faces when Patrick announced that I signed."

Carrie refers to Patrick's two older sisters as the Furies.

"Okay then, it's your life," I conceded.

"It could stop before it starts!" She moaned.

"Have you called?"

"Every hour."

"Have your parents called?"

"Every half hour, they have nothing better to do."

"Are they calling Patrick?"

"He promised to screen his calls, that's a start. He's met them, he now knows what they are capable of."

"I don't see the problem."

"He's screening my calls too."

Chapter Thirteen

"I really do think they are dying." Sarah whispered into the phone receiver.

Her grandparents would not hear her over the blast of the 6:00 news, but she kept her voice low anyway. The commentary on the broadcast rankled, but her grandfather loved the hysterical conservative views that Sarah found repugnant. But since Sarah insisted on helping her grandparents fill out their absentee ballots, her liberally inclined conscience was clear. Grandpa could rant all he liked; he had voted Democrat in the last three elections.

"Honey, haven't they been dying for years now?" Her mother's voice both weary and indifferent.

Sarah glanced into the living room. Her grandparents had sunk so thoroughly into the sprung confines of their matching recliners, she couldn't tell where the chairs ended and their collapsed bodies began. She could hear her grandfather's labored breathing from where she stood in the kitchen.

Sarah sensed her mother rolling her eyes. The few hours her mother wasn't high, she was cynical and angry, especially when the discussion centered on her parents. The only reason Sarah ever called was to deliver an update on those very parents. The conversations were rarely cheerful.

"Come on, do I have to? Didn't I see them at Christmas?" Her mother whined like a teenage girl.

"No, you did not see them at Christmas, you had an emergency and couldn't come down." An emergency for her mother was running out of gas so she couldn't drive down to visit, and by the time Sarah sent up the money for gas, her mother had run out of drugs and subsequently used the gas money for more drugs. And then had no money for gas.

It was an effective system for avoiding the parents.

Sarah rubbed her eyes and leaned against the doorframe. Dorothy Gale had a whole village of people to take care of her, watch after her. Sarah relished that role, the role of the girl who had people willing to help her: The Tin Man, the Cowardly Lion, the Scarecrow. Dorothy had friends, even at the end of her adventure. What did Sarah have?

"Don't do it for them." Sarah said, her last ditch effort to actually be the adult even if her mother, and grandparents for that matter, refused to co-operate. "Do it for yourself. You can't afford the amount of drugs it will take to wipe out the guilt you'll feel if you don't visit one last time."

She knew what it was like to miss the good-byes. She liked Danny Timmons and his friend Jimmy. Even though they were much older than she, they had always been nice to her. And suddenly they were gone, just like that. No final words, no good bye. You can't live that way. If you can, say good-bye. Sarah knew that.

"Just for the afternoon, I think it's important," she begged her mother.

"I could probably fit in something during an afternoon. I'll have to check my schedule."

"Oh sure, your schedule." Sarah did not bother tempering the sarcasm in her tone.

"Sarah, we can't hear the TV, they got all quiet on us again! These men need to speak up."

She hung up the phone. "I'll be right there."

Tom stopped by right after Ben left.

Prue offered him coffee and a place at the table, Tom gratefully accepted.

"Help me out here. What did Mattie Timmons mean when she said Lucky killed Danny?"

"The insulation in those homes is flammable." I said. Someone had to say it out loud but Tom did not seem particularly surprised.

He nodded. "We think so too, but since the proof went up in flames as well, there's little to go on. No records, Lucky destroyed all his records prior to 1995."

"Mattie has proof, from Danny." I offered.

"I also heard rumors he started the fire."

I thought so too, but I also knew Danny had raced back into the conflagration to save someone who was at least more innocent than Ben, or me, and lost his life in the effort. However that fact was tempered by the fact that Danny was also willing to sacrifice Ben in that same fire. He was about morally even in my book.

"I don't have anything to say about that," I said virtuously.

"That's fine, don't. Penny filed a restraining order against Mattie Timmons. She was up at the house this morning."

"Mattie was? Was she threatening Penny?"

He nodded. "Mattie Timmons is also a member of the shooting range. She was a crack shot in high school; they started a High School team just because she was so good. I talked to George out at the range. He said she came there a lot right after the divorce. It's a great way to let off steam."

"So I hear."

"How about recently?" Prue asked. Tom nodded in her direction.

"I asked too. A couple times this month."

"Who monitors the sign in sheet?"

"Honor system."

"Of course."

"Is Mattie a suspect then?"

"She makes a great suspect," Tom admitted. "But we have no proof and I can't arrest someone on rumor."

For which we all should be very grateful. I glanced at Prue, who looked as pious and innocent as she could, which is to say, not very.

"Lucky organized the range so there was a membership fee and more control. He used to bring Penny out here, a real father/daughter activity."

"Was Penny a good shot?"

"Not really, she wasn't as enthusiastic about the sport as Lucky. Since her mother died, they really didn't get along."

"That's why she had that house on the hill and Lucky lived in town," Prue commented. "Lucky always liked being in the center of things. The new house was too far away for him."

"Still is," I agreed.

Tom took his leave. Carrie helped Prue upstairs for a nap and I started calling local real estate agents. For the right price, people will sell their homes, even if the home is not officially for sale.

"Anything can be had for the right price." I pressed the keypad on my phone.

Carrie appeared downstairs. "What about love?"

After a gratifying short time, Ben returned. "Are you up for a social call?"

I was alone in the kitchen, Carrie followed Prue's example and was upstairs resting with her eyes closed. An hour earlier I checked on both of them and covered each with an extra quilt.

"Sure. Who are we calling upon?"

"Mattie Timmons, I cannot believe that she is as bad as Penny says."

"Penny was ranting about Mattie? I would think Mattie would be too small a fish in Penny's pond to even merit notice."

"Nothing is too small for Penny's consideration." Ben closed his eyes. "No wonder the woman never married, I don't think I could get through even a whole dinner with her."

His admission cheered me no end. "Sure, I'll come with you, but, full disclosure, I am not her favorite person."

"I know," he agreed. "She must realize by now that you and Danny were a long time ago."

"I hope so."

Mattie lived in one of the suburban tract developments popular in the sixties, before historic homes became all the rage in Claim Jump. The house had been well cared for at some point in the past. Danny must have come by even after the divorce. But now that he was gone, the house was started to fray at the edges. The grass was uncut, the windows were dusty and a number of roof tiles were missing.

Mattie answered the door looking much calmer and dryer than when we last saw her. Her crinkly blond hair was well fluffed; the black strands underneath contrasted starkly against the blond.

"Oh, it's you," she frowned, her expression falling into well-grooved lines on her face. "Come in then." We followed her past the kitchen to a living room decorated in bold beige that overlooked a bedraggled lawn. Red dirt showed through where the grass had worn away. A wooden swing set stood forlornly in one corner.

"I'm sorry about the funeral, but no one was saying it." Mattie perched on the edge of the beige sectional. We chose to sit on the two remaining beige chairs.

"Saying what?"

"That Lucky Masters was a first rate bastard."

"That is exactly why he donated heavily to the community, so no one would say it out loud," I pointed out.

"Then why didn't he buy me out?" She whined, suddenly petulant. "Danny was almost killed twice by Lucky's shortcuts."

"Did you know what the shortcuts were?" Ben asked quickly.

She crumpled and slumped over the ottoman. Some of her self-righteousness and thank goodness, whining, stopped. "It wasn't until after the divorce. We didn't talk much, and Danny kept to himself, I suppose I don't blame him for that. Lucky promised him job after job and that was enough to keep the poor bastard quiet. But it's not right, Lucky owes me and now Penny owes me."

She was right; Danny had tried to tell me. The insulation Lucky used for his tract homes was cheap, but not safe. It was in fact, flammable; one small kitchen fire hitting a wall, any wall, and the whole house would go up like a firebomb target. Most communities banned the product, but no one here knew about the insulation in the first place. Plus, Lucky's work was never that closely monitored. Danny discovered it and was killed before he could bring it to anyone's attention. But Danny was not killed by Lucky directly. Mattie was wrong about that.

"Do you have any proof?" Ben asked.

She slumped even further forward, her raw rough hands dangled between her knees. "Danny didn't share that much with me. He always gave me child support; he was good about that. But now? Nothing. I had to go back to work . . ." she trailed off. "I hate Penny."

"That's understandable but it doesn't sound like much of a case."

"Now you sound like Tom Marten."

"Tom Marten is right, you may want to keep your distance from Penny." Ben counseled.

I glanced at him, he was more than serious; he was warning her.

But I could not tell if Mattie was really listening.

We returned to the car and I threw it in second to climb Mattie's steep driveway.

"Do you remember we picked up all that insulation I had on my hands?"

"After you pulled the door off the hinges to escape a fiery death? That insulation?" That was the last time Ben had visited Claim Jump, Danny, ironically was part of the problem then. At the time, Danny mistook Ben for a housing inspector, and Danny did not want to take the fall for Lucky's shortcuts. So he decided on the spur of the moment that Ben should take the fall.

"You make it sound so melodramatic," he teased, "It was a flimsy door, and the fire was at least five minutes away."

"Thanks, that makes me feel so much better."

He waited. I turned the corner and headed back to Prue's. "Check the glove compartment."

He did, after pulling out handfuls of unnecessary AAA maps of places I no longer visited, three emergency lipsticks, a small travel size hand lotion, gum, mints, notepads and scratched New Century name badges, he found a flattened baggy wedged in the back corner of the compartment.

"Don't you think it's a little risky to just drive around with a baggie of white powder in your car?" He waved the folorn thing at me.

"Not really, it's not pretty and sparkly enough to be coke, it looks more like corn starch and that's not yet a controlled substance."

He hefted the bag. "We can tell the story, but that won't hold in court or in favor of a class-action suite"

"No, no it wouldn't."

"I'll take it down to a friend of mine in Davis, he can be the expert witness, if it comes to that. Will you be okay if I'm gone overnight?"

"It's Claim Jump, I'll be fine."

"Just stay off the shooting range, and out of Penny's way, and don't sell any home filled with this," he rattled the bag then slipped it into his pocket.

"I'll be careful." I promised.

Chapter Fourteen

I should have been worried that there was a murderer lurking around the community, ready to strike again, but I was pretty certain this was a one shot deal, so to speak. I was still convinced that a whole group of residents were responsible for Lucky's death, which meant the whole town was crawling with would-be murderers. Perversely, I felt safer for it.

I picked up my phone and walked around the apartment until I found enough bars to make a call.

Tom answered on the first ring. "It's after hours."

"This is not official business."

"Allison." His voice held a note of warning. I had no rights, Lucky wasn't my father, but Penny wasn't asking questions, so I would.

"Was the body tied up?"

"No, but we did think of that," he said with exaggerated patience.

"Do you have any leads?"

"Would I tell you?"

"No, but you may as well."

"We have no leads, it's a bizarre accident, we may never know."

"Aren't people clamoring for justice?"

I heard him blow out a breath. "We're talking about Lucky Masters here. Penny isn't pursuing the situation and Summer just discovered the theater will be generously endowed. No one is protesting anything."

"So you are going to write it off?"

"The mayor would like that. Just bury the whole event along with Lucky and, as she put it, allow his good works to stand for themselves."

"Or not."

"Or not," he agreed.

"Did you get very far with the cause of last fall's fire?" I switched subjects.

He paused and then cleared his throat. "We hit a dead end there too; no evidence."

I thought of Ben driving to his friend's lab in Davis. I did not bring that up, I don't know why.

"If you had evidence, would you open the case again?"

His pause was even longer. "Lucky's insurance agency would like to know, and a pack of attorneys would like to know. But you know if there is a class action suit, like the kind Debbie is working to organize, all Lucky's money will go to the plaintiffs."

"Instead of the theater?"

"Instead of the theater." He agreed. "Instead of the Children's Festival, Instead of the music hall for the high school, instead of the tympani drums for the symphony, instead of overtime for the police to organize the Constitution Day parade. Instead of a long list of things."

"Thanks."

"Stop calling me at home."

I returned to the deserted kitchen in the main house to work on my computer, the apartment was out of Wi-Fi range. I skimmed the web for further reports on Lucky. As annoying and sometimes scary as our receptionist Patricia was, she was excellent at researching the web. I had half a mind to call and ask for her help, but there was no excuse I could use. Lucky was not a New Century client.

"What are you doing?" Carrie padded down wearing a pair of my grandfather's thick socks.

"Looking up information on Lucky Masters, what are you doing?"

"Mourning what could have been."

I wondered, did they say anything about finding a cane at the scene? I scrolled down and read the local news report and blog but there was no mention of a cane.

"He always carried his cane," I said out loud.

"What does that have to do with anything?" Carrie snapped.

"Someone needs a cookie." I continued to stare at the rows and rows of sentences and letters willing them to form an answer to questions I didn't know yet.

"It has to do with Lucky's ambulatory status at the time of death," I finally said out loud.

"What?"

"Did he walk out to the shooting range himself or was he carried?"

"Like tossing kittens in the lake," she said unexpectedly.

"Yes, yes. It doesn't say if the body was tied or bagged. Tom said it wasn't tied. Did the killer find him napping and without waking him, dragged him to the shooting range so a good twenty or so citizens of Claim Jump could plug him full of holes?"

"Drugged?"

"Doesn't say."

"Sometimes they don't," she pointed out. She was right, it used to be that the fourth estate would helpfully print everything about a murder or suicide or killing of every kind. Now reporters were more circumspect. Evidence was withheld so the real killer could be discovered; I had run into that technique myself before.

The sky was dark and forbidding on April Fool's Day, on odd day to schedule an event, but I was not in charge.

Patrick did fly in for the weekend; he and Carrie were as frosty as the weather. But we loaded them into the back of my warm car anyway, ignoring their sidelong glances and glowering expressions.

I felt like a mom with recalcitrant children who minutes before boarding the car, refused to participate in the field trip. The good news was that I found a great new dress to wear. The bad news was that like a ballerina who has to wear a sweater over her costume for trick or treating, I had to pair the light jersey dress with winter black boots and my heavy coat. I was cranky, the weather was oppressive and cold, and Patrick and Carrie did not utter a word the whole trip up the mountain.

Ben's news didn't do much to cheer us either. He returned Friday afternoon just a few hours ahead of Patrick. Carrie and I were oddly unenthusiastic about our loved one's homecomings.

"Thirty voice mails from my parents." Carrie announced. She deleted them all. "I don't know what they want from me. I don't know what Patrick wants from me. Some kind of happy reconciliation? They won't change, and I wouldn't trust them if they said they had."

"A note from an AA sponsor?" I suggested.

"Even more than that." Carrie was my fabulous, liberal, caregiving, kitten saving friend. She makes Mother Teresa look like nothing more than a publicity hound. Carrie saves everything and everyone who crosses her path. But her charitable propensities did not begin at home.

"Maybe they just want to reconnect."

She gave me a withering look. "I've been drinking Cooper milk all my life, this is not lost on my parents. They want a cut, they want money."

"Can you give them enough to get make them stop harassing you?"

"There will never be enough money for extortionists," she said. "They would never leave me alone. I already know that."

"What about Patrick?"

"He's coming."

That was all she said on the subject.

Ben's news wasn't remarkable or dramatic or even very helpful. The insulation was flammable. Great. We knew that. We had a signed statement from a real research professor, but we still did not know what the hell to do with the information. Especially since no one really wanted it.

It was a low point in our visit. Patrick, who burst into the house with a blast of icy air, was a welcome distraction. To her credit, Carrie immediately greeted him in the hall.

Ben listened to for a moment. "I think we should all take Prue out for dinner. No one can misbehave in the presence of a grandma figure."

He was right of course. Patrick would never make a public scene, and Carrie wouldn't put Prue through anything embarrassing, not in such a small town. We grimaced and made small talk and chatted as much as we could to get through the evening.

The open house event was a relief.

Penny's house, built on upper Gold Mountain, was located in an exclusive area called Oak Glen. Lucky developed it and sold it as the only place anyone who was anyone could possibly live. I remember reading the ads in the Sunday *Chronicle* when I was little, even then I remembered thinking, Claim Jump? Exclusive?

But enough wealthy former Bay Area residents took the bait in the eighties and built their monstrous dream homes with views well under 380 degrees. Penny's house was the crown jewel in the development.

We drove though an elaborate iron gate, open for this event, and past dogwood trees covered by delicate pink and white flat flowers. Penny's house sat at the top of a crest surrounded by similarly sized homes: some built in Tudor style, some built to resemble Queen Anne, all pretentious, none very funky. One prairie style home was enhanced by a blue Coldwell Banker for sale sign waving next to the mailbox built into a stacked stone pillar. I could show that to Scott tomorrow. I squinted at the front door.

Ben saw what I was doing, and dashed to the house.

"What are you doing?" I called after him.

"Checking for a lockbox."

He quickly returned. "There is one on the front door. You're good to go."

Penny was stationed at her front door, greeting the guests like the good hostess she was, or at least aspired to be.

"I want you to sell my father's house." Penny stated right after I said hello to her in her foyer. "Ben says that you are the best."

She batted her eyes at Ben as she said it.

"Yes, I am, but what about Lucky's friends? Your dad was in the business, he must have a number of Realtors who could help." Good, Allison, now you're deflecting business. What was wrong with me? But I couldn't snatch a listing from someone like that nice Coldwell Banker guy, Leonard. Leonard liked Lucky, and he'd probably do a great job at selling the place.

Would Scott want Lucky's house? It was only a few doors down from the library, short commute, beautiful place, historic as all get out, riddled with character.

She ignored my suggestion. "Will you do it?" she continued to squeeze my hand, not hard, she wasn't capable of that, but insistent. I suddenly understood Ben's position better. Penny didn't give a person much time or space to consider her proposal or even say no.

"How much do you want for it?" I acquiesced. I agreed with Leonard, there was no way to comp the house, and no way to put a price tag on the former home of the murdered Lucky Masters. I would either have a stampede on my hands or I'd have to call in professional psychic cleaners to run around the house with smudging sticks. I was already mentally ordering the plastic statue of St. Joseph to bury in the back yard.

"Lockbox?" I asked, hoping I could borrow one from the New Century office; maybe they could share Inez's percentage if they helped me.

"Of course," agreed the daughter of a developer. She knew the score; I'll give her points in her favor for that.

"See me tomorrow." Penny dropped my hand and walked away. Her work was done. I wasn't sure if I was flattered or deeply insulted.

"See?" Ben came up behind me. "There is nothing you can do, resistance is futile."

"What just happened?" Carrie asked.

"I just got a listing." I said, still feeling a bit stunned. "This will make Inez and the national office happy." And at least this time the dead body was not located IN the house.

"You're selling Lucky's place?" Carrie asked. "Won't people just be curious and tramp all over the house?"

"Of course they will; I would. But morbid curiosity can sell just as well as perfection, and Summer is practically across the street at the theater, she can shoo away the merely curious."

"What about privacy?"

"You don't buy a huge house like that and expect privacy," I lectured. "You live up here for privacy. The buyer can always plant laurels in the front yard."

As if on time, I spotted my client, Scott Lewis. Sarah Miller was with him, not holding his hand, but hovering close by. I wondered what the members of the Brotherhood would make of that.

"Hi," I greeted them both.

"Hi Allison, this is Sarah Miller."

"Hello Sarah." I shook her hand, it was rough from housework, but she returned my grip with equal strength.

"Hospice is with my grandparents, or rather Melissa is with them, I didn't leave them alone just so I could come to this," her words tumbled out as if I had accused her of neglect and I was thinking nothing of the kind.

"You have a great reputation for caring well for them," I soothed.

"I wanted you to know that Lucky's house is officially for sale," I told Scott.

"I remember his house," Scott said. "Dad and I liked walking around the town when I was a kid, just imagining the lives of people who could afford just marvelous places. Dad said that Lucky's house reminded him of the movie *It's a Wonderful Life*."

I wondered if it was the house, or Lucky's attempt to turn Claim Jump into Lucky Town, just like Potterville.

"Yes," I agreed. "It does have that feeling of a grand house. I have a couple of calls in for Gold Way."

"Thank you for letting me know. Hey, how about a breakfast restaurant?"

"No."

All the niceties, the greetings and business accomplished, we split up. Ben took Patrick's arm and they wandered off to the right, Carrie and I wandered to the left. The house itself was beautiful with Craftsman flourishes, tile and enough wood paneling to reforest Stern Grove. Lucky had removed most of the surrounding forest to build the house, it was a small comfort to imagine he had put all that wood back into the house.

As naturally stunning as the place was, what was more eye catching and impressive were all the quilts. The house was packed with Penny's hand sewn quilts. I recognized them; they looked like the ones hanging over the library shelves and gracing the brick walls of the theater. Red and blue quilts covered bedroom walls. Green and umber quilts doubled as shower curtains. Quilts lined the upstairs hallway. Every bed in every bedroom was covered in an elaborately pieced, perfectly color matched, hand crafted quilt.

"These are fantastic. Look at the variation in the Wedding Ring pattern; I've never seen that. And the gradations in the Log Cabin." Carrie put her hands on her hips and surveyed what was the smallest guest room. It looked like the guest room in my house - unused.

"These are amazing," Carrie stroked the quilt. "Where did she get them?"

"She makes them." It was one of the few pieces of information I was certain of.

"Really? The woman who owns the house?"

"Incongruous?"

"She doesn't strike me as the domestic type."

We listened to the other guests in adjacent rooms oohh and ahh over the quilts. We slowly threaded through the crowd and made our way back to the main floor. We met up with Ben and Patrick in the living room. It was a large space with a soaring 20-foot ceiling dotted with glass. Very impressive, but it held no charm.

To the right, over by the front foyer, Summer stood at a table piled with quilts. A hand lettered sign announced the quilts were valued at $500 apiece, checks to be made out as a donation to Summer Theater. She was doing brisk business. Now there was a good fundraiser. Carrie and I approached, not able to resist something for sale.

Summer looked much better this afternoon, her hair was slicked back in a more restrained bob, her lipstick was bright red and mostly intact. "It's about time, Lucky never allowed her work to be sold, as if they couldn't leave the family! But now, this will make Penny's reputation."

"Did she ever enter in the fair?" I thought of the banners of quilts hanging along inside the Lucky Masters Building.

"All the time," Summer confirmed, "She told me she started making quilts right after her mother left, in the early eighties. It was terrible. Her mother died soon after."

Summer shook her head. "I just can't imagine, the poor thing. You know what Lucky told everyone? That his wife was unstable."

Unstable: as if life was only about successfully balancing in your first pair of high heel shoes.

"She used to decorate the house on Main Street for every holiday, Lucky was once very proud of her, but gradually things became worse and worse and she had to go away, but to lose your mother." Summer shook her head.

I did not have an answer to that, because I had no reference. Two women clutching three quilts each pushed up against me. I stepped aside. "You look busy, I'll catch you later."

Carrie paused next to the huge river rock fireplace and frowned. Considering how much surface area in the house was covered by quilts in one shape or another, the area above the fireplace was conspicuous by its lack of decoration.

"A quilt must have hung there." Carrie gazed up at the bare space.

"It didn't necessarily have to be a quilt," I pointed out. "Penny could have just retired a very large, aggressively poor painting. Maybe Lucky gave it to her as a gift and she was finally able to throw it out of her house."

At that moment Penny entered the living room. She was dressed in a deep brown sweater and matching slacks, the color complimented her auburn hair and pale skin. She marched over to our little group.

"What happened to the quilt that hung up there?" Carrie asked Penny.

Penny's eyes traveled up to the blank space and then quickly looked away.

"Damaged. Careless of me, but there you go, sometimes things get hurt."

The fireplace was cold, scrupulously cleaned, my mother would approve, all ready for summer. Except it was only the first of April. There was still a chance for snow. Penny must have an efficient central heat system; maybe she didn't need the fireplace except for show.

We all stood and gazed at the fireplace for a moment, then Ben and Patrick exchanged glances. "Okay, let's go, we have appointments to keep, people to call, deals to make."

Carrie and I both looked at the men in surprise, but we kept our mouths shut.

"But you'll miss the luncheon," Penny protested, "Stay, you won't be sorry."

With that order, she left us again.

I glanced around the crowded living room. The house was now packed with people huffing and puffing, dressed for the cold outside and overheated in the warm house. I recognized a few locals, a couple Brotherhood members. Suzanne Chatterhill stood in a corner quizzing poor Scott and Sarah. I made a move towards that group to save the kids when I caught a glimpse of blond hair and bedraggled ski parka.

"Come with me," I whispered to Carrie. She followed me without a word. Patrick and Ben were still standing in the living room; Patrick was muttering something about his phone. I could have told him there was no reception up here.

"Mattie," I greeted her as quietly as I could.

"I tried to talk to Penny about the you know what," Mattie whispered.

"What are you doing here?" I demanded. "There's a restraining order out on you."

"This is a public event," she pulled out a damp ticket stub. "I paid the entrance fee."

"Oh, good, especially since it's for a worthy cause." I glanced around. Carrie, skilled in years of fundraising experience, knew a pending crisis when she saw it. She moved forward and took Mattie's arm. We both hustled the woman into the kitchen. The Sacramento caterers ignored us.

"What are you doing here?" I whispered, trying to sound fierce and stay quiet simultaneously.

"She won't answer my calls." Mattie whined. She shrugged out of her damp jacket and held it in front of her like a cloak of invisibility – it wasn't working.

"Oh, you think?" My frustration with the woman was rising along with my heart rate.

"She knows, but won't admit it." Mattie shook her jacket for emphasis.

"Admit what?" I grabbed a shrimp wrapped in prosciutto and pesto off a passing tray and popped it in my mouth.

"That she knows about that cheap flammable insulation Lucky blew into every house, probably even the one she's living in, the bitch."

I didn't think Penny was a bitch for living in a beautiful house, but she could very well be a bitch for the covetous eye she kept casting in the direction of my, let's try it again, fiancé.

But I did not burden poor Mattie with that information.

"She said I couldn't prove it, and Lucky already gave us money."

I swallowed too quickly. "Wait, he gave you money? Why didn't you mention this before?"

She shrugged, her bra strap slipped down below her tank top. For the occasion she wore what must be her best tight Wranglers and paired them with a massive silver colored belt buckle.

"He already paid you?"

"Yeah, right after the funeral he came to the house and wrote me a check for $10,000 as a condolence for Danny's death."

"He didn't have to do that you know," I pointed out. "You were divorced, you weren't the beneficiary or anything." As if I knew all about those details.

"But," she said, reasonably, "the money is gone now."

I groaned inwardly.

"And Penny told you, no more," I confirmed. I took a slice of bruschetta as it passed by. Now I needed a drink.

"Can you believe it?" Mattie demanded. "And here I have, what's the word, incriminating information, proof of that negligence."

"Did you learn that word from Debbie?" I guessed

She nodded. "We could get all those home owners to sue, it's called a Class Action lawsuit."

"Where's the proof?" I asked, suddenly tired of all these accusations that didn't add up to anything. Ben and I did have proof, yet it didn't really help the situation, not when Tom spelled out some of those, what do you call them? Unintended consequences.

"I have proof." Mattie said suddenly, her expression was smug. "I have it where no one can find it."

"That is never true," I said automatically.

"In comming," Carrie sang out.

"Come on," Carrie and I steered Mattie from the kitchen; we each grabbed another prawn on our way out. A light dusting of snow covered the back kitchen garden. I swallowed my prawn, delicious, and looked at the snow again as if it was a new experience for me.

"Where's your car?" I asked moving Mattie around the side of the house. She slipped on her jacket; tiny dots of snow decorated the surface. She nodded to a pick up parked a half a block away.

"Stick with Debbie," we all moved towards the vehicle. "Just do what she says and stop working on your own." I helped Mattie unlock a faded red Toyota truck a stand out among five different models of Subarus, and bundled her in. "Debbie clearly knows more than we do."

She nodded and threw her car into gear.

"Out back," Carrie said quietly. We both pasted big grins on our faces and enthusiastically waved good-bye to Mattie's parting car.

"Good bye, thank you, we'll be in touch!" We called various versions of sentiment as the car careened on a slippery spot, recovered and pulled out of sight.

Penny marched up just as Mattie disappeared.

"Possible donor for the theater," Carrie said immediately.

"From out of town," I explained quickly.

"The prawns are fantastic. Who is your caterer?" Carrie took Penny's arm and hustled her back into the house. "I'm getting married this fall," I heard her begin to explain. But I didn't know if we got to Penny soon enough. She may have recognized the car.

I trailed behind. I knew enough not to interfere with Carrie when she was on her concerned philanthropist roll. Her propensity to help others at all cost almost got me killed over Christmas, but that hasn't slowed Carrie, and truth be told, I don't retain many lessons I've learned through experience myself. So I followed.

"Tell me more about the quilts." She had linked arms with Penny and the two walked back towards the house. The snow increased, the tree tops, what was left of them, were obscured by low clouds.

"My father didn't approve," Penny confided.

"Parents can be quite a problem," Carrie pulled open the kitchen door and we once again disturbed the caterers.

Penny must have heard the sincerity in Carrie's tone, I sure did.

"Do you know what he did once?" She paused before entering the living room. "My mother had to go back to the hospital for a rest and I was all alone, again. I found this cute kitten, its mother was gone too, so I thought we could keep each other company."

Carried gripped Penny's hands.

Penny drew in a breath. "My father thought it was too much trouble, he grabbed it from me and got rid of it."

Carrie's eyes opened so wide she looked like a waif painting.

"Oh my God, you poor thing." Carrie spontaneously hugged Penny. The sudden contact startled her, but slowly, slowly, she responded. She awkwardly patted Carrie's back.

"What kind of monster does such a thing?" Carrie asked quietly.

"A successful one." Summer had snuck up on the scene and whispered in my ear.

"Here," Penny marched into the living room, pulled a quilt draped over the couch and bundled it into Carrie's arms. "For you, take it."

"But I couldn't!" Carrie immediately protested. "It's too beautiful, you can sell it along with the others."

"It's okay, we've already sold twenty," Summer announced happily.

Carrie looked longingly at the substantial quilt sagging in her arms.

Penny nodded and tossed a folded quilt at me. "There, now you each have your own."

Startled, I glanced down at the purple and red colored fabric swirled around a center of gold. Carrie was right; these were stunning, certainly original.

"Think of them as lovely parting gifts" Penny smiled ironically. "I can't use them all."

We took the quilts, bowing gracefully, exiting quickly.

Chapter Fifteen

Ben and I couldn't help overhearing the two of them. I didn't think Patrick ever raised his voice; he probably never had to. Even now Carrie was doing the job for both of them.

"Unstable? Unstable?" she shrieked. "That's all you think they are? What the hell do you know?"

There was a murmur from Patrick but apparently Carrie was not mollified.

"I'll tell you, Mr. Perfect, my father molested me! Are you satisfied? Is that the answer you expected?" Her voice cracked. "That's not unstable, that is criminally insane."

Another pause then Carrie started up again. I know it sounds like the rest of us, the three left in the house, were eavesdropping, but the sounds were coming at us at an assault level, there was no escape. And it was snowing outside, it's not like we could take a nice walk around the block.

"What was there to report? I was sixteen, who would believe me?"

She was right. Plus, in the past, like just last week, if a girl was the victim of abuse or rape and she did manage to work up the courage to report it, all it accomplished was to put her on an endless loop of telling the horrible story over and over to ostensibly caring adults who only wanted to hear the gory details. Carrie long dismissed the practice as barbaric and prurient. She told me she just refused to participate.

"And now they think they can get away with anything. It stops now!"

"Wow," Ben breathed. "Did you know this?"

I shook my head. "Part of our pirate code is to never force your friend to relive the painful parts of her past." I looked down the dark hall. The snow outside fell faster, the wind knocked at the windows. "All I needed to know was that she had a bad childhood and her parents were awful, that was enough for me."

"You aren't damaged, that's ridiculous." Patrick had finally raised his voice.

"When do we tell him the roads are closed?" Ben asked.

"They may not care," I said.

Ben squinted at the snow piling up outside. "Think we'll lose electricity?"

"It's more romantic that way," I acknowledged.

The snow in the foothills doesn't rage. The snow doesn't cascade down in a sudden blinding white storm. We don't live that far in the interior of the continent. We are still west of the Sierras. Here, the snow is slow, but unrelenting. It just floats down like a slow man paid by the hour, just doing his job.

For the intrepid and those who are comfortable with installing snow chains, then removing the snow chains, then installing them again, snow is not a real problem. The snow piles up just gradually enough to give even the most reluctant of us about an hour to get out of town and head for lower, snow free, altitudes. The other option is to give up completely and blame your own inactivity on the weather.

"Stay in the big house," Prue commanded. "I don't want you freezing to death if the electricity goes out."

"This place is rather fraught with natural disasters." Ben commented.

"No earthquakes," I pointed out.

"That's why we have gas heating and a gas stove," Prue shot back. "But the apartment is all electric. Remember that," she addressed me with the kind of authority I save for my first time homebuyers. "When you buy up here, remember to get a gas heater and a gas stove, you'll thank me for it."

"I am not moving up here." I protested.

"Go make up the back bedroom," Prue instructed. I wondered if Patrick would need his own room.

Carrie and Patrick strode into the kitchen. Patrick looked pretty commanding given he was dressed in jeans, sweater and was barefoot despite the cold. His normally coiffed black hair was in complete disarray. He looked rather irresistible.

Except for the fact he was really pissed.

Carrie, to her great credit, did not back away. She followed closely behind him.

"Thank you for your hospitality," he said formally. "But I need to go now."

"Nope," Ben said cheerfully.

"What?" No one says no to Patrick Sullivan. I could tell.

Ben gestured to the snowfall outside. "We're stuck and with any luck," just as he said that, the electricity did indeed go out.

If this were a murder mystery, someone would scream. But I controlled myself.

Chapter Sixteen

Patrick stopped as if we hit him with snowballs, not just simple information.

"Stuck?" He repeated into the dark.

Prue flipped on two electric lanterns, on hand for just such a contingency. I trip over at least one of those things every summer. Now, I will no longer complain.

She flipped them on and bathed the room in dim yellow light – not flattering to any complexion. I took one of the lights and handed it to Patrick.

"Stuck, as in no one gets out, and no one gets in."

Carrie carefully approached Patrick from behind. Her ring glinted even in the low light.

"In times like this, it's best to just go to bed," she offered quietly.

Patrick wrinkled his handsome face, then just as quickly, relaxed. "Okay then, it seems I have little choice." He studied me for a second. "Did you plan this?"

Ben laughed. "She would be queen if she could."

I would very much like to be the queen and run the world as it should be run. But not tonight, I did not manage the snowstorm all by myself. But it was a pretty great idea.

Carrie slipped her hand carefully into Patrick's. "Come on, I know the way."

He followed her; the light disappeared as they made their way upstairs.

"Now that was romantic," Ben said with approval. "I'll get our stuff."

He took the second lantern and plunged my grandmother and me into darkness

"You should marry that boy." Prue called out of the dark.

"Because he's a Stanford man?"

"That certainly helps." Prue acknowledged. "But I've never seen you this in love, you get upset if he looks at you cross-eyed."

"Do not."

"Yes, you do."

"Okay. Okay."

I glanced outside searching for the wavering of Ben's lamp. Brick and Raul had hunkered down in the guesthouse as soon as the weather turned. Pat had called but knew the house was full of helpers, so there was no need to come up the street.

"So you'll marry him? Have the wedding here. In June, that's enough time. Pat and Mike can help."

"Not this June." I gestured upstairs even though Prue couldn't see me. "She comes first, her wedding is the first week of October and then we'll go from there."

The lantern illuminated the kitchen as Ben struggled for the door. I leapt up and opened it. Ben wanted to cohabitate, as an advancement towards the abstract and far in the future idea of marriage. He had not agrees to a wedding, we had not discussed a honeymoon, we did not have a ring. And since those were more or less hard facts, I didn't think it was wise to engage a caterer quite yet.

Sarah loved the snow and was ready with extra quilts and a small fire in the freestanding stove in the living room in case the electricity went out. It was a pellet stove; ugly, but did the job when the electricity went off. She stoked the fire, and covered grandma and grandpa with the thick down quilts she bought at Costco a few years ago.

"You're good to us," Grandpa murmured. "Everyone who listens to Lucky is good."

"You are very lucky I'm here." Sarah said briskly. Every once in a while she said it out loud, but knew they weren't listening and couldn't really hear her even if they were.

She kissed their heads with dry lips and hurried upstairs. Some evenings she was able to stay awake long enough for an hour or two for herself. She kept a battery-fueled lamp in her bedroom and planned to read into the night.

The light still glowed strong when she woke hours later. She glanced at the clock; it was black. She listened. Absent power, the house didn't hum with the accustomed background noise. She only noticed how noisy her life was when all that ambient sound went missing. No refrigerator motor, no electric heater, no TV, no hum of the digital clock. The streets were silent; there was not even the usual low level humming from the streetlights.

The silence grew around her.

She listened for a second longer, then tossed off her covers. The satin quilt cover made a huge noisy scratching sound in the silence of her room.

She picked up the lamp and quickly padded downstairs.

The pellet stove was dark, no glowing embers. The room was chilly but not freezing, she was thankful for that, she hadn't let the stove go for too long. She automatically stoked the stove and re-lit it. She turned to her grandmother to adjust the quilt, but then quite suddenly realized how silent the room really was. It was the complete lack of sound that woke her. The snow muffled all the sounds outside, like insulation. She lifted her lamp higher and carefully placed a hand over her grandmother's slack mouth, and felt no breath.

She did the same with her grandfather, no breath, no sound.

The stove clicked as the metal warmed up again.

"It's too late." Sarah said out loud.

She moved towards the phone, but the hand-held was dead. No charge on the set.

Sarah did not own a cell phone. There was little point. Her grandparents always knew exactly where she was and what she was doing. The gossip in town was more effective than a GPS chip. Sarah pulled her robe closer around her throat. There was nothing she could do at this hour in the morning.

She slowly climbed the stairs back to her own bed, now cold.

Sarah woke to the snow. She allowed a sigh to escape as she regarded the empty street, decorated with wet, March snowfall. Did she want it to all change? It would change, she knew. A flood of activity was banked up, ready for her to say the word and allow events and activities and expectations to engulf her and carry her forward. She wished she had some idea what she would do when she hit land.

She glanced at the clock, still black. She was unable to remember what was scattered around her small apartment: a tiny kitchen she did not use; a living room decorated with a love seat and a television for the odd nights when she didn't drop to sleep as soon as she climbed up to her rooms; a phone, that's what she was thinking of, a phone. She rose stiffly and dragged the heavy, slippery quilt from her bed. She wrapped it around her shoulders; it trailed behind her like a colorful train.

She picked up the handset of the avocado green princess phone sturdily connected to the wall. She dialed in the first memorized number that came to mind.

Scott watched the snow fall from the library windows, it was early morning again, he was quite the morning person now. The light was a gentle white color a bright wash over all the empty shelves and old flooring in the former children's area.

He flipped on the lights but the white light didn't change. He flipped the switch back and forth like a meditation. Ah, the power outage ploy. He had only visited Claim Jump in the summer months, he never experienced this kind of weather, but he had heard the stories from his dad.

Scott turned and trooped back down the stairs and regarded his little car. Sporty, red, low to the ground, the car would be perfect if he was still living in LA or in Dubai. An inch of snow covered the car; it looked very picturesque. He kicked the tires, as pretty as it was, it would not get up the hill to where Sarah was surely stranded with her grandparents.

He turned up his collar and trudged carefully down the slushy sidewalk of Main Street. He'd walk to her. At least the walk wasn't all uphill. He glanced around the stores as he walked. It was too early for even the tiny grocery store to be open. Did they open with the electricity out?

There didn't seem to be that much snow, not enough to cause a power failure. But the consistency was, he noticed, more slushy and heavier than the powder at Tahoe. Maybe it only takes a couple feet of this weighty snow to pull down the power lines.

Sarah's house was not very far. Scott turned into Grove Street. The narrow street was choked with cars and snow. The small driveway was just large enough to host an old brown Oldsmobile. The car was covered in three inches of snow.

He glanced at his phone; it was barely seven o'clock. Were there rules about early calls? Was he crazy to think that she'd even be up? What about those grandparents? He hadn't heard much about them. Sarah always deftly turned their conversation away from her and back to him and his travels with his dad. To Sarah, Scott's peripatetic lifestyle was romantic, interesting and far more elevated than he deserved. It was not of his doing. Very little in his life was of his doing.

But he was doing this.

He banged the doorknocker. The sound was muffled by the snow outside, but echoed through the house well enough.

Sarah jerked the door open, the knocker swung and banged for one final time.

"You came! I just called. There was no answer. Then I couldn't remember if the phone at the library was connected to the wall or if it was a handset and if the charge had gone out. You can call out of course but what if the other phones can get it? And how would you know if someone is calling? I couldn't even leave a message. I'm so glad you're here." She backed up and he stepped forward out of the chilly air.

"Are you okay?" He stomped his boots on the mat, water puddled around his feet.

Sarah looked terrible, her blond hair was matted and messed, she had grabbed a ripped sweatshirt that should have been be tossed in the trash years ago; it wasn't even good enough to donated. Under the threadbare sweatshirt, she wore a yellow tee shirt with a neckline that was stretched and thinned. Her sweatpants were stained, and she shuffled down the hall in socks three times too big. If he didn't know better, he'd say this is what a person looks like after surviving a real tornado, class four hurricane, or an earthquake, not just a night without electricity.

She must have noticed his expression. She deliberately ran her hand through the tangle of her hair and made a gesture towards straightening her sweatshirt.

"I really didn't sleep," she admitted. A long stairway rose up to the right. To the left, a narrow wall separated the entryway from the living room. Since he had viewed a number of homes in the area, he knew that originally there was no wall dividing the front door from the main living room. The whole room welcomed the guest at the front door.

This home had been divided into apartments.

"Sorry, I didn't mean to wake your grandparents." He lowered his voice. From what he gleaned from her and her nervousness when she spoke of her guardians, they weren't the most forgiving or flexible of people. Yesterday, he delivered her back to her house just five minutes late. It was because of the increasing snow, so not her fault, but she was frantic none-the-less. He didn't want to get her in trouble again.

"I wanted to see if you needed help, you know, because of the electricity." He finished awkwardly.

She wrung her hands and stared at the closed door.

"My grandparents died last night," she blurted out.

He took a step back. "Both of them? Oh my God, Sarah, I'm so sorry, what can I do?"

That was the right thing to say. She brightened a bit.

"Do you have your cell phone? Does it have a charge?"

"Do you have reception?" He was learning about the foothills. He pulled out his phone and squinted at the tiny bars. He was good to go.

"Who do I call?"

"Suzanne Chatterhill." She rattled off the number from memory and he dutifully punched in the numbers. He handed the phone to Sarah so she could do the negotiating. He wasn't quite brave enough to take on Mrs. Chatterhill so early in the day.

I woke to the sound of the ringing phone; no ring tone can replicate the sound of a real phone rattling off in an empty kitchen. Or not empty, the phone stopped on the third ring. Prue was up? I groaned and rolled over and grabbed Ben's phone, seven fifteen. Rather early for a social call, but sometimes the calls in Claim Jump were not social.

I struggled out of bed, leaving Ben where he was. He smiled in his sleep and rolled into my abandoned spot. Now he could rest comfortably.

I pulled on what was handy and staggered downstairs. It was only when I reached the dim kitchen that I realized there still was no electricity.

Shit.

"No, no, you're right to leave them there, the coroner can take them. Do they have insurance? Plot picked out? Ah, good."

Prue limped to the calendar hanging on her now silent refrigerator. "Tomorrow? Are you sure that's not too soon? Oh, they have an opening. Of course."

She listened for a minute and nodded to me with a finger on her lips. "I'll bring the deviled eggs. No trouble."

Prue gestured to a cabinet and I pulled out a classic two-cup espresso maker, Italian, lifesaving.

"I told you, the gas still works." She flipped on the stove to demonstrate. I packed in espresso grind, filled the base of the coffee maker with freezing cold water and prayed to the Starbucks gods to forgive me.

"Who was that at such an ungodly hour in the morning?"

"Suzanne Chatterhill of course. The Millers passed away last night."

"Because of the cold?"

"Because they were old."

"I thought they were younger than you." I blurted out, which demonstrates why I should not operate my life before a good amount of caffeine is delivered into my system.

Prue ignored me and gestured to the refrigerator. "Get out the dozen eggs and we'll boil them up right now. I'm bringing eggs to the funeral service."

"Which is?"

"Tomorrow. The church had an opening."

"Difficult to schedule funerals." I pulled the eggs out of the dark refrigerator. "Death can be so last minute."

"You have no idea."

"Whose funeral?" Ben blinked and automatically glanced at the espresso maker. I pulled it off the gas and poured three cups then refilled it so we could do it again.

"Sarah Miller's grandparents. Suzanne called all the right people so the girl will be taken care of. They can't reach the daughter, the lines are iffy on the Ridge and she may not have a real phone at any rate."

"Most of us just use our cells." I said, a small defense of Sarah's mother.

Ben emptied his mug of coffee and held it out for more.

"Not yet."

I loaded the eggs into a pan with water and set that on the stove while the second round of coffee was percolating.

I looked out the window while I waited for water to boil, I knew enough not to watch the pot. Outside about five inches of snow glittered in the growing morning light. Cars came down the street slowly, chains clanking, clanking. The outside was muffled in cotton. The whole world looks so pristine before the first shovel takes to the driveway, before the first anxious path is cleared to the car. Snow is so lovely in those first precious minutes before we have to get organized and figure out how to get to work. But in this minute, there was a soft peace all around us.

"Do you think they made up?" I asked.

"Yes," Ben yawned, "about as well as we made up."

Chapter Seventeen

The hearse blocked the whole street. Neighbors who in the past just nodded to Sarah without saying anything more, helped direct traffic and explain to the drivers of two trapped cars that it will only be a another minute or so. The trapped drivers, neighbors as well, abandon their cars to watch, their feet getting soaked in the slushy road snow.

Scott started out by just holding Sarah's hand. He felt it was an important job, and he was right. As a gurney loaded with a black bag pushed through the front door, Sarah cried and sagged against him. Scott held her close, his arm around her, his other hand steadying her as best he could. It was cold, but he knew she was colder inside than outside.

Hell of a thing. He wished he didn't know exactly how she felt.

The second bag was rolled out, Suzanne Chatterbox following close behind.

"Here," she handed Sarah a list; bullet points for emphasis, many items already check off and completed.

"I called most of the Brotherhood. You don't need to worry about food for the service, just come at two o'clock."

"They didn't want a service or anything." Sarah said faintly.

"Nonsense, the service isn't for them anyway," Suzanne said firmly. "Do you want to call your mother or should I have Maria Johnson continue to call?"

"That would be good." Sarah's voice was small and faint.

Finally Suzanne turned her attention to Scott. "Here is your copy." She thrust the list at him and he took his obediently. Suzanne took in the two of them; Sarah leaned against Scott who, for the first time, looked like an adult and able to handle his responsibilities.

"Take care of her," Suzanne instructed. "Remember, the funeral is tomorrow at two o'clock, Methodist Church."

"They were Baptist," Sarah's voice was a little stronger.

"The Baptist minister will be there," Suzanne checked another list. "The Methodist church is easier to get to in this weather."

Scott's phone beeped. Suzanne looked at him disapprovingly and she marched off.

"That was the Northern Queen. They have power."

As if in answer, the living room lights in the house flared on.

He squeezed her hand and gently pushed her to an upright position. "Do you want to stay here?"

She took a deep breath. There was nothing left to do but weep. She squinted at the house and considered her position. She squared her shoulders and marched back inside. She flipped off the lights avoiding the two chairs. She found her purse and her keys, slipped on her grandfather's galoshes and walked back outside to Scott.

"I'll come to your place."

Prue took an envelope from Maria Johnson who had her cell phone glued to her ear and couldn't stay for coffee. She just waved and moved on intent on whatever Brotherhood task she'd been assigned.

I made up another batch of coffee for Carrie and Patrick. They emerged on cue, Patrick looking adorably disheveled and Carrie just looking adorable because that is her job.

She still wore her ring. I could shine a flashlight through it and light up both our kitchen and the kitchen across the street. So the behemoth diamond was still with her. At least all was well in that department.

Prue made steel cut oatmeal on the aforementioned gas stove, because everyone knows to buy a house with a gas stove in case of a power failure.

I asked the obvious question in order to banish the elephant in the room.

"What are you going to do about Carrie's parents?"

Patrick took a sip of his coffee, grimaced. Carrie pushed the carton of milk towards him and he glanced at the label, and then poured it into his cup.

"Clearly, we can't ignore them. So I called them yesterday and invited them to participate in the wedding, you know fully as the bride's parents, and gave them an estimate of what their half would cost. Just the rough numbers, we haven't firmed things up with the caterer yet."

"Who's catering?"

"Thomas Keller, he's doing it as a favor to Dad, but I added in what he normally would charge, if you could get him to do it."

"Of course." Thomas Keller was such a famous chef I was surprised he even had time to cook anymore.

"What did they say when explained the price of being part of the family?"

Carrie grinned. "Patrick was wonderful! There was this big silence, so Patrick talked about how much he respected their desire to be part of the family and be full partners in the wedding process, and of course they should be in the wedding and Patrick could help Dad buy a tux because the rentals never fit quite right."

"Do you think that will do it?"

"Not at all." Patrick drank up his doctored coffee. "So I brought up our own family tradition: if the groom's family pays for the wedding, then the bride's family pays for the honeymoon."

"You're the first to be married in your family," I pointed out to Patrick.

Carrie nodded. "They don't know that. So we began making suggestions for honeymoon destinations, like Istanbul or to the Galapagos or I suggested a cruise to Easter Island on a private yacht.

"What did they say?"

"Nothing. They got off the phone in a hurry."

"It's not the end."

"We know, but we won a battle, and that's important."

Once we ate, and washed up with cold water, the question was, what can be accomplished with no electricity? I could make phone calls, and intended to, but my unfortunate habit was to shower and be clean before I worked, and I felt grimy and gritty and unwashed. I was not taking a cold shower. What Prue did not mention is that even though the water heater is gas, the pilot light is electric.

"Poor Sarah." Prue finished rinsing the last oatmeal bowl and handed the chilly bowl to me to dry.

"Will she be okay?"

"Yes, but she is such a lost soul."

We stood around while Patrick called the airport. "They have electricity, I'll need to leave."

We waved him away. He opted to shower at home.

Just when I was considering which book to read, we were interrupted by another call.

"Who?" She paused then handed the phone to me.

"Have you seen Mattie Timmons?" It was Maria Johnson, who would run out of cell charge soon if she wasn't more careful with her calls.

"Why would I know where Mattie Timmons is?" I responded.

"We saw you talking with her at the funeral, then at Penny's open house." Maria said, matter-of-factly. "Have you seen her lately?"

"As in yesterday?"

"Yes. Her babysitter called and Mattie hasn't picked up the children. Of course the phone isn't working. School is closed, but still, three more children is a lot more children."

"I'm not taking the kids," I defended myself immediately.

She paused. Ha! I knew it. I stood my ground. "I have to work with Sarah to figure out her house plans." I offered, just so she knew I was contributing to the general community effort.

"I'll call Michelle," Maria said after a minute or two.

"Thanks for letting us know." I hung up the phone. "We should visit Mattie Timmons."

Prue stayed home, I gave her the job of sitting by the phone in case anyone called. What an antiquated concept, sit by the phone. The power came on just as the three of us left. I felt we were abandoning Prue but she waved us away. "Just come back quickly, I want a hot shower."

The drive was slow; we all seemed to want to silently regard how the white and pink dogwood, once confident of spring was now weighted down by wet snow.

"Good thing it snowed after the house tour," Ben remarked.

The house looked the same. I could see the wood ripple under the eaves and grain of inexpensive lumber emerging from under an increasingly faded coat of paint.

"Not the best side of town," Carrie concluded.

"No, but she was keeping it together."

Carrie squinted at the shabby house. "Wasn't her husband in construction?"

"Not so you could tell." Ben confirmed.

"She works at a dentist office." I remembered Danny told me she had a job but still bled him dry for alimony anyway. His passing did not make her life any easier. It was enough to drive a woman to murder.

"What if she's dangerous?"

"Oh please, with three kids?" Carrie brushed past me and banged on the door.

My phone buzzed, on cue. I glanced down. It was my mother. If she wanted to call the house, she could. Then I realized Mom probably had called the house and Prue, true to her name Prudence, had not picked up. My grandmother did not have anything as high tech as caller ID on her wall mounted princess phone, so how she knew not to answer her daughter's calls was nothing short of voodoo magic. I shook my head in awe of my grandmother, and let my mother go to voice mail.

"Hello! Anyone home!" Carrie banged the door again then pushed it open.

"You can't," I started to say, just walk in, but changed my mind. Ben and I trailed behind her.

The short hall branched to a kitchen on the right and the living room on the left. I remembered the long sliding glass doors from the living room led to the back yard. I glanced at the dimly lit yard. Ben flipped on the kitchen lights and they blazed in white-hot fluorescent splendor. A second later the TV in the living room popped on, three lights down the hall turned on.

I felt like primitive man, look fire! Look moving pictures!

"Mattie!" I called, "the power's on." Just in case she was hiding in her bathroom and needed to use her curling iron for a hair styling emergency.

"Mattie!" I called again. Ben walked to the back of the house and quickly returned. I held my breath for a minute; I do not have good luck with master bedrooms and bodies.

"Not there."

I let my breath out. I turned towards the living room. There was no one in the living room to appreciate the morning news (top story, power outages across the tri -county area). Ben picked up the remote and snapped off the TV. I glanced around. I saw a few toys, a video game consol on top of the TV, a DVD player. I was surprised the TV wasn't a new flat panel model. People may not be able to pay rent, but they manage to pay installments on what is really important, a big screen. Not Mattie. I kind of admired her for holding out.

"What's that in the back yard?" Carrie asked.

"A swing set," I replied. "Toys."

I glanced out the window. A lump the size of a person was awkwardly positioned on the back lawn. It was covered by an inch of snow. The back outdoor lights cast a yellow glow on the figure, making it look almost human.

It was human.

"Oh crap," I said out loud.

"Better call your friend," Ben said.

Tom Marten made good time.

"I suppose you are here under the auspicious of the Brotherhood?" He was justifiably suspicious.

"This or take the kids."

He tucked his notebook back into his jacket pocket. "You chose wisely."

Tom didn't try to keep us away, but did politely ask us not to muddy the already muddied and snow covered body and surrounding muddy evidence. I didn't see why we couldn't stomp around; kids, animals, and the weather had already effectively destroyed what was left of the yard.

"The killer could have come in the back or the front." Tom observed unenthusiastically. "Shit, and those kids." He dragged his hands down his face.

"The front door was unlocked." I pointed out helpfully.

"No one locks their front door in this neighborhood," Tom said dismissively. "Too much trouble to remember to bring along a key. I keep telling people if the door's not locked, it's harder to collect insurance if they're robbed. But they don't listen. Especially if we went to school together." He kicked at a soggy clump of grass.

"She had evidence. She told me." I said.

Tom looked at me with a gimlet eye. "She told everyone."

"Didn't that bother Lucky or even Penny?" I asked.

"Debbie was prepared to do something about it, but I don't know if Mattie ever gave Debbie her evidence. Maybe not." The grass clump broke free and he pushed it aside.

"Summer is depending on that CRT," I pointed out.

"A lot of people are depending on the largess of Lucky, now that he's gone," Tom responded.

"Is that bad?"

"I told you, it makes it more complicated."

If a class action suit was successful, there would be nothing left for the town. Without Lucky's money, Summer may have to shut down the theater, the Brotherhood wouldn't be able to afford more books; the police wouldn't get any more laptops.

It was very complicated indeed.

"Then who?"

Tom squinted at me. "Everybody?"

Mattie did have family; there were people, other than us, or the members of the Brotherhood, who could take over. Tom looked more haggard than usual. I told him so.

"Lots of dead bodies."

"At least the Millers died of natural causes," I commented.

"Debbie actually confided in me that she thought they were killed to keep them quiet."

I frowned. "That is a stretch, even for the most wild imagination. The Millers were already quiet. Prue says they haven't attended a Brotherhood meeting in months."

He nodded. "I agree, but you know Debbie."

I just looked at him. "Oh," he amended. "You don't know Debbie."

He shuffled his feet and gazed up at the unforgiving sky. It had stopped snowing but black clouds hovered between us and the spring sun like a bully blocking the path to the school restroom.

"She moved here, what?" he calculated. "About ten years ago. Had some trouble when she first arrived."

"What kind of trouble?"

"Well, she was from the city."

I nodded, that summarized so much. So many people moved to the bucolic mountains without really thinking it through. They quickly become disillusioned; the late paper deliveries, the lack of shoe stores, no Costco close by. City transplants even complain about the lack of traffic. Claim Jump residents encourage as many of these unhappy residents as they can to go back to where they came from as quickly as possible. Some of the displaced city folks end up in Sacramento, which, at least, has proper shopping malls.

"Her apartment burned when she first moved in."

"Arson?"

"Probably bad wiring," he scowled at his phone and texted something back. "But ever since the fire, we get a call from her about every six months, she's convinced that she's being followed or spied on by a deranged arsonist."

I thought of Raul and his ubiquitous web cams. But I did not share that with Tom. I was uncertain about the legality of Raul's activities and I didn't want him in trouble. Raul, not Tom.

Was Raul keeping tabs on Debbie? Especially since she beat Prue in the City Council race? I never knew with Raul. His background was obscure at best. Sometimes he claimed he was from Russia and sometimes he spoke of happy years in San Francsico. Raul mentioned he knew or was acquainted with Penny long before he ended up in Claim Jump.

"Let's get back to the Millers, why would anyone want to keep them quiet? Especially now, I'm sure they've blurted out everything they intended to blurt out."

"I don't even care. Natural causes." He nodded to the back yard. A body bag was suspended between the corner and the other officer. The ground was too rough for a gurney. "Unnatural causes."

"Was she shot?"

"I'm surprised you didn't look."

"I'm not that hardened," I admitted. Ben frowned as the body bag swung between the two struggling men.

"Boyfriend?" Tom switched subjects.

"Fiancé," I sighed.

"Good. He looks capable enough to distract you. Try to hold off finding another dead body for at least 24 hours, I have work to do."

Other than power failures, funerals were my next most exciting activity in Claim Jump. Big fun here, nothing but big, big, fun. The summer season is less hazardous.

We attended the Miller funeral out of solidarity for poor Sarah and for the Brotherhood at large. We all stood around the damp basement of the Methodist church sipping bad wine and circulating the same stories around and around. I've been here before; I've had these discussions less than a week ago. The church basements in Auburn are identical to the church basements in Claim Jump.

But this time I had my favorite secret weapon. Ben Stone, Rock Solid Service is irresistible to women of a certain age. And every single member of the Brotherhood was of a certain age. It didn't make them any less dangerous or treacherous. But it did make them susceptible to Ben's charm.

While Ben charmed the Brotherhood at large, Prue pointed out Sarah's mother to me. Sarah and her mother shared the same feature I shared with my own mother: we are nothing alike. Sarah's was an unfortunate exercise of effort over skill. She had let her hair go years ago and it stood out from her head in an uncontrolled gray frizz. Old cake eyeliner emphasized how tiny her eyes were and how much sun damage she had sustained. Her dress ended in a limp, uneven hem that hovered over the preposterous heels. I got a vertiginous thrill just watching Ms. Miller right herself on her staggeringly high platform shoes, and I use staggering in the literal sense of the word.

I glanced at the former Dorothy of Oz. Sarah must have shopped the same store where I found my black slacks and black sweater (now classics in that I wear them to all occasions, many being funerals). Thank goodness the storeowner talked Sarah into buying the sweater in midnight blue not black. Sarah's new sweater clung to her slender curves and brought out the ice blue of her eyes. The matching blue skirt and high heel boots transformed her into the most elegant woman in the hall.

I glanced out one of the clear, high windows. Debbie Smith, dressed in an easy to spot tie-dyed shirt bounced across the street carrying a small occasional table to the theater. Ah, looting Lucky's house already. I assumed she had Penny's blessing, and if not, the table wasn't being carried very far.

Scott was disinclined to leave Sarah alone, even for a minute. She looked wonderful, all Technicolor, a woman of his fantasies. His heart started beating faster every time he looked at her. She looked even better today than when she was costumed as Dorothy.

Sarah's mother approached, and Scott automatically hummed the theme music for the wicked witch of the west.

At least the woman wasn't fat. Before she died, Scott's mother told him to always look at a girl's mother to see how she'd end up. So, not fat. And he assumed the woman's hair looked that way on purpose.

"The term," a man placed a hand on Scott's shoulder and whispered in his ear. "Is rode hard and put away wet."

Scott nodded not turning to look at his new friend, he was too focused on the women plowing through the crowds towards Sarah.

If the rumors were true, and to date, all the Claim Jump rumors were true, this is what Sarah would look like if she had about 30 years of hard drugs, and he assumed, less than salubrious living conditions, behind her. In the hard drug department, Sarah was not keeping up.

Lizzie Miller squinted at Sarah and then at Scott.

"So you finally got a boyfriend." She shook her head. "Your grandfather is probably rolling in his grave."

"Is not," Sarah denied hotly.

"Scott Lewis, nice to meet you." Scott held out his hand and shook Mrs. Miller's limp one.

"And what do you do Scott?" She swayed, and then righted herself with only a bit of arm waving.

"He owns the library," Sarah quickly answered. "You must be starving." She took her mother's arm in a heavy grip and led her away from Scott, she glanced back and he nodded. He understood completely. Lizzie Miller looked a little drunk.

"She never met a controlled substance she didn't love." Prue Singleton placed her hand on Scott's arm to steady herself. She had a more legitimate reason for tipping over. According to the rumors, she tripped in her own greenhouse. There was something about the green house that was important, but he didn't catch that part of the story. He automatically helped her.

"But Sarah is not her mother," he pointed out unnecessarily.

"Or her grandmother, for which you should thank God. I think you're safe." The perky little old lady winked at Scott and limped away. Now, she would have been a good grandparent for Sarah Scott mused.

Allison Little approached him and blocked his view of Sarah and Lizzie.

"What do you think of a pizza parlor?" he asked automatically.

"No."

"Pet store?"

"No."

"Thank you for taking such good care of Sarah," Allison changed the subject.

"Care? Oh, yes the grandparents." He took a breath. Maybe his father had passed down some valuable qualities after all. That would be nice. He missed his father. All these funerals were difficult, but he couldn't not show. He cared too much for Sarah to blow her off just because he still felt sad about the loss of his father.

"It was the least I could do."

Allison Little nodded and looked at him thoughtfully.

"I was the first person she called," he blurted out.

She smiled, she had a really dazzling smile. He almost thought she would be so pretty if. . . he stopped that speculation, it was an insult to who she was right now.

He smiled awkwardly, "is it that obvious?"

"Only to the people who care."

He glanced around the sparsely populated basement.

"Okay," she admitted. "Everyone here probably cares."

"Look what I found." Another man, tall and broadly built, joined Allison. She took the plastic cup of wine from him and glanced up with deep gratitude. Wow, Scott considered the couple. He had feelings for Sarah, but these two were so in love it radiated from them like, what was that called? Like an aura, Scott could almost make it out in the dim yellow light of the basement. It was almost shocking.

"At least the snow stopped." Allison Little took a sip of the wine, and stepped back an inch or so to make room for additional guests to join the conversation.

"Yes, that's a relief," the man said. "I hear you bought the old library. What are your plans?"

"Plans?" Scott automatically shrank from the question. Plans. Adults were always asking about the plan. What are you going to do with your life Scott? What are your interests Scott? Sometimes he had no answer; often he had no answer. Why does everyone need to know his business?

"Scott is going to help me for a while." Sarah returned sans mother, just in time to save Scott.

Allison nodded with some private satisfaction. "That is very generous of you Scott."

Damn, she saw right through him! "I still want to know about those houses."

She took another sip of wine. "Don't worry, I'm on it."

"What about my grandparent's house?" Sarah asked. "Should I put it on the market? Mom wants her half of the money."

Allison narrowed her eyes. "Isn't that house for you? So you have somewhere to live, always have a roof over your head?"

"She wants her half of all the money," Sarah repeated miserably. "She said I'd have enough to rent an apartment for at least a few years. And I can work."

"Rent!" Allison snorted.

"Honey," Lizzie lurched back towards them. "I want you to meet my friend Jack, he's here to help me with your grandparent's things."

"Sure mother," Sarah peered around her mother, but saw no one she didn't already recognize. Was Jack an imaginary friend?

"He's over there," Lizzie said impatiently.

Sarah dutifully detached from their small group and followed her mother's swaying figure. Apparently this Jack was best met one on one.

"Sarah has good instincts," I noted out loud.

"But a terrible upbringing."

"I'm inclined to disagree," Scott started.

"No, no, she is lovely, clearly," Prue said quickly. "But those Millers, all Fox news and Republican boneheads." She shook her head, as if being Republican was the worst thing a person could be. I held my tongue.

"She shouldn't lose the house," Scott said hotly.

"No," I watched the mother and her new boyfriend bend and sway towards Sarah. "No, she shouldn't. Is there a will?"

Scott nodded. "Their lawyer is Buster Porter, he'll read the will later today, just family of course."

Buster Porter; Lucky's lawyer. That was interesting.

"Did Mr. Miller work for Lucky?"

"In the seventies," Prue confirmed.

Chapter Eighteen

One would think that after a funeral there would be time for contemplation, for ruminating on how short life really is, and wondering what the hell a person was doing with her own life. That's what I thought, but when I watched poor Sarah Miller walk stiff legged with her mother (with what must have been Jack trailing behind) to the Miller's Oldsmobile, I knew that in their case, contemplation would be more along the lines of financial remuneration, not big-picture spiritual questions.

"Damn, I wish there was something I could do." Scott stood next to me in the doorway of the basement and watched Sarah firmly take the keys from her mother and climb into the driver's seat.

"Just be by your phone," I counseled. "She's going to need a friend after this session with her mother."

He nodded.

"A good friend," I emphasized.

Her mother did not waste any time. She rolled out of the back of the Oldsmobile and scurried into the house as fast as her high heels would allow.

"No rush babe, they're already dead." Jack, as grey and grizzled as Lizzie, followed her inside. Sarah waited for about ten seconds. She could hear the sound of the door to her grandparents' apartment rattling from her relatively safe position inside the car.

"Fuck! Who locked the door?"

Sarah smiled. Her mother was no match for the members of the Brotherhood of Cornish Men. Yesterday, despite the power failure and treacherous road conditions, three Brotherhood members had arrived at that same door minutes after Suzanne Chatterhill made her calls. They spirited away the remaining silver, three books they deemed "rare", all the jewelry and two original watercolors by local artists. Suzanne made a list and handed it to Sarah.

"After the it's all over, here's where you can pick up your things."

The list was in Sarah's purse.

She slowly exited the car and took her time walking over the ice and sludge covering the driveway.

"I locked it of course," Sarah said coolly. "The whole town knew about the funeral. You wouldn't want to risk someone stealing grandma and grandpa's stuff would you?" Sarah handed her mother the key and opened her blue eyes as wide as she could. She played an orphan in *Annie* a number of years ago.

"Wow, we don't even have locks on the Ridge." Jack reached to rub his nose. It was bulbous, pockmarked and looked too fragile for such rough handling. Jack rubbed and then thought better of it. He saluted her with a smile that was blackened by years of home cooked smack. Lovely, her mother certainly knew how to pick them. This Jack made Scott Lewis look like a god, but that comparison wasn't fair to Scott.

Her mother grabbed the key and jammed it into the lock. She stalked in.

"We need the TV," she announced immediately.

"Sweet," echoed Jack.

"I'm sure you do." Sarah trailed behind as her mother weebled and wobbled through the tiny apartment.

"So, what about the money?" Lizzie paused in the kitchen just long enough to reject the stacks of Blue Willow plates and bowls.

"What money?" Sarah had an unexpected advantage; she didn't know what her mother was talking about.

"You don't know? Who has been taking care of the money all this time?"

"We get a check from Social Security every month and I make that last." That should be pretty obvious. The TV was small, the house was small, they had lost the tenant downstairs last year and never replaced the rental income. They got by, that was all.

"Well, then who gets the benefits?" Her mother kicked off her shoes. One made a dent in the wall. Barefoot she trolled through the house again, opening drawers and testing the cushions on the loveseat and matching rocking chair.

"What happened to their chairs?"

"I threw them out." Sarah explained.

"Why? We could have sold them!"

"No," Sarah pointed out, keeping her voice low and moderate, Suzanne Chatterhill would be proud, "No, they died in those chairs."

Her mother paused a moment. "Oh, I guess that wouldn't have   worked."
She lurched towards the back door. "What did they keep in the basement?"

The house Sarah grew up in, the house her mother grew up in, was three stories, and like all the homes on Grove Street, built on a hill that sloped down to the creek. The basement was actually a full apartment. But the tenant complained about the old-person smell and the TV noise all day, and moved.

Sarah could hear the banging and clanking as her mother prowled through the empty lower apartment with the focus of a women determined to find gold bullion stashed somewhere obscure.

"There is nothing here, they had nothing," Lizzie finally emerged and stalked back through the kitchen.

"They had me," Sarah said quietly. But her mother didn't hear.

I knew what the members of the Brotherhood of Cornish Men were capable of, but on days like today, they always exceed my expectations and assumptions.

We returned from the funeral and found Carrie alone.

"Bad?"

She shook her head. "Not bad, better. We're working on it."

"Good, you two can now concentrate on Sarah. Here." Prue thrust a safety deposit box key at me. "This is Sarah's, she's on the card. Take her down on some excuse before her mother gets wind of it."

I glanced down at the key.

"It was my turn to keep the key," Prue said innocently as if it was her turn to bring the deviled eggs, oh yes, she did that too.

"In other words, before the IRS gets wind of it?"

"The electricity has been out." Prue expression was guileless. She should try out for the theater's next production.

I glanced at my watch. I called Scott and gave him instructions. "We'll walk, it will be less obvious." Carrie nodded and pulled on her boots.

Sarah left her mother as soon as she got the text from Scott.

"Mom, I'm going to pick up some of the food from the reception we forgot," she searched her mind for a plausible food. "The deviled eggs."

Her Jack and her mother had dived back down to the basement and the crawl space unconvinced that it was full of little more than cast off furniture and an ancient electric stove. Sarah shook her head and quickly walked down the street to the massive brick Bank of America building on the corner of Main and Kentucky.

Scott, Allison and another woman greeted Sarah as she entered the bank.

"Mom and Jack are probably loading the TV into the Oldsmobile as we speak," Sarah announced. "There really wasn't anything more valuable than that in the house."

I gestured to the bank teller who offered Sarah the signing card. Sarah scribbled her name and we headed to the vault.

"Is your mom keeping the car?" I asked.

Sarah nodded. "And she still wants to sell the house. We'll split the money."

I did not say anything. The teller tried to keep me out of the tiny room for viewing the safe deposit box contents, but I brushed her aside the same time Sarah said,
"Oh for heaven's sake Suzie, she's with me."

Suzie stepped aside and I wedged myself into the private viewing closet to privately view whatever it was that the Millers wanted to keep private.

Carrie waited in the lobby with Scott.

The safe deposit box was crammed with stock certificates, two insurance policies and cash. Cash. Jesus. Or maybe the cash was for Jesus. I had no way of knowing. I immediately took the cash and stuffed it into my purse; Sarah nodded and shuffled through the colorful papers.

"It's all Lucky's company." She fanned out the stock certificates.

"You have a lot there." I looked at the certificates in her hand and started mental calculations but I didn't know any current valuations.

"Grandpa must have bought them when he worked for Lucky. That was before I was born."

I pulled out my phone and called Ben, who quickly called his stockbroker. Ben has his stockbroker in favorites because he is in constant contact. Ben doesn't just fix plumbing, he just likes to make people believe that's all he does.

"Rough estimate?" Ben called me back within minutes.

I tried to get comfortable in the tiny room. "Rough is fine."

"All in all the stock is worth about $500,000, a lot really, considering Lucky's recent setbacks, but he probably had more going on that any of us know or want to know."

I clicked off the phone and considered Sarah's options.

Thanks to the quick and, I suspected, practiced efforts of the Brotherhood of Cornish Men, Poor Sarah was no longer poor.

"Your mother wants to sell the house and split the proceeds." I tapped the certificates and considered the options.

"Yes, mom thinks it's worth $500,000 at least."

I shook my head. "Not anymore, what has she been smoking?"

"Everything," Sarah said glumly. "She's determined to get a quarter million, that's how she says it, a quick quarter million. Jack is all over it. The quicker the better."

"Your grandparents left you the house?"

"Yes," she ran her hand over the colorful stock certificates.

"Okay, listen to me, my grandmother is a member of the Brotherhood so you can trust me. Do you trust me?" I lifted the girl's chin so she could meet my eyes.

She nodded.

"He could turn it into a spa," Carrie suggested. "He could sell those lavender infused soaps and sachets, like that adorable store down the street that sells only white things. He could sell all purple things."

"No."

Carrie twisted her ring. "Patrick said he'd take care of my parents. But how? They'll just want more money, there's no paying them off."

"I know."

"I know, you know, but I'm not sure Patrick knows. I don't think he's a match for the way they work. He lives in a beautiful home, and has a great job and doesn't have people coming at him all the time, you know, savage, mean people."

"Maybe he'll surprise you." Although I was not really convinced myself. Sometimes street smarts can outwit education. I've seen it before; our business is loaded with street savvy survivors. Naturla sales people take on real estate with no formal educational background save for the training their own offices cram down their throats, and they are magnificent and astonishingly wealthy. Sometimes success is a triumph of experience over education.

In Patrick's case, I hoped I was wrong.

"What do you think happened to that Lucky person?" Carrie asked.

I sagged down in my seat. I had calls to make on Gold Way for Scott, Penny wanted to talk to me about lowering the price of her dad's house and she wanted to sell off his rentals, which was idiotic but I wasn't ready to tell her so just yet.

"I've been too distracted to consider Lucky's murderer."

She nodded. "Understandable. You did a good thing for that Sarah Miller."

"Thanks. I think I convinced her to not sell her own house. Where would she live?"

Scott walked Sarah back up to her house. They took their time, Sarah was in no hurry to confront her mother again, Scott understood.

"I feel so alone," she finally said out loud.

"Are you kidding, the whole Brotherhood has your back."

She gave him a pained looked.

"Maybe that's a mixed blessing." He reviewed the cast of supporters from the theater. She had twice as many people as Dorothy, any number of scarecrows, tin men and cowardly lions. She had a whole village at her disposal. But that's not what she meant. He knew that.

"When my dad died," he watched where he stepped on the slippery uneven sidewalk. "I thought my life line, my whole life, was over. I was officially an orphan."

She sniffed loudly and wiped her hand over her mouth and nose. "Did you get over it?" The safe deposit key weighed heavily in her pocket. If she didn't have enough to worry about; she had to pull off this plan.

"It's only been six months." Scott said.

"So no." She kicked away a ball of snow and it shattered in the street.

"The Shah sent me a plaque, an acknowledgment of Dad, he said he would do anything he could for me."

"Well that's nice, is he rich?"

"Owns the whole damn country."

She nodded, but wasn't all that impressed because she had no point of reference. He liked that about her.

"We're both orphans. We really are alone."

"I still have my mother." From her tone, it was clear the woman didn't really count.

"But she's still like a barrier, between you and death." Scott moved a wet branch out of the way. "She will probably go first. It's like she represents time. She stands between you and eternity." He stopped climbing. She paused to rest with him.

"Maybe we have each other?" she suggested tentatively.

He held her hand and gave it a tug. "Come on, let's review the damage."

The apartment where Ben and I camped was an after thought. Grandpa converted the space above the already-converted dance studio to a handy apartment where the dance instructor could live. A dance studio is not terribly practical, but he and grandma wanted to give their friend, Rachael, a chance to turn her life around and Rachael danced in the Sacramento Ballet and so, a dance studio. They paid her to give me lessons, which validated the program and they encouraged other mothers to follow. A good dozen families offered up their daughters on the altar of good intentions.

It didn't last long, but grandma and grandpa never found another use for the space. The large dancing space, the practice bars, a full wall of mirrors were all still there, with a fine layer of dust on the walls adding to the nostalgia. Nostalgia is always dusty or sepia colored.

I moved around the floor remembering the ballet, tap and modern dance classes grandma enrolled me in. Was I good? No, but I was busy I think Prue convinced Mom that I could dance my way to a more beautiful, slender body. But even at a rate of a class a day, the workout made no dent in my solid figure. I was better at playing the rock in a modern dance number than I was dancing any number of snowflake positions.

I raised my arms, took a few running steps and executed a perfect tour jete landing so heavily the whole barn shook.

"Tell me again why your ballet career was cut short. Shin splints? Tragic love affair?" Ben lounged against the doorframe, arms crossed.

"More tragic that I was encouraged all those years," I retorted.

The last of the spring sunset illuminated Ben. The windows, dirty and opaque, filtered the light so it was rose and gold, beautiful.

"You ran away again." Ben looked calm, sounded calm, but I knew he was agitated. If he were a king in the Middle Ages, his name would be Big Ben the Agitated.

And who was responsible for his bulging eyes, wild hair and heart palpitations? Me, and I wasn't even in trouble yet.

"You have to stop running away." He raked his hands through his hair.

"I'm not running away, I'm helping my grandmother," I held my hands before me in a pious position.

He ignored me and slipped off his shoes, took a quick couple of steps and slid across the wood floor. Two even tracks in the dust followed his progress. "This is what wood floors are for."

"There is usually furniture in the way," I agreed.

"Yes, there are often many things in the way when all you want to do is slide freely across the floor, unfettered, alive."

"Is that a metaphor?"

He circled the dust with his toe - his own crop circle. "I'm staying until we fix this."

"You know, you are wonderful." Why don't I just acknowledge that Ben is the best thing that ever happened to me?

"Yes I am. Which means you should just marry me and get it over with."

"What?" I stopped admiring my lifted arms in the mirror and let out all the air I was sucking in to be thinner with a big whoosh.

"We will. You know you love me, and God help me, I love you. Let's just get married, after Carrie and Patrick of course, let them be first. I'm tired of introducing you as my serious girlfriend who I will probably marry someday but not right now because she can't make up her mind over a fucking house!"

"You have a point." I said breathlessly. "But I'll be more trouble as your wife than as your girlfriend."

"Keep your name. In case of an emergency I'll pretend I don't know you."

Was that the answer? First comes love, then comes marriage, then comes Allison pushing a baby carriage? No.

"We'd have to choose a place to live together, that's what married people do, live together." He pressed his advantage.

I paused; I couldn't see my reflection in the fading light.

"But where?" I finally blurted out.

He gave me an astonished look. "Oh my god, that's your problem? It's not me!" His relief was palpable.

I considered that for a minute or two, he may be right.

"Would you like to live here?" He finally suggested.

"But what about your business?"

"Rock Solid guys can live anywhere. And you already have business here, right now, which is impressive."

"I don't know." I admitted.

"Let's sleep on it," he suggested.

"When do you need an answer?"

"After you find Lucky's killer of course."

"Look what I found!" Raul dashed into the kitchen clutching his laptop.

The screen came up to reveal Lucky and Summer standing by the theater stage. The quality was not as good as the video of the actual production.

"Years ago," Raul muttered as if reading my mind. "Equipment is so much better, I replace those cameras twice, you know, upgrades."

"What do you care?" We watched a jerky Lucky Masters as he tore down a colorful quilt off the stage. "I'll pay top dollar for it, and you get the money."

"But it's so beautiful, it's art. You don't destroy art." Summer protested. Her hair was blond in this video, I wasn't sure if it was a better look for her or not.

Lucky bundled the purple, red and black colored quilt into a large awkward bundle, he staggered a bit under the weight but didn't let go.

"It's stupid, it's like those isolated Amish women with nothing to do but to make stuff people don't need."

"I'm surprised you even know that. It's a respected art form, some end up in museums."

"The Amish? I bet they never made a dime. My daughter is an idiot for wasting her time on something that doesn't matter."

"Art always matters." Summer said quietly.

"Only if it gets you what you want." Lucky staggered out the door with his heavy burden leaving Summer in the empty theater. She clenched her fists, and then burst into tears.

"That is all," Raul said, exiting the program.

"But what does it mean?" I protested, "We already know Lucky was mean to Penny and now he's rude to Summer, not that big a revelation."

"She always won at the fair but no one could ever buy her work." Prue leafed through a magazine on the top of the pile designated for the library. "Lucky always came in and bought all her quilts before the fair opened. I should read that article." She pulled the magazine and tossed it towards her place at the table.

"I have one," Raul said. "I bought it before the fair, she was happy to sell it to me. We usually don't talk." He mused, "she does not like me."

My phone chirped. It was the office.

"Have you seen the inspection papers for 305 Skilling Court?" Inez said without preamble.

"In my office computer, probably on the desk top." Patricia keeps copies of all that information, Inez did not need to call me.

"I'm working on two sales and two listings. And I may have two more," I announced instead, knowing that was the real reason for her call.

There was some silence at the other end of the line. "That is good."

"I thought so," I confirmed.

"Then you'll be up there for a while."

"Just until I get these in escrow, I'll come down soon and check in," I promised.

"No, as long as you're working. Stay up there as long as you need to."

I looked around the kitchen. Raul was working on the computer. Brick opened the wine and Carrie and Prue hovered together in a tete-a-tete over the newest issue of *Brides Magazine.* The scene was begining to feel familiar: it was staring to feel like home.

"Okay," I took Inez up on her offer. "I'll stay as long as it takes."

Sarah surveyed room number 245. "This is nice."

"You've never been here?" He pulled in her stuffed duffle bag and an old hard sided brief case containing her computer.

"Why would I stay in a hotel in my own home town?" She waited for him to push her luggage inside, then followed.

He moved the briefcase to the low table by the window, next to his own lap top. "I'm sorry about your grandparents." He opened his hands in offering, as if it was the best he could do.

She knew it was probably *was* the best he could do and accepted his gesture for what he meant rather than whatshe thought should be expressed. Her grandmother had always insisted that people say and do things the way SHE thought they should be done. And she was always disappointed. "Thank you. Is it all right if I take a shower?"

He gestured to the bathroom and she scurried quickly in as if he may suddenly change his invitation

"I'll just be a few minutes."

"Take your time, they told me we have hot water."

The shower started up, but it wasn't loud enough to muffle her sobs. He understood and didn't try to come in and hold her, or get into the shower fully clothed, any of that. She needed some privacy.

Scott rubbed his face and allowed the warmth of the room to sink into his bones. True to her word Sarah was quickly out of the shower. The whine of the hair dryer started up.

What was he doing? Did he even want a house here? How could he support himself? He shook his head again; he didn't have to worry about supporting himself. He could sit right here, in this room forever, not do anything at all. Except now that supporting himself was no longer an issue, it was exactly what he wanted to do. That must be Dad's ghost extolling Scott to take action. What kind of action? Scott had no clue.

"You just lost your dad," Sarah stepped out of the steamy bathroom dressed in jeans and a flannel shirt that was too big for her, but made her look pretty wonderful. He realized, as he gazed at her, that no matter what she showed up wearing - oversized shirts, crappy stained sweats, she would always look wonderful.

"Was he old?" She lifted her still damp hair and expertly wound a rubber band around it, without even looking.

"No, he died while building an indoor water slide."

She dropped her arms to her side. "At least that's interesting."

"More than you know."

"I was thinking." She tossed the towel back into the bathroom, hesitated, then ducked in, picked up the towel and smoothed it over the rack.

"I was thinking I could sell the house and use the money to help you."

"I thought your mother wanted half."

She emerged from the bathroom, considered what she would say next, then blurted it all out anyway. "Two minutes after you dropped me off at my house, my mother insisted on going right back down to the bank. She figured I was up to something, I'll give her credit for that much consciousness. We got there just as it was closing."

"What did your mother find?" He had no idea what had transpired in the bank vault, just that his real estate agent looked pretty happy with herself, and Sarah was decidedly relieved. He felt the less he knew, the better for Sarah.

Sarah, for her part, knew she'd eventually tell Scott what transpired between she and this remarkable woman, Allison Little. But for now she reiterated the official version. Her grandfather saved his stocks in Lucky's company - totaling as close to $250,000 as she and Allison could count out. Later that afternoon, as she and her mother gazed into the now familiar safety deposit box, Lizzie had reacted exactly as Sarah predicted. She pulled every stock certificate out and just tossed the insurance folders at Sarah.

"Here, that's for you. Keep the house, I'll take this." She fanned out the certificates and waved them as if to cool herself.

Sarah nodded and pulled out a release form dotted with arrow shaped sticky notes pointing to where her mother was to sign and initial. After Lizzie signed over the house to Sarah, Sarah in turn, gave her mother the name and number of a stockbroker in Auburn. Lizzie and Jack loaded up in the Oldsmobile (the TV just fit in the back seat) and soon to be richer beyond their most wild, drug fueled, dreams, they drove into the sunset.

"We think the certificates are worth about $250,000." Sarah explained to Scott, omitting that she held the other $250,000 in certificates, not to mention the loose cash.

"That's more than half your house value." Scott felt he was qualified to make that call, having hung out for almost a week with a Realtor.

Sarah laughed. There were wads of hundred dollar bills in her backpack, more at Prue's house. Allison took the rest of the stock certificates to give to a friend who would invest the whole amount into something completely different. Sarah didn't understand how different, but she'd get income from the investment, more than the income from Lucky's company, that was for sure.

"Don't worry about it. Should I sell?"

"Where do you want to live?" Scott asked reasonably.

Sarah stopped laughing. "Here. With you."

For my next big project, I was presented with more buyers. A new and very happy couple looking for new digs, that it was still Scott Lewis and he was just still looking for a place of his own reduced the excitement somewhat, but what else was I doing? Nothing. I still had calls out for sale possibilities on Gold Way, but so far, no response.

"Are you sure you want to sell your grandparents house?" I asked Sarah again.

"Yes, I'd like to start over, with my own place, or with Scott." She glanced at the boy, who put his arm protectively around her shoulders. It should be as simple for Ben and me. I envied them.

I was back on top, I was in the game. I had listings! I was too busy to call Rosemary and gloat. I had a listing on Grove. I had the Lucky listing on Main and I had a buyer, now two buyers but together, which of course is more annoying than both listings combined, but that cannot be helped. And Penny kept calling and leaving messages about Lucky's other properties. I promised to work out of the New Century office up here and ordered signs with a local phone number that would roll over to my cell.

Lucky owned many properties, but Penny directly inherited her home and three more: the Main Street home, Lucky's office building and a rental on the other side of town.

I visited Penny at her house and immediately suggested she keep the rental to earn easy, passive income. "I noticed they are long time tenants, it seems a shame to move them."

"I don't give a damn about the tenants. I want the money from the sale," she narrowed her eyes and glared at me. "Do you have any idea how annoying tenants are? Always calling about problems you have to fix, always demanding things, as if you owe them a living space."

"They can be a hassle, true. But monthly rent is great steady income."

And she may want that steady income. I had no idea what would happen if the class action lawsuit went through. Ben's broker was busy selling and re-investing Sarah's stock as we spoke. We did not want to take any chances with her future. But what about the other stockholders? Even if the plaintiffs just got a little bit each, the lawyers would take the rest, and no matter how the money would be distributed, Penny would be left with nothing.

As if reading my mind, Penny replied, "the lawsuit will take forever, and I want the money now. Mattie Timmons had no idea what to do and that Debbie Smith has even less savvy, Dad told me so."

"They could have help," I pointed out, usually the barest rustling of a class action suit alerts dozens of gun toting attorneys who are perpetually loaded and ready to fire.

"From whom?" Penny sneered. "No one touches Lucky Masters, just ask him."

I ducked my head so not to really gaze directly at her.

"Oh," she turned and rearranged a collection of little glass ornaments on the table. "I forget. You forget a loved one is dead, don't you?"

I don't forget. I remembered the death I'd have seen in person and I work hard to push away the images and the horror. I would love to forget, but I can't. I'm not cut out to be first on a scene. I'm a fragile delicate flower, ask anyone.

"Do you want to sell that rental or not?" she demanded.

"I'll sell it," I assured her.

Chapter Nineteen

"I'm pleased you have some listings," Rosemary called.

"And buyers," I pointed out, just to make me sound busy.

"Oh, buyers," she uttered the word with the same tone as if she were describing dog turds in a backyard.

"So, things are interesting up there?" Rosemary couched.

"Tell Inez I am not moving out and I'm not switching offices with you."

"How did you know that's what I was asking?" Rosemary demanded.

"You should have burned more incense to cloud my perceptions or something," I suggested.

"Humph." Rosemary hung up with no good bye.

Penny and I agreed that a full week would be enough time for her to clean out Lucky's house. To help move the project along, I contacted Summer and suggested she could borrow some of Lucky's furniture for the next theater production (besides the furniture that had already mysterious appeared in the theater). Summer took immediate action and asked if we could meet at the house in five minutes. I countered with ten, Summer had an unfair advantate, I had to drive all the way down two hills.

"I'm monitoring the tryouts for *You Can't Take it With You.*" Summer announced before I could even exit my car.

I slammed the door and locked it out of habit. "And is the irrepressible Sarah Miller slated to play the ingénue? Who is the ingénue in that play?"

Pat pulled up behind me in his white Mercedes and helped Mike from the car. "The daughter of slightly insane parents."

"Sarah is not at the theater." Summer swept into the house and the rest of us followed. The three immediately scattered as if on a scavenger hunt and only had five minutes to gather everything they needed on their list.

"Are you taking this breakfront?" Summer called from the dining room.

"Not the breakfront, but you can have the sideboard." Mike dashed off to prevent Summer from putting a particularly good piece in the spotlight of Act II.

"Hideous piece." Pat clattered down the stairs to check on the sideboard, gestured his blessing, then ducked back upstairs.

Pat and Summer carried the sideboard out the front door and across the street. At least it wasn't raining, which is why they all came so quickly as soon as I called.

"Is Penny too busy to be here?" Mike stepped around the front parlor. He carried a pad of yellow sticky notes.

"Everything we want, we'll mark." He slapped a sticky on a cane back rocking chair. "The movers will come tomorrow."

"I can handle furniture. It's not the most odious thing I've ever done for a client." My tone was mild.

Mike pulled out a stool, climbed up and attached a sticky to the chandelier.

"Can we keep that for now?"

He glanced down at me, arm still raised, barely reaching the lowest glass pendant. "Only because it's you."

"Thank you."

Summer and Pat reappeared. "I need a bed." Summer announced.

"The guest room." I directed her upstairs.

"Not the master, choose anything else." Pat called up.

Pat looked around, rubbing his hands as he considered the furnishings. "I can't believe Penny is not here. She should be here, haggling over every cent. Getting the maximum value for every stick of furniture in the place."

They nodded solemnly and said together, "that's what Lucky would have done."

"Do you guys rehearse this stuff?"

"We've been together forever," Pat explained briskly. "That's what happens. It's like when you end up looking like your dog."

"Not a good analogy," Mike staged whispered. "We want her to marry the man remember?"

"I can hear you."

"Sorry, we want the breakfronts for sure, but not the crap inside. Help us empty them out."

For the next hour the two experts trolled briskly through the house. Every once in a while they obligingly helped Summer drag a chair, a desk and the guest room bed across the street, apparently abandoning the furniture in the lobby.

The boys tagged what they wanted with yellow sticky notes.

"Anything you want?" Mike asked me at one point.

"No, I'm more of a Danish modern kind of girl." I have no interest in any furniture built before the Arts and Crafts movement. I've been known to pick up chairs at the Laz-Z-Boy furniture store. I am a big fan of comfort.

Pat and Mike however, are all about style and high value, which is great for them. But I may not ask them to decorate my next house.

"When's the open house?" Mike brushed his hands with satisfaction.

"Sunday, in two days."

"We didn't see it in the paper."

"That's because I didn't list it in this paper." I explained. "I bought the *Chronicle* and the *Bee*. Locals already know about this house and have made up their minds, I wanted a minimum of looky loos."

"You'll get them anyway, at least everyone who wasn't invited to the post-funeral party."

I nodded. "Summer will hang out in the front yard distributing flyers for *You Can't Take it With You*."

"The movers will be here tomorrow. Let Penny know."

"Are you sure you don't want any of these?" I gathered up as many breakable, sharp edged, crystal, porcelain, figurine stuff I could, and only then did I glance around for a place to stash them.

"No, the markets are crammed with that stuff. Maybe Hospice?" Pat suggested.

"I need a few boxes." I took the offending items to the kitchen and carefully placed them in a jumble on the kitchen table.

The boys did not take any furniture from the great room. I had forgotten to turn on the heat but at least the west facing kitchen felt a few degrees warmer. It must get pretty hot during the summer months. I stepped outside to check for, and found a retractable awning. Good Realtors notice those details. I didn't recall if there had been more personal things around the back room or not, we hadn't been allowed to linger here. Certainly the flat panel TV screen spoke to a more modern life than the museum quality front rooms.

"But that piece would be perfect, you can't take it." Summer protested. Her voice became stronger the closer she came to the back of the house.

"Oh grow up, Penny gets 30% of the sale. What are you giving her?" I heard Mike demand.

I decided to meet Summer halfway. I rounded the corner to the hallway. Summer glared at Pat and Pat glared back at her. Debbie now appeared on the scene, now that all the heavy lifting was finished. She stood two steps behind Summer.

I didn't think Debbie was the best kind of friend for Summer. I come to this opinion honestly; I quizzed my grandmother. She told me Debbie is about fifty years old. And fifty does not look good on her. Coco Chanel said that by fifty, you get the face you deserve. If that is true, Debbie had been a very bad girl indeed.

"Debbie used to live on Gold Way." Prue commented. "There was a fire."

"Did Lucky own the building?"

"It was a house," Prue corrected. "There are no buildings on Gold Way."

I kept quiet and let her continue.

"I don't know why she came up here, following up on something she had going in Sacramento I suppose."

"Was she working for Lucky?" It was a good guess, so many people were.

"I don't know. Raul?"

Raul shook his head, his eyes glued to his computer. "After the fire she claimed she was almost was run off the road." He flapped his hand in the general direction of down hill. "On the way to the river. No one believed." He paused and hit a few keys. "Her," he finished his thought.

"Locals pass on that road all the time, then run out of room," I mused. "It could have been local versus flatlander."

"That's what we all said. But she claimed that someone was after her."

"I'm certain she is not that important," I retorted. Raul snorted. See? Even the funny man with thousands of hours of video in his library agreed with me.

"Tom Marten said she was just paranoid," Prue said.

"She's seems healthy enough," I said innocently.

"I offered to set up cameras and video tape, but she refused," he said sadly.

At least the woman had some common sense.

"It was so popular for a time, people watched the lives of other people." Raul was lost for a moment in the hazy nostalgia of three years ago.

"Why would anyone do that?" I asked.

"Because it was new," Raul looked as severe as someone who resembles a cartoon character can look.

"When she won the council seat this fall, she seemed to calm down a bit, then again I wouldn't really know, I tend to avoid her, she's rather intense." Raul brooded over the screen. "I recognized her when she first came. But now, now I'm not sure."

"Recognized her from where?"

He shrugged. "Where else? The City. You know what happens in the Castro, stays in the Castro."

"That's Las Vegas."

"The eighties were very interesting," was his cryptic rejoinder.

Since I'm not conversant with the ways of gay men in the Castro specifically, nor the eighties in general, I did not particularly have any reference point nor did I want to know more about what or why Debbie was hanging out in the Castro, shopping? The restaurants? I am more hopelessly bourgeois than I thought. I dropped it. I did wonder who bankrolled her sudden and wildly successful campaign against a local woman who knows where all the bodies are buried, so to speak.

"If Lucky was bankrolling her campaign," Prue read my mind. "He got a rude surprise, Debbie has been battling him ever since. She's belligerent about everything just like that last lawyer the city hired, he was bad news." Prue shook her head, dismissing all lawyers, as she tends to do.

I knew more than I should about that last scenario and wasn't interested in a replay of those painful events.

"Oh, all right," Summer glared at Pat. "I'll find something else. Honestly, you people.   Come on Debbie." She stomped into the dining room. "Can I have this hutch?"

"Be our guest." Pat called back.

Normally I would hire a Stager to take care of my listing, my favorite owns a warehouse filled with appropriate furniture guaranteed to make the house look desirable.   But one seller didn't have extra funds for such things and the other seller didn't give a damn. There would probably be just enough original furniture left to make the house appear slightly a little less cavernous. I could imagine the front rooms decorated with my own furniture, mentally eliminating the heavy, gloomy Victorian original furniture and just seeing the big bay windows and high ceilings, but few buyers could visualize their life and their belongings in an empty house. A few chairs and tables scattered about help immensely.

Once Summer took her stage props, she optimistically labeled another half dozen pieces with her own orange sticky notes, to be picked up later, and she and Debbie were ready to go.

"We'll come tomorrow to get the rest of the furniture." She called over her shoulder, halfway across the street. I waved from the front door like June Cleaver and disappeared inside.

Once the troops retreated, I was left to execute Plan B: the un-glamorous job of clearing out the closets. Penny instructed me to throw out anything that didn't move, and if anything did move, call the exterminators. I had no problem tossing unwanted items, but I was careful about disturbing any small, animated residents.

By the time I moved upstairs to the bedroom closets it was starting to get dark, five o'clock. I dragged a big garbage bag into the guest bedroom and began emptying out the tiny closet. I piled discarded clothes, blankets and quilts into the garbage bags: most was destined for Hospice, I would relinquish very little to the garbage. As Prue would say, there was still some good left in the stuff.

I found a stash of five more of Penny's beautiful quilts and immediately called Summer.

She crossed the street seconds after I hung up.

"You found more? Oh my God, those are exquisite, just look at her workmanship."

Summer put her hands on hips and shook her head. "I can't believe he just hid them here, they should be appreciated, they should be used."

I folded them carefully, they were stiff and a bit awkward but that was due to the batting and all those stitches. Penny sewed the quilts by hand; Carrie showed me the tiny, more uneven, stitches. The batting was so thick it must have been a tremendous project to make so many tiny stitches on such a big quilt.

"There are already a couple on the upstairs guests beds. Why don't you take these for more fundraising or decoration?" I handed the heavy pile to Summer who almost dropped them.

"Don't you want one?" she offered.

"I have one," I reminded her.

"That's right. You know, Penny doesn't give those away to just anyone."

"I consider myself special," I reassured her.

In the typical Victorian, the master bedroom is located at the front of the house, overlooking the street. But that position is terrible feng shui, not to mention just noisy. So Lucky created a master bedroom across the back of the house, with a narrow porch attached that perched over the downstairs great room and overlooked the rest of the garden.

I would have expected someone like Lucky to re-create the halls of Versailles in his bedroom, something along the lines of a kingly canopy over the large bed, long silk curtains held up by gilded cherubs clutching huge ostrich feathers in their tiny chubby fists. Something appropriate for his station in life.

Nope, his bedroom was decorated in late Mission, a man with style after my own heart. The head and footboards for the bed were made of thick, straight slats. His king-size bed would need to be winched out through the large French doors off the porch. Three big deep chairs, all accompanied by reading lamps, were scattered around the room. Filled bookshelves lined two of the walls. Chris and Pat's yellow stickies fluttered from the bed, chairs and end tables. All of this would go.

I automatically approached the bookshelves. No yellow or orange stickies here, Pat and Mike didn't deal in books.

I pulled out first editions of *Tom Sawyer*, *Vanity Fair* and *Little Women*. Not bad. Claim Jump hosted the most bookstores of any town in the state, someone would be able to sell these, or at least appreciate them. I hefted the Alcott volume. I appreciated it. I wondered if Penny would sell these to me, or trade against my commission. It wouldn't be the first time I indulged in a trade of that nature.

The three front rooms and two baths were either empty or tagged. One room still held a cleared desk, his office at home. But Lucky also kept an office in a building he owned in downtown. The same lawyer, Buster Parker, asked me to list the commercial building on Kentucky Street, apparently Penny didn't want the rent from that either. Silly woman.

Selling Luck's commercial building was easy. I called Pat and Mike first, and they immediately gave me an offer. "This will be just delicious," Pat crowed. "We've wanted this building since we first moved here. But Lucky outbid us. So we bought the place down the block, which turned out beautifully, make no mistake, but still, that was always such a great location, and already wired for internet and the like. Does the furniture come with it?"

"Probably. Do you want me to call Penny?"

"No, I will. We'll draw up the paper work whenever you're ready."

I was relieved they wanted it. Too many buildings already stood empty in Claim Jump's downtown. That bothered me, as the unofficial Miss Chamber of Commerce of Claim Jump I don't like to see empty buildings or faltering businesses. We now had Lucky's office, and the Library, plus this house that could not be used for commercial purposes. So many possibilities, so little time.

In honor of the inaugural Lucky Master's Personal Home Open House I dressed in my now familiar funeral ensemble, something I'd have to rectify soon. I didn't care how casual Claim Jump was, I was personally opposed to wearing the same outfit to every event. In my funeral black and Louboutin high heel pumps, I was the picture of prosperity. My goal was to attract potential clients loaded with money to lavish on an old (sorry, antique) house, that for its part, would accommodate a large income by always needing repair.

The photos I posted on the web site showed the house to advantage, both enormous and elegant. Not many homes could claim to be located smack in the middle of town. Most homes in Claim Jump were "close to town" or "walking distance" which was a relative and often flexible term. I mentioned that the theater across the street offered a limited run of performances so prospective buyers wouldn't think their front stoop would be overrun by rowdy patrons of the arts on a nightly basis. As usual, I had the web site, the flyers, the ads, the Facebook postings, everything that I knew would be effective.

And I anticipated that the outcome of all my hard work would result in a Sunday afternoon spent alone. I wandered around the house for a good hour, alert to the creak of the front door hinge or the squeak of the loose board on the third porch step.

It was already April 14th, I had been up here for three weeks. It felt like a lifetime. My shoes clacked back and forth on the hardwood lined second floor. Like Prue's house, Lucky's had one of those superfluous widow's walks perched on the roof like a third layer on a cake made with a left over batter and an odd sized pan. But while Prue's widow walk was reached by a pull down ladder, Lucky's widow walk was equipped with stairs, albeit very narrow stairs. Ben and I had noticed them during the funeral, but that would have been presumptuous in the extreme to disappear and climb up to take in the view. But not today.

I risked missing a guest and potential buyer, and cautiously steped up the narrow creaky stair. The tiny room was enclosed with dirty glass, but the floor was stable, a person could just fit a tiny table and chair up here. A person could pretend she was Louisa May Alcott writing in the attic.

The bare branches of the huge maple tree in the front yard arched over the top of the roof creating a tree house effect. I was enchanted. I could see the front stoop from my perch. Debbie walked over to the theater and disappeared inside. Tourists paused at the fence, then moved on. I could see up and down Main Street. I could stay up here all day. But no, I must play Realtor today.

I turned and took a step back to the narrow opening leading to the stairs. My foot caught on a floorboard and I almost sprawled down the stairs. I caught my balance and leaned over to push back the floorboard. It resisted. I pushed it again, there was something wedged under it.

I glanced back out the window. So far, no one approached. I fully expected Debbie to march over here after her visit with Summer, doing the rounds, intent on due diligence.

I tentatively pressed on the floorboard. The only time something interesting is found under the floorboards of an old house is when they are found between the pages of my favorite mystery novels. In real life, discoveries are pretty mundane.

I stepped on one end of the board to lift the opposite side enough to wedge my fingers under it, very carefully of course, no treasure is worth a trashed manicure.

I pulled and board came up with a shriek of nails. I glanced outside again. Good, no one heard, although a haunted house is popular. I wasn't up for a ghost story, and Lucky would have scared off ghosts a long time ago, unless they materialized monthly with the rent.

I pulled out a thick shopping bag. It was printed with a sewing needle and thread logo and an address in Sacramento. I would not be familiar with a fabric store of any ilk but the bag was nice. I opened it cautiously, old fabric? Pins and needles set to explode?

At first it looked like a jumble of charred plastic. I gingerly pulled out the top item and immediately dropped it. It bounced grotesquely around the tiny room and rolled right to my foot. It was a charred baby doll head, burned beyond recognition.

The whole bag was filled with mangled, melted baby doll heads.

Chapter Twenty

"Helloooo?"

Debbie on cue. I glanced back down at the bag and decided quickly that discretion was the better part of valor and shoved the bag stuffed with the rouge burn victims back under the floor and stomped the floorboard back down.

"Hi," I called as I carefully staggered down the narrow stairs. "I'm up here, come on up."

I landed on the second floor just as Debbie emerged up the stairs: wild hair, followed closely by a full-blown nineteen seventies psychedelic green caftan. I did not know caftans were made anymore. She must have rescued it from the Hospice store in town.

"So, how's it going?" As if she somehow missed a horde of prospective buyers stomping through the bedrooms.

I kept my eyes on her face and away from the widow's walk stairs.

"It's going well, this is the first open house of course, it takes a while to get some traction."

She nodded to the stairs. "That's going to give you some trouble."

"What?" I looked back at the stairs half expecting to see escaped baby doll heads bouncing down the stairs. No, all was quiet. Perhaps they just rolled around at night.

"You don't want people to climb up those stairs, it's too narrow, probably not up to code. Do you have homeowners insurance?"

"Penny does," I reassured the lawyer. But I was happy to move her away from the stairs and the potential danger. I made a mental note to post a sign with a photo of the view with a warning to not use the stairs.

"Good, we wouldn't want anything to happen."

Anything more to happen, I thought. I gestured to the upstairs bedrooms but apparently Debbie had seen enough. She abruptly turned and banged downstairs, her clunky, probably comfortable shoes, made heavy thudding noises on the hardwood stairs. Like Herman Munster. He would fit nicely in this house, come to think of it.

I took one last look at the narrow staries and followed Debbie down. I found her lecturing Scott and Sarah by the front door.

"I like to keep an eye on everything that is going on." Debbie crossed her arms under her low slung breats.

"Of course you do," Sarah smiled quite sweetly and I could actually see Debbie's shoulders drop an inch or two. Wow, maybe I underestimated Sarah, I should stop assuming that just because a girl is pretty, she doesn't have skills or guile.

"Are you looking for a house as well?" Debbie squinted at Scott, who, after a month of exposure to the Brotherhood, was able to hold his ground.

"Yes, I think I'll settle here. You seem to like it." He nodded at Debbie.

Debbie sidestepped that loaded question. I looked out the front windows. What I needed were potential clients from out of town, not these uninterested locals staring at each other, taking up space.

"This place will take a lot of work," Debbie commented, as if her job here was to talk potential buyers out of considering the house.

"Are you in the market?" Scott asked innocently.

"Hell no, I've had it with these old houses - dangerous - I have a place in the co-housing up the street."

I knew that co-housing place. "And that of course is all up to code." It had to be, they got government funding to finish the project. It was a lovely idea, a group of strangers all wearing sensible shoes, living cozily together and cooking dinner every night in the big communal kitchen. Shoot me.

"Not only is it up to code, it's sustainable housing." She scowled and her shoulders hunched up again. She must have been Nurse Ratched in another life. "We are very green, we live responsibly."

"I'm sure you do," I said soothingly. "Is there anything I can tell you about the house?"

I created a brochure with the help of Prue and the historical society, many of who were also members of the Brotherhood. If anyone had the goods on the house, they would. And if I really want to sell an old house, it must have history. I handed Debbie the brochure and she took it without much enthusiasm.

"I suppose this place isn't up to code at all." She brightened at the thought and glanced around with a renewed vigor, ready to find violations, ready to file a new report.

"It was built before the code was written." I glanced at my watch. I wondered how Carrie was doing, and Prue. I needed to close up and get back to them.

I shooed Scott and Sarah upstairs to look at the bedrooms and warned them not to hike up the stairs to the top of the house. Debbie planted herself in the hallway, her substantial butt precariously resting on a narrow antique hall table. An orange sticky note fluttered from the leg. Good, it wasn't valuable.

I was defeated. "What brings you to Claim Jump?" I glanced at my watch again, fifteen more minutes and I could legitimately close up the house and rescue what was left of my Sunday.

"I moved up here to supposedly save my soul,. I was really good at what I did, made a lot of money in the 80s, but it wasn't working too well. I had health problems."

"What kind of law?" I asked tentatively. I did not know if I really wanted the answer.

"Real estate law."

I stifled a groan. Real estate lawyers think every real estate agent they meet is a crook, a shyster and ready to debunk every client who signs a listing agreement. To real estate lawyers, Realtors are the enemy. I had a client/evil lawyer once berate me saying I was just out for the money and didn't care about him or his family at all. I finally broke down and pointed out that I make one percent of the sale price and he was buying a condo and if I wanted money, I'd go into banking and bleed customers slowly through more traditional methods like torture and predatory interest rates.

I don't like lawyers, and I did not think associating with Debbie was going to change my mind.

"Are you still practicing?" I did not want to antagonize her, these lawyers can blow at any minute. One little crack in the sidewalk or evidence of suspicious behavior hidden in the attic, and it's lawsuit city.

"I work on our garden. It's organic," she added unnecessarily.

"That must be more relaxing that litigation."

"Yes." She gnawed at a fingernail. Scott and Sarah banged down the stairs, circled us and headed to the kitchen.

"You do know to tell people they can't turn this into a bed and breakfast. We have too many bed and breakfasts, you know there is a new ordinance." She said it with great pride so I could guess who was the author.

"People can't convert, maybe you should put that on the flyer?" She was quite helpful and clearly did not understand sales. I smiled and said nothing.

Debbie found another errant fingernail to tortue. "Isn't your grandmother running a bed and breakfast?" She was good. Her tone stayed conversational, and she looked me straight in the eye. I did not blink.

"I assume that by bed and breakfast you mean paying guests?"

"Of course." She went for another nail.

"I can assure you that my grandmother's guests do not pay a penny." Extortion, trade and the occasional distribution of controlled substances do not count.

Debbie dropped her hands. I waited. She waited.

"You never married did you?" I was willing to fire a direct hit just to get her out of the house. She was not going to be my friend. I had nothing to lose.

She shook her head.

Of course not. Maybe there was a nice woman she could meet. I don't know why that was important, but recently I have found the tumbling and polishing of a relationship had worn down some of my own sharp edges, or maybe that was just the result of regular sex. Maybe both. My mental message to Ms Smith; lighten up and cut your hair. But I did not express that thought out loud, she may sue for wrongful beauty advice.

Scott and Sarah returned. "Thank you, I always wanted to see this house. Grandpa talked about it all the time. He worked on the plumbing for extra money."

"Ah ha." Debbie brightened up considerably at that news, amateur plumbing, non-union, payments under the table, no permits. "I better be going, there is so much do." And with that, she launched out the door and down the front steps.

"She's spending too much time with Summer," Sarah noted.

"We ordered pizza." Carrie announced as I let myself into the kitchen.

"How are you doing?"

She shrugged keeping her expression netural. She glanced around the kitchen as if looking for hidden cameras, as well she should.

"I should be going," she finally said. "Patrick is back home. I should be with him."

"What about your parents?"

That broke her. "I don't know!" she wailed and ran to the front parlor. A good escape from possible calls from those very parents we are all so concerned about, but not a very effective escape from me. I followed her.

"It isn't that difficult is it?" I thought of Scott and Sarah, the perfect couple, probably because they were young.

"Easy for you to say." Carrie stood off in the far corner of the parlor. This room hadn't seen this much action since the seventies.

"Not really," I countered.

"We know what I want," Carrie deftly turned the tables on me. "What do you want?"

Not fair, she knew my favorite subject was me, but this time I was having none of that. I resisted the urge to make it all about me again and turned the tables again. "What do you want?"

"I want to marry Patrick."

I was relieved there was a name at the end of that sentence. If she had said, I just want to get married, I would have been sad, suspicious and even more depressed than I already was.

"Then don't let your parents come between you and your happiness." It was at once a simple solution and a complicated answer.

"Did you read that in some horrible inspirational blog?"

"No, I think it's embroidered on a pillow, somewhere around here." I cast around the parlor littered with antique chairs and tiny pointless pillows - many of them gifts from my mother who never knew what her own mother would enjoy. I keep suggesting books, but Mom thinks books are educational and thus not very festive, so she never gives books as holiday gift. Plus reading interferes with a person's golf game.

I like to give my mother books on golf. But we are discussing Carrie.

"What did Patrick say before he left?" I asked, fluffing a tiny pillow that read *Eat Dessert First*.

"He loves me," she said sulkily.

"See? Even after blurting out your past, he still loves you." I picked up another pillow, read it, and tossed it on a narrow love seat.

She ignored me, as if her past, because it was now so public, was no longer an issue. "His mother will insist on sending them an invitation because it's the right thing to do and Patrick will not tell her all the sordid details to protect me because he says it isn't anyone's business. But then how will she understand why I hate them so much? And I know they'll say something, something about how damaged I am, how lucky I am, how they are so pleased I can afford to support them in the manner they'd like to be accustomed." She trailed off the fight abruptly drained from her.

She picked up a pillow, *Well Behaved Women Rarely Make History*. I found that for Prue myself. "That's really what's bothering me." She squeezed the pillow, and then let it fall back to the needlepoint chair seat.

"That they will spend the next thirty years at your back door with their hands out?"

"I thought it was the past, that when I ran away, it would all be over. I mean, who does that to a child?" She demanded, but did not, fortunately, wait for an answer. "But I know what really will drive me crazy is their constant begging, constant asking." She rubbed her eyes. "Patrick is so easy to find."

"I don't have a creative answer right now." I admitted.

She nodded, "You usually need about 24 hours to come up with a miracle."

Pat banged on the kitchen door then let himself in. "So, did you hear?" He flopped down in the kitchen chair, one of the few floppable pieces of furniture in the house. I think at one point in the seventies, my grandfather staged a rebellion against fussy Victorian furniture and moved in kitchen chairs designed in the audacious service of comfort. Of course, they don't match any other furniture in the house – no one cared.

"I was down at the bank yesterday and you will never guess what happened!"

"Go ahead," I set down a glass of wine for him and kept an ear out for the pizza delivery, what an indulgence, I would have picked up.

"That Lizzie Miller, with this horrible boy friend in tow, came down to the bank with one of Lucky's lawyers."

"Was Sarah there?" I asked.

"Sarah was sort of hovering. Buster Porter and Lizzie opened the safety deposit box and you should have heard her! Shrieked so loudly it could have shattered the windows."

"Was it a good shriek or a bad shriek?" I asked tentatively. I did not meet Prue's eyes.

"Both. Lizzie was angry that so much stock was in the safe deposit box, that she could have used this kind of assets when she was young, they were terrible parents, withholding assets withholding love, the usual."

"What was in the safe deposit box?" Prue asked innocently.

"It was crammed with stock certificates, worth about $300,000 or so, Buster could only estimate. And a couple of life insurance policies that the lawyer insisted Lizzie split with Sarah. Oh, and Lizzie signed over the house to Sarah. Right there, Sarah seemed rather prepared." He looked specifically at me. I smiled and said nothing.

Ben interrupted us. He slumped in the kitchen, shoulders hunched, head down. He looked more dejected than Summer in her best funk.

"Where have you been?"

"Bar."

"Tom Marten doesn't mean anything to me," I quickly protested. The rumors started at bars around here will follow you forever if you're not careful and quick on your feet.

He smiled wanly and dropped heavily into his chair. "This is not about you."

How is that possible?

He dragged his hands through his thick hair. "I was just down at Hank's Roadhouse, place was packed."

Of course it was, it always is.

He rested his elbows on the kitchen table. "It seems most of the gun club members head over to the Roadhouse after they've spent the afternoon target shooting."

I slid into the chair next to him. I still had no idea what disturbed him, but I was relieved it wasn't about our so-called engagement or me.

"They are torn up about it," Ben said simply. "No one knows who did it, who fired the first shot, who fired the last. They are sick about being part of something so ugly. They never knew, why should they? Who would do such a thing? Who would allow innocent men to kill?"

"A whole group of elderly genealogists?"

He refused to take my bait. "But they don't have specific arguments with the gun club members, quite the contrary. So why?"

I placed my hand over his. There wasn't a single person in Claim Jump, including my own grandmother, who had not, in some week or another, loudly complained about Lucky, publicly threaten to kill Lucky, wanted to kill Lucky, expressed out loud how easy it would be to kill Lucky, and how much pleasure they would derive in Lucky's untimely demise. More than enough Claim Jump citizens exchanged stories about the various ways a person could kill Lucky and get away with it. The number of potential suspects was staggering, the field crowded with possible culprits.

And here were the murderers: innocent. Someone drove Lucky to the shooting range. Someone dragged Lucky's body behind the targets. Someone hoped for the best.

"Just listening to them broke my heart. People are so sweet up here," he mused. "And innocent."

"Not that innocent."

Scott walked Sarah to her house and after making sure she really was okay, and not just saying she was okay, he wandered back downtown in the fading afternoon light. He liked the Sunday evening feel of the town, the shops were closed, the bars quiet. He was growing quite fond of Claim Jump. The ladies of the Brotherhood were relaxing a bit, especially after their first meeting under "new management" as he was introduced at the meeting, and the members were particularly pleased with his offer to allow them full run of the place until he decided what to do.

"Yoga Studio?"

"No."

He had left the ladies alone during their meeting and spent the time walking around. He walked back towards the grammar school, three long indiscriminate blocks to the right of Lucky Master's house, then two blocks to the left just before the big walled schoolyard. Gold Way stretched across the back of the school, a dead-end street on both ends, he entered in the middle. The street was the perfect location for a kid to play ball out on the street or build things in the driveway. No wonder his dad remembered it so fondly.

The trees were valiantly displaying flowers and new leaves under the heavy wet. In the summer, he imagined the towering elms would be leafy, verdant green. He admired big, he understood his dad's propensity for large, which is why Dubai was just a good fit for dad. Big, bigger, best. Dad understood the Shah, Dad understood elaborate. Yet, he never stopped talking about this street and this town.

Scott stood in the chilly air and took measure of the houses. He knew the one his dad spent summers in had been long sold to another couple, and they kept it up fairly well. The fence needed painting, but everyone's white picket fence needed painting. Must be that time of year.

The house to the right belonged to Mrs. Legson. Scott actually remembered her, nice old lady. She was always an old lady. By now she must be a thousand years old, if she was still alive.

The house on the other side of his grandparents' was painted with bright colors; the fan carving over the door was painted red, the gingerbread trim, yellow and the main house was colored purple, fading now, but probably pretty spectacular when fresh. Faded Tibetan prayer flags waved from the front porch.

The house next to the colorful house was painted a simple green and white, it looked reproachful in its simplicity as if to say, look at those gaudy colors, look at that hippie house, look how they show off and make a scene when the rest of us are so sensible..

Scott sympathized with the plain house, but he liked the gaudy house too. Didn't matter, none were for sale.

Why wasn't Sarah involved with some nice local boy? It was the first question that popped out of his mouth the first night they spent together. Way to go Scott.

"A nice local boy?" She snuggled next to him and pulled the bright colored quilt she brought from home over them more closely. It was heavy and marvelously warm.

"There were a couple of boys, when I was in high school of course, but my grandparents did not approve of me dating, probably because of my mother. She dated seriously, like it was a contact sport. That and other activities," she trailed off.

"So you're a paragon of moral rectitude."

She frowned. "Maybe. I really didn't have the friends to do bad things with. And once I started caring full time for grandpa and grandma I didn't have time at all. So there you go."

She was matter of fact about it, but it still made him wince to think about all those good years, all that wild fun, lost.

"And I'm the first," he confirmed unnecessarily.

It had been simultaneously an honor and horrible. She had not really elaborated the situation until it was too late. Of course, he hadn't pointed out how long it had been for him since his last encounter either. To be honest, his last sex had not exactly been a prelude to a relationship, or to cement a relationship, or to consummate a relationship or, never mind.

With Sarah it did feel like the beginning of something, maybe something big.

He rolled on his back and stared at the Northern Queen ceiling. Allison said she might have a lead on a house on Gold Way.

He pulled Sarah closer, her slender body fitted against his as if she were made for just that purpose. "So, how are you feeling, now that your grandparents are gone?"

"Honestly?" She rested her head on his bare chest.

He rolled his eyes, "Well sure, honestly." What was left but honesty?

"I feel free."

Chapter Twenty-One

That night, I curled up with my own good man. We snuggled down under Penny's heavy quilt and felt comfortably insulated from the cold and rain whipping outside the tiny windows of the apartment. At least it stopped snowing.

"Isn't this fun? Just you and me." I pulled up the quilt over our heads careful not to disturbe the candles on the head board.

"Do you like it that way? Just you and me? I mean, is that enough?" Ben's face was carefully composed.

It was the closest comment he had ventured to make about my hospital stay. I blinked. He reached over my head and pulled the candle closer to see me. The power was restored, but we had discovered the romance of candlelight the night before and I could use all the romance I could muster.

"Yes," the word was heavy in my mouth and heavy in my heart. Was two enough? I never doubted it until last month.

He nodded. "I think we can make it enough." He gently stroked my lips. "You, of course, are more than enough."

He pulled me close and I flung my arm around him brushing the candle.

The candle tipped over and hit the edge of the quilt, tented up around our heads.

"Crap." I automatically pushed the quilt down and patted the scorched marks. It was so lovely, it was a shame to mar it. While I patted, I considered ways to mend it, would Penny take it back and help repair it? Could I pay her to do it?

My efforts and plans did not affect the quilt in any way. Instead of behaving like a good, thickly sewed cotton quilt, the scorch mark bolted down to the center of the quilt and burst into flames as if fueled by a stream of lighter fluid. I yelped and threw the whole thing to the bare floor. The weight of the quilt should have smothered the fire, but it started to blaze up like eucalyptus branches on a bonfire (you only do that once, then you learn). I pulled off the wool blanket from the bed and threw it and myself on the flames, I couldn't think of any other way. I was so involved that I forgot about Ben who had, in this tiny nanosecond, found the fire extinguisher. He pushed me off the rapidly heating wool blanket and covered the whole mess with foam.

"My God," I panted. "Was that thing possessed?"

Ben pulled on his jeans and quickly dragged the sodden, foam-covered quilt down the stairs, the stuffing falling out to the walkway outside, oblivious to the rain and cold.

He paused and sniffed the air. I found an umbrella and followed. I was as lightly dressed as he was, but I didn't care, the rain felt good. Immolation was not something I aspire to.

Ben leaned over and pulled out a handful of stuffing from the inside of the quilt.

"I've smelled this before." He ground the stuffing between his fingers. I couldn't see things very well, but the stuff in his hands had a glow of its own.

"Is that," I tentatively touched the material, now taking on rainwater and swelling in Ben's hand.

"I think it's the insulation, the famous or rather infamous insulation." He dropped the stuff and dusted his hands.

"She stuffed this quilt with the illegal insulation Lucky used on all his homes?"

"I bet not just this one." Ben contemplated the soggy mess.

Visions of charred baby heads danced in mine. "Carrie has one."

"Let's go."

The kitchen door stays unlocked just in case any of us, that would be Raul and Brick, Pat and Mike, Ben, or I need to get into the house.

"You get Carrie's and see if your grandmother is sleeping under one," Ben instructed.

I nodded and dashed upstairs.

Grandma was snoring peacefully under her own quilt, made in the seventies when quilt making was all the rage. Grandma's masterpiece looked worse for wear, bedraggled and unmatched. I think it's called a crazy quilt pattern. But safe, that one will not ignite. She must not have taken her quilt when the brotherhood closed shop at the library.

The Brotherhood. I froze on the landing. Smoking in bed under this quilt would be like dragging in kerosene soaked kindling and lighting a few matches over it to see what would transpire.

"We're thrilled to finally be able to take these home." I remembered a member commenting. "They were certainly good insulation in the library, kept us warm."

Those quilt kept every neighbor warm.

I cautiously stepped into Carrie's room. This was easier since she was alone. The beautiful quilt lay on top of her recumbent form, too much like a colorful shroud. I gently pulled it off, and tossed a nearby afghan back over her for good measure.

She frowned and stirred but didn't wake. I hefted the quilt and peeked into the guest bedroom, a crochet monstrosity covered that double bed.

"Any more?" Ben whispered.

"Just this one, Penny gave these to just Carrie, and me."

"She didn't offer me a quilt, " he mused.

"She must really like you," I snapped.

Ben and I did not sleep well. We were cold and not even tangling our legs and arms helped warm us. We abandoned the bed as soon as it was decent to do so. We shuffled to the kitchen and made coffee while we waited for Carrie and Prue to wake.

Prue was unsurprised, Carrie was skeptical.

"How could Penny do such a thing? You don't just take insulation for houses and stuff it into a beautiful handmade quilt," she protested. "A person doesn't do something like that."

"Apparently Penny did." I didn't counter her argument by insisting a sane person wouldn't do such a thing.

I refused to let the quilts back in the house. We trooped out like a funeral procession to where Ben and I tossed the quilts. I wielded a huge sharp scissors I found in Prue's antique sewing basket. As I pulled out the shears, I recognized thread and scraps from that crazy quilt still on Prue's bed. It must have been the last thing she made by hand.

"Just cut off the bottom section," Ben micromanaged.

Raul appeared with a small video camera. I didn't stop him.

Carrie crossed her arms, huddled against the cold morning air. "I don't think the quilt is like a bag you can cut and the contents pour out, it's all carefully stitched together."

"She's right." I paused, scissors in hand. Damn.

"Then we default to plan B." Raul rolled the video. Ben flicked a thick kitchen match on the side of the box and tossed it into the center of Carrie's quilt. The quilt was soaked with rain so I didn't think anything would happen. I was wrong.

In seconds, a streak of black snaked from the center of the quilt permanently marring the beautiful colors, a second after that, flames roared up from the quilt and engulfed the fabric, insulation and our quilt below it like a roman candle. It burned out just as quickly and before we even registered or were able to express our dismay, the quilts were gone, nothing but ash on the walkway.

"But why?" I breathed. The air was toxic with the smell of spent insulation.

"For the same reason people put razors into apples and give them away for trick or treat." Ben's eyes locked onto the black mess, a curl of smoke rose up, just as it must have smoked right after burning poor Elizabeth, who everyone knew, smoked in bed.

"You know, I never, ever picked up a razor infested apple when I was a kid, and I was an excellent trick or treator." I couldn't look away from the pile of ash, of death.

"You lived in a classy neighborhood." Ben squatted down and tentatively poked at the ash. "Come to think of it, I never heard of anyone who ever actually found a razor blade in an apple."

"Maybe a kid made that up so he or she would never have to eat fruit, just pre-wrapped Snickers and Mars Bars."

Ben dusted his fingers. "It worked, smart kid."

"The poor woman." Prue backed away from the mess as if it was contagous.

"Who, the dead Elizabeth?" She was on my mind.

"No, Penny, what would drive her to do such a thing?"

I had no answer, but those burned baby doll heads came immediately to mind. Crap, Penny was not stable at all was she? Did her father's death finally unhinge her? I looked at the charred, curling remains of the quilts. No, she had been doing this for a very long time.

And Mattie? Was Penny unwilling to wait for Mattie to do herself in, death by quilt smothering? Should I call Tom Marten? Sure and explain that the flammable insulation that no one believed in was stuffed into beautiful collectable quilts that no one could buy? Did Penny even know what she was doing? Wasn't that part of the quilting tradition: make do with what you had around the house? Or in between the walls of the house?

Should we talk to Penny? What possible good would that do? Particularly since I was selling three of her buildings a situation that Inez christened as "fabulous." I was back in the good graces of the company, did I want to risk that?

I took a deep breath. Who knew? That was the next question. We saw Summer on video. She was clearly unaware, but what about the ladies of the club?

Ben shoveled the remains of the quilt and loaded it into a black garbage bag. The rest of us trudged back to the relative warmth of the house.

We all needed as much coffee as the coffee maker would produce.

"What about the Brotherhood members?" I helped Prue up the back steps. "What do they know?"

"I'll ask them. I'll make calls."

"Are you going to contact the police chief?" Carrie asked sensibly.

"Right after I contact a little old lady," I replied.

Finding a house for sale on Gold Way was more difficult than I anticipated. I called and called, because that is what I do, it's my job. Finally one person responded to my message but only because I was Prue's granddaughter and she loved my grandfather. Mrs. Legson was 98 years old, and just got around to calling, she explained on my voice mail, because she only checks her message machine once a week.

"Why don't you come over for some tea?" Her voice was quivery but from age rather than lack of personality.

"Prue, do you know Mrs. Legson?" I hung up the phone.

"Everyone knows Mrs. Legson. She walked neighborhoods for me during my run for City Council. She thinks Debbie is an idiot and is still upset over the election."

"Member of the Brotherhood?"

"She's not a joiner."

Mrs. Legson sounded interesting. I presented myself at her door as soon as I could.

Mrs. Legson was a round, pleasant woman shaped like a sticky bun. She answered the door and gestured for me to come in. "I'm too old to get out. You can come to me."

I complied. She led me through the hallway to the kitchen in the back. The kitchen overlooked a ravine that may or may not brag a creek. The term, seasonal creek, can also be code for winter flooding.

"What can I get you?" She toddled to the old gas stove and pulled the whistling kettle off the burner. She poured the hot water into a teapot in the shape of a bright-eyed Asian; his long braid was twisted to make the handle of the teapot.

"I understand you have someone interested in buying a house on this street?" I picked up the tray with the pot and chintzware cups and followed her halting steps into the living room.

"You must know Debbie Smith, the person on the council now." Mrs. Legson continued. "She wanted to buy a place here too. She rented from Lou Ellen; back when Lou Ellen was more involved. But there was a fire and she had to move out. I heard some of the locals said she was bad luck, no one wanted to rent to her."

I couldn't see the house from the living room windows. Fire damage did not sound promising.

"The place needed work anyway," Mrs. Legson sipped her tea and made another face. "Needs something. Honey, can you reach that bottle there?" she gestured to a sideboard loaded with silver framed photos of people in various stages of life. I plucked a brandy bottle from the clutter.

"That's it, bring it here."

Of course I obeyed, who wouldn't serve a nice little old lady her brandy at 11:00 in the morning?

"Perfect, thank you dear, have some yourself."

"No, I'm good, thanks. You were talking about the fire."

"Oh, that's all fixed, but I don't know how Lou Ellen manages. There's far more money going out than coming in. If at all." She added darkly, just in case I didn't get it.

"And where did Debbie move?"

"Her next house was one of those awful tract houses up on the hill, above your grandmother. She was in Sacramento the day of that horrible fire, good thing, her rental burned like the rest of them."

"Not very good luck around here," I commented.

"You would think she'd take the hint, but she stayed and fought." Mrs. Legson sighed, poured herself more tea and doused it with more brandy.

"Are you interested in our little street for yourself?"

"I have a client interested in buying a house here on Gold Way," I explained.

She shook her head. "I'm not selling, I'm only 98, not ready to go to a home like poor Lou Ellen."

"So Lou Ellen doesn't live in her house?" I sat up and sipped my tea. It was horrible, no wonder Mrs. Legson masked it with brandy.

"No, she's been renting it out for what, five years? I really should go to see her, but she's all the way in Auburn."

I nodded in sympathy, Auburn is about forty minutes away, a great distance for the residents of Claim Jump, nothing to residents of the Bay Area.

"Who lives in her house now?"

"Hippies. Artists, it's amazing Lou Ellen gets any rent at all, but she needs anything she can get, the poor dear."

I did not pursue the poor dear comment, at least not yet. "They rent?"

Mrs. Legson nodded. "Of course, some ridiculous amount. But the place is too big right now because some of their friends," she rolled her eyes, "have left and the rent is apparently too high. They're talking of moving and then where would poor Lou Ellen be?"

We finished our tea and I learned more about Debbie, and Penny who, because her mother was unstable, was never really accepted into the soft bosom of the Claim Jump elite.

I took my leave and hiked quickly over to the hippie house, as Mrs. Legson called it. The house was old, of course, they all are. This was in worse shape than most, the wear and tear more than just the regular suffering through a cold, wet winter. The door was warped and unpainted. The elaborate detailing on the roof and porch were faded and flaking.

A woman answered the door, looking much like Debbie's twin. "Yes?" She wasn't friendly but at least she wasn't scary.

"Hi, my name is Allison Little, I understand you rent this place?"

"Since 1996. What of it?" She narrowed her eyes. "Are you with the government?"

"No," I said quickly. "Happy here?" I peered behind her. The hallway was short, a tiny parlor to the left and a minisculre dining room to the right were empty of furniture. The windows were dirty, filtering what little light there was and dimming it to shadows before it could illuminate the rooms and reveal if the original hardwood floors were still in good shape.

She shrugged, "the rent is good."

"How good?"

She named the price, the total, which if they were splitting it or subleasing it, would be manageable for a group making their living on selling stain glass and original woven wall hangings at farmers markets and crafts fairs. But bearing the full amount? From the deferred maintenance and lack of immediate amenities, this house was clearly wearing on both the renter and the landlord's resources.

"Would you consider a rental on Grove Street? Three separate apartments, backs into the creek."

She shrugged and eyed me suspiciously. I tried my best to look innocent and small town, non-government. It was easy to do dressed as I was in my all-purpose black funeral ensemble.

"Those houses never rent, or go on sale, they're passed along to the kids. We've looked."

"I happen to know there's a chance to rent a whole house for less than what you are paying here, and it's all fixed up, no deferred maintenance. Interested?"

Her stiff posture relaxed a in inch or two. "Get us out of the lease?"

"Let me work on it."

Mrs. Legson did happen to have the name of the rest home where Lou Ellen currently resided. I checked on Prue and Carrie, they were involved with something Raul was showing on his computer. I did not have time to look. I hoped they were comparing wedding dresses.

I found Ben in the garage, building more shelves to hold more magazines and recyclables that still had some good left in them, and pried him away to visit yet another little old lady.

I took Ben because little old ladies love Ben plus Ben commanded an impressive number of contacts in the attorney world. Ben considers the species a necessary evil.

"Third party," he explained, dialing up one of the creatures as I drove to Auburn. "We can't do this unless we bring in a disinterested third party."

We found Happy Homes Retirement Village fairly easily. The parking lot asphalt was worn, shallow puddles reflected the gray sky. The impression did not improve as we entered the facility. My first thought was here was a fierce advertisement for in home care.

"Oh man." Ben breathed. We passed through a bare, undecorated lobby. The walls were painted a neglected beige with white trim that failed to make the forbidding double metal doors that led to the resident's room look like anything more than an emergency room entrance. Three small, elderly residents sat propped up in their wheel chairs. Their heads were secured to an upright position, but their eyes stayed downcast, afocused on the scarred linoleum flooring.

A phone sat at the abandonded receptionist counter. I stated our purpose and Lou Ellen's name. A voice promised to be right with us.

We sat in the only two available seats, hard plastic chairs that reminded me of third grade. We waited for ten minutes before a young girl, pulling off yellow latex rubber gloves, slowly pushed open the double doors just enough to slide between them and beckoned to us to follow, as she was too exhausted to push open those doors twice in one afternoon.

We followed her slouching frame to room 1034. She gestured without a word and returned to whatever domestic purgatory she inhabited. The TV volume was turned up so loudly I didn't think I could hold a conversation. But that's how cowards think. No excuse for me.

Lou Ellen's name was printed on a piece of binder paper and thumbtacked over her hospital bed. It helped distinguish her from her roommate, whose name I did not seek out. Fortunately the TV belong to the roommate, I didn't want to interrupt the woman's shows.

"Lou Ellen?" I said loudly.

I could hear her sigh from where I stood; the pathetic sound was stronger than the incessant blathering from the talking heads on CNN news. The least they could do was air cartoons, more cheerful.

"Hi," I moved closer, Ben stayed at the foot of the bed and took in the room's accoutrements. I could tell from his expression that he was not impressed.

"My name is Allison, I'm Prue Singleton's granddaughter."

The woman regarded me suspiciously. I can hardly blame her. She closed her eyes, and then opened them. "I know Prue, still growing?"

"Uh, yes," I glanced around to see if anyone had heard, but we were alone except for the roommate, who was not paying attention.

She nodded. "Those brownies really helped my Hank. She wouldn't even let me pay for the stuff you know, she said she was happy to help."

"That would be Prue," I agreed. All compassion: little profit. Then again, her pot growing was just an entertaining sideline, sanctioned and encouraged each time she helped another cancer victim in pain. It was, as you can imagine, quite the family conundrum, my mother becomes frantic and wild-eyed just thinking about it. So she doesn't.

"And what are you doing visiting an old lady?" Lou Ellen got right to the point.

"I'm here because someone wants to buy your house," I obliged her directness with my own.

She shook her head. "I need the rent, it keeps me here."

Ben sucked in his breath. I agreed.

"Yes, that could be true," I kept my tone as neutral as possible. I cast around for a good argument, the best argument. "What about your kids?" If she had kids, they should be shot for leaving her in a place like this.

"Didn't have any, we had kids in the neighborhood, that was enough." She smiled at the memory.

"Then when you go, the house will go to the government," I pointed out.

"Hank will inherit," she said.

"Hank is gone," I reminded her gently.

"Oh." She thought for another minute, possibly getting her head around Hank being gone, I hated being the person to remind her of that.

"Who is that?" She finally noticed Ben.

He moved towards her and took up her thin, blue veined hand in his huge strong one. "Ben Stone." He glanced at me, daring me to say it.

"My fiancé," I complied, after all, he was helping me.

"Ah, good," she squeezed his hand, and then fell back exhausted by the effort.

"And you want to buy my house?" I had to lean over the bed to hear her.

"No, I have a client, friend, who wants to buy your house."

"I need the rent," she repeated.

"You'll do better if you sell," Ben pointed out.

She shook her head.

"My friend is Scott Lewis, George Lewis was his father. Scott wants to buy a house on Gold Way, it's his way of remembering his father."

"George." She gazed off, remembering. The TV turned up louder; we were interrupting her roommate. Sorry about that.

"He built a suspension bridge over my back fence. Had to take it down, the cats used it as an access. He was a lively little boy. What happened to him?"

"He died on one of his jobs. He built big bridges." that was all I knew, that and Scott Lewis could pay for both a decommissioned library and a house with the cash from the insurance policies.

"Too young," the elderly woman breathed.

"Yes," Ben and I chorused.

"But I need the rent you see? I can't afford this otherwise," she waved a purple veined hand in the air. "The house is all we have. You know we paid $30,000 for it. That's only two years here." She nodded wisely; she had done the math in her spare time.

I could feel Ben grinning behind me. I wasn't the one who would actually make her world better, but I took some pleasure in bearing good news.

"How about a little more than $30,000 for the house?" I suggested. I planned to take my time, I would return if need be. I did not want to rush this poor, abandoned woman.

"No, no, that's silly, it's not worth more than that."

I looked around at her grim space. "He'll pay you a million dollars," I offered with confidence.

"A million. . ." she worked out that new number, catching her bottom lip on her dentures. "I could use the money."

"Yes," Ben had the same thought I did. "Yes, you could."

She looked at me and at Ben. The thought of money simultaneously energized her, and made her suspicious, which happens a lot. "Why the hell should I trust you?"

"Because if I'm lying, the Brotherhood of Cornish Men will have my ass," I said succinctly.

"They say it needs some repairs," she was looking a little better already, her cheeks showed some color, her eyes were a bit more sparkly. There must be nicer rest homes, perhaps the best rest home. I'd ask Prue.

We didn't need one of Ben's attorneys. We asked the receptionist/cleaning woman to witness the signature. Lou Ellen signed both the listing agreement and the purchase agreement. Scott could sign tonight. I know, I know. Don't do as I do, do as I say.

I called Scott.

All the members of the Brotherhood of Cornish Men gathered at the library. They sat in their usual chairs arranged around the table designated as the conference table. Suzanne Chatterhill presided at the head. On-line they had a following, but at home they were ignored, not even the alternative paper carried their stories and meeting times.

Sarah found the ladies in full throttle. They were arguing about something, old scrapbooks or a new biography or who would take on an elaborate indexing project or something like that. Sarah rarely paid attention.

She rounded the corner of the main library room and they all stopped talking. "I'm sorry, I was looking for Scott."

"He left us to ourselves dear." Suzanne Chatterhill spoke for the group. "You look lovely today, new lipstick?"

Sarah blushed. "Thank you."

"Scott will be back to lock up." Suzanne checked her watch, "in about another half an hour and we were about to break for tea, join us?"

Sarah didn't feel she had much of a choice and it was still too chilly to sit in the shade outside of the building and wait for Scott there. Plus, it would look silly.

And she did not want to look silly or pathetic. She was painfully aware she already held the title of Most Pathetic to the good women of Claim Jump. She'd very much like to change that. Today would be the day to begin.

"Thank you all for attending the funeral, Mom and I really appreciated it."

"Oh of course, you are like family to us."

And like family, Sarah knew that they would bestow a multitude of advice on whom she was seeing and what she should do with her life now. An absent mother was difficult, only because she then inherited a dozen mothers, which was eleven too many.

"Okay!" Scott bounded up the narrow steps and skidded around the corner. "Wow, great to see you all again! Sorry for the interruption, Sarah and I have more business to attend to!"

He whisked Sarah back down the stairs and out to the brisk afternoon.

"What was that all about?" She demanded, not unhappy with the sudden save.

"You have the distinct glow of a woman in love and they can tell, they are far smarter and craftier than they look, they've been outmaneuvering me since I arrived here." He said it without rancor or judgment. "Plus they are up to something - very agitated, I don't want you in their sights."

"They invited me to stay for tea."

"I bet they did."

The two walked past Lucky's house, the New Century For Sale swayed in the light breeze.

Scott took a breath, the thrill of the rescue embolden him. He never did anything without carefully thinking it through and more importantly carefully thinking out an exit plan and by then the plan didn't seem worth implementing in the first place. Nothing was permanent, nothing was good enough, so he always approached his life with the idea that he better leave his options open, another great opportunity could be around the corner, another, prettier girl might be waiting in the next bar.

But the better thing never materialized, the prettier girl never showed up. In the last few weeks he considered that he might be staring right at the next great thing: the last great thing. So he plunged ahead. "Want to see my new house?"

"Are you kidding? You bought a house, with what? You just bought the library."

"Allison Little found a house for me on Gold Way. Dad spent all his summers on that street. I just signed the papers. Do you want to see it?"

"Your dad?"

He paused. The snow had finally melted; the yellow daffodils, most barred behind picket fences, bowed as the couple walked past.

"My dad built buildings, bridges and sighs." Scott cleared his throat. "Dad died while on a job in Dubai."

"I remember you telling me." She kept pace with him. He turned down the street and headed towards the elementary school.

"He was building something that was the largest, longest, highest, coldest. I didn't realize it at the time, but people who are in charge of projects that include the terms biggest, longest and highest, take out enormous insurance policies on the principals of the same."

"So you got a lot of money from the insurance?"

"That and some other investments."

He stopped, stepped over a deep crack, and paused. "My father will never be a grandfather because I couldn't settle soon enough. My father will never be able to marry again. He'll never see me marry. Never see me finally get my act together." Scott smiled faintly, "He will never know I bought a house on his old street."

He took her cold hand and tucked it into his jacket pocket. They turned into the narrow street that ran behind the school.

"I'm selling my house," she hesitated. "I can help you know, with money for the repairs and stuff."

He reached out and squeezed her hand. Was it possible to find someone so generous, so genuine, so flippin' naive? It was like dating Dorothy.

"Thank you, but there's no need." The narrow street dead-ended into Gold Way. Three small moving vans hovered over the most colorful house on the street. A young couple watched from their front porch next dor. Maybe the young couple would let Scott see the house that Dad stayed in, so Scott could feel, for a second or two, exactly what his dad experienced.

"You know, I don't have to work."

"That's a lot of insurance," she hazarded.

"The Shah is a generous guy." Scott drew in a ragged breath. Had he made a mistake? Would he miss his father every time he turned the corner to the street? Would he cry every evening at the front door?

Sarah squeezed his hand.

"All my life I did nothing; just drifted around. And now I want to do something. Anything that will keep me busy."

Sarah eyed the peeling paint on the house Scott had indicated. She saw five loose roof tiles just from the street. "I'll think of something," she volunteered.

Ben answered the call from Penny to come and look at a few things. I suggested he discover what he could about Penny's quilting/immolation hobby. I suggested he take his fire extinguisher with him. Maybe a switchblade. He assured me he would be fine and would stay out of her bed, particulary one covered with a hand-made quilt.

"You cannot imagine how relieved I am to hear that," I drawled.

He waved and climbed into his truck.

Carrie offered to come and help me clean and take photos of Sarah's soon to be former home. The renters of Gold Way had dissipated so quickly I did not get a chance to nail down the terms for rental, so Sarah won, I'd sell her house.

"What kind of life did she have here?" Carrie stood in the center of the faded harvest gold carpet and surveyed the tiny living and dining room. The kitchen was so small I had to back into the door to get a good photo. *Efficient kitchen.* I scribbled in my notebook.

"She apparently was okay for the most part. Prue told me the Millers were quite odd, strict, and secretive, they were friends with another couple, the Sisleys, who lived over on Uren Street. The Sisleys had a daughter, Sheldon, but she's older than me, I don't know her." Meaning that Sheldon didn't spend her summer afternoons along the banks of the Yuba River, the one place a person could let her hair down and strip her clothes off without censure from the Brotherhood. "According to Prue since the Mr. Sisley died, that friendship fell off." I shrugged. "What's more important is she and Scott found each other."

"You are a closet romantic, you know that," Carrie accused.

"Don't tell anyone, it will ruin my reputation."

"Sarah probably just wants a new start."

"It is much easier to start a new relationship in a new house, the house you shared with a former lover just doesn't cut it. I even think you should buy a new bed. But that's just me."

"And have you?" Carrie asked.

"Have I what?"

"Bought a new bed?"

I angled away from the pellet stove and took a shot of the living slash dining area. *Intimate living area,* I wrote down.

"No." I knew I had a problem, but I was more concerned with firestorm-level batting and Ben hovering around Penny like an agreeable Labrador. I couldn't figure out if the baby doll head art project belonged to Penny or to her mother. That distinction alone could make quite a difference. Especially since I prefer to think of Penny as the guilty party.

The full apartment down stairs was accessible by an outside stairs. *Possible rental/in-law unit,* I wrote down. It was unremarkable, a sofa that will have to be thrown out and a tiny kitchen featuring an old electric stove. I scribbled, *move-in ready.*

The upstairs, where Sarah lived, was tidy, thank goodness. It boasted a miniature efficiency kitchen that was crowded into one end of a living room area. The walls up here were decorated with posters from current films and Summer Theater announcements. A single bed and nightstand was all that furnished the tiny bedroom; one window was tucked under the sloping roof. This room overlooked the creek that tumbled with melting snow and defined the back boundary of the property. Nothing was in bloom, but the creek was clearly visible. It was not a good time of year to take pictures of the yard, but that creek access would be an excellent selling point. *Your own private creek.* I wrote.

"She doesn't have any shoes." Carrie peeked into the closet.

"What do you mean no shoes? What kind of barbaric, deprived life did this girl live?"

"Maybe she packed them all. She's staying with Scott at the Northern Queen."

"And, how do you know that?"

Carrie gave me a pitying look. "I just spent an hour with Prue at the beauty salon, how do you think I know that?"

"Of course, silly me. Hear anything about the listings?"

Carrie thought for a moment. "The general consensus is that Lucky's house is overpriced, but that didn't surprise anyone. They are glad Mike and Pat made an offer on the Kentucky Street property and without money from Lucky's estate, the theater will definitely have to shut down."

"Do you think Summer is capable of killing Lucky to make sure the CRT doesn't get changed?"

Carrie shook her head. "Summer may not dress her age and her hair color is all wrong, but I don't see her as murderer, neither does any one else."

Generous closet space, I wrote in my notes. *Private back terrace, Price to Sell!*

A good day's work. I ordered the signs through my new "home" office.

"Why doesn't she want to keep the house?" Carrie asked, "besides wanting to live with her new found love?"

"Memories? It's also really small, she may want to have a family." I said.

Carrie stepped closer to me and put her arm around my shoulders, not easy for her to do, her arms are short and my shoulders are wide, so I doubly appreciated the effort.

"She may, or she may feel she has enough family." She patted my arm and returned to the closet.

"Maybe," I echoed.

"What are all these?" Carrie backed out of the closet pulling out half a dozen quilts.

God, more of the damn things. "They look like Penny's."

"But simpler. Could be early work, are you sure Penny made them?"

"I'm not sure at all." I punched in Scott's number and asked for Sarah.

"Sarah. Where did you get all these quilts?"

"Oh, I found them at the thrift store. Someone told me an anonymous donor dropped them off, but they were so nice and warm, and they looked a lot like Penny's work, you know the ones in the library and the theater? No one will sell them, and I found them for five dollars each. You can have them if you like."

Carrie hefted one as I listened to Sarah and shook her head.

· "Uh, no, no, I don't think that's a good idea at all. Thanks." I flipped the phone closed.

"Do you think she was trying to kill off the homeless as well?"

Carrie shrugged, but stuffed the yellow and blue patchwork quilts into one of the black garbage bags. "Doesn't matter, does it? Maybe she didn't know and wanted the homeless to be warm. You know, that's not a bad thing."

"Well my blanket delivering days are over," I announced.

Carrie winced and focused on the full garbage bag, not at me. "Are you still mad about that?"

During the Christmas holidays I delivered blankets to the homeless as a favor for Carrie. That the homeless person in question almost attacked me was not really Carrie's fault.

"I am not mad, I would never be mad at you. Unless you break up with Patrick."

She dragged the plastic bag to the head of the stairs and let it bounce down the steps to the entryway. "Fair enough."

Chapter Twenty-Two

Carrie volunteered to drive Prue in her car to do errands. Tom called just as I finished up the listing agreement for Sarah.

"I'm going out to the range again." Tom's voice was weary, and rather defeated. "I figure I may as well ask you to come with me, so I can keep an eye on you."

"I never asked to see the shooting range," I protested with false sincerity.

"It was only a matter of time," Tom insisted.

The shooting range was only five minutes by car, as has been discussed, and distressingly close to Prue's house.

I pulled up next to the Claim Jump squad car.

"We've temporarily closed down the shooting range, sort of out of respect for Lucky." George, the manager of the shooting range, was a sweet looking man of about 75 who offered to show me his automatic machine gun collection. I declined. Disappointed, he went ahead and opened a locked gate to the range for us. "Between the snow and the rain you aren't going to see much."

Tom acknowledged the futility of our mission and we walked through the gate to the range.

"I hear you're selling every house in town." George called out to me.

"Three is not every," I pointed out. But that was a good rumor, Allison Little, selling out Claim Jump. No, that didn't sound right.

"Any bites on Lucky's house?" Tom asked idly. He marched through the slippery mud with more aplomb that I was managing.

"No bites, it's kind of big and will need constant repairs, you know how it is."

"I do know how it is. What about the library?"

"I'm not selling the library."

He rolled his eyes, "no, but you know this Scott guy. What does he want to do with the library?"

"The jury is still out. So far, I've convinced him to not open a massage parlor, tea house or yogurt shop."

"Thank you," the chief of police said.

"Or bordello."

"That would bring in the tourists."

"And bring down the wrath of the Brotherhood of Cornish Men."

"True, too bad. Watch your shoes, its all red dirt and mud out here."

Indeed. I came prepared. I had packed a pair of very cute shiny waterproof boots I rarely had cause to wear. The boots were decorated with big red roses on a black checked background. I brought them because they were impervious to rain, sleet, snow and cheered me up in the gloom of night, and the old hydraulic mining site was pretty gloomy.

The red dirt gripped my pretty boots and threatened to hold me in place. How could anyone drag a body all the way out here?

As if reading my thoughts, Tom commented. "It was dry the night Lucky was dumped here. The storm started up only after he had been left."

Dragged, carted, God help us, did the murderer use a wheelbarrow?

I stood in the chilly air, the stripped monoliths of ripped mountainside blocked what was left of the sunshine. The damp air brightened the striations of yellow, rose and tan that made up the surrounding bare hills. The area was fascinating if you were a geologist, depressing if you loved trees.

We stepped just past the creepy human silhouettes decorated with shredded black and white targets. Shattered shards of plywood littered the rough ground. I staggered and the mud sucked at my feet as I took slow monster steps to the yellow caution tape.

I had no idea what I was looking for. I had a vague idea that I'd just lean over and pick up the definitive clue to the murder, just like on TV. But even if such an item existed, the weather would have deleted any telltale signs. If the killer did use a wheelbarrow, there were no signs of a deep track or groove.

There was nothing at all save for a couple of flattened Scotch Broom bushes.

Defeated, I asked Tom what he thought.

"I think he or she dragged the body out on a black tarp and then left the body here, right behind the targets. It wouldn't look like much, just another hump of built up debris and mud, and more important, since no one expected to find a body out here, they didn't see it. We found a muddy tarp in the recycling bin, but there was nothing on it."

"How about a quilt?" I asked suddenly. A quilt was not only sturdy, if Penny made it, the evidence would flame up and disappear in a matter of seconds. We would never recover it. Clever, I had to admire that approach.

"What about the quilts?" Tom asked.

"Penny's quilts are stuffed with flammable insulation," I blurted out.

He raised an eyebrow and waited for the punch line.

"There is no punch line, that's it." I freed one, then the other boot so I wouldn't be stuck out here forever like poor Lucky. "Ben and I almost went up in a fireball the other night. The quilts are as flammable as the houses above Deer Creek."

He blinked. "Are you telling me Penny Masters is a mass murderer?"

"I don't know what it means," I admitted helplessly. "Maybe she doesn't know. And it certainly can't be a focused kind of vendetta, how can she control who uses the quilts and what they'd do in bed?"

Tom shook his head. "She can't be that dumb."

"But she can be in denial." It's a popular river in my family; my mother floats down De Nile on a regular basis.

"I'll look into it," he promised. But I knew he could do as little with the information as me. A quilt is not a weapon. A person would have to wrap him or herself into the quilt and ask someone else to torch it. Not very dependable as far as murder weapons go. Better to drag the body out to a firing range and let the community take care of the murder.

It was not a cheerful meeting.

"I'm back," I called to Prue, but there was no answer. I wrestled off my boots outside and left them by the door. I padded into the chilly kitchen and called again. Where was my grandmother? It was past five o'clock and she usually hosts the cocktail hour during the week. Pat and Mike take the weekend. I stood in the cold room and called again. A little wave of panic snaked up my spine. She was injured after all. No, no, she was fine. I dashed upstairs to check hoping she was just napping. She was not.

I took a deep breath. First thing was to contact those very cocktail buddies. Carrie and Prue probably stopped by Pat and Mike's after picking up the groceries.

"Nope, she's not here," Pat said. "Did you lose her?"

"Ha ha, very funny, no I'm just checking around."

I smacked my phone in my hand. Just checking around.

I prowled through the house. Carrie wasn't in evidence either, which made sense, she was with Prue. I dashed outside, soaking my socks in the process, but no Prue.

I walked back to the kitchen door; it had the best number of bars for my phone service. I pulled off my sodden socks. No messages from Carrie, if they needed to stop somewhere, why wouldn't they call?

Thank goodness Ben picked up.

"I'll come right," and then he faded out. He must be back out at Penny's. She does not have great cell reception at her magnificent house.

I was too worried about Prue to worry about where Ben was spending his time. Besides, he said he was coming. It would take him fifteen minutes to drive back down Penny's mountain and back up this mountain. I wanted to wait for him outside so I could look for the car, but it was too cold to stand outside.

"Where is spring?" I demanded to no one in particular. "Where are the darling buds of May?"

It was only April, perhaps spring did come in May. But I needed spring now, right now. I pulled my boots back on over my bare feet and stomped around the yard. I wanted to find something, but at the same time, I didn't. I couldn't help thinking of Lucky wrapped in a tarp, Mattie Timmons wrapped in nothing atb all. Teenage boys running across the fireing range. My own search produced nothing of interest: no signs of struggle, no bodies, and the greenhouse was locked. The boots sucked at my feet, I couldn't feel my toes. I abandoned the boots again at the door and marched barefoot back into the house. I found Prue's cell phone in the knife drawer. The charger was in the liquore cabinet. Her purse was gone. Who had taken Prue, had the same person taken the purse?

I called Carrie's number, but she didn't pick up. Some joke? An accident? I groaned, and envisioned the two of them, run off the road, crashing down the side of the mountain, broken bodies, broken phones, unable to hit 911. Tom said that Mattie was run off the road. Here were my two favorite people, completely out of range. If they crashed on the side of the highway, they wouldn't be able to get through, even if they could manage to raise a broken finger to hit send.

Ben startled me. "I came as soon as I could get away from Penny."

"I can't find my grandmother!" I tried to get the vision of crumpled cars and bloody steering wheels out of my head. I was only moderately successful.

"She must have fallen!" The thought was awful. I've heard of old people who fall and can't get up. "And," I warmed up to my second worst fear, " old people lay on their sides for days in the dark, hungry and stiff and all the blood pools in their arms and they can't move and it will be my fault for not finding her in time!"

Did that high pitch wail come from, me? I believe it did.

"Okay, Okay," Ben tried to pat my arm, hug me, rub my back, all in an ineffectual attempt to calm me down. "Where was she last?"

I sniffed and dragged the back of my hand across my nose.

"I don't know," I admitted. "She and Carrie went out earlier, I thought they'd be back by now. I had a chance to see the shooting range and I didn't pay attention to their plans, if they even mentioned what they were doing."

"Okay, where would she likely be? Did you search the house and the barn?"

I gave him my best withering look, but didn't hold it for long; he was, after all, trying to help. "Of course I did, it was the first thing I did. People fall in their home all the time, I even checked the bathtub although she never takes a bath, but you never know!"

"Carrie, did you call her?"

"Not picking up. I left a voice message."

"And where have you been again?" He finally circled back to that fact.

"I had a chance to go see the shooting range," I admitted.

"So you aren't going to say much about me helping Ms. Masters because you were outstanding in your field with the chief of police with whom you had more than a passing acquaintance," he correctly summarized.

I stopped my blubbering for a second or two.

"Oh my God, that is the most complimentary thing you have ever said to me. Except for the Mitchell brothers wet dream compliment, but that was just to my breasts."

He dragged his hands through his hair. "You are welcome. Come on, did you call the hospital?"

"They would have called me," I explained. "I'm the number on her call sheet."

"And you say I baby my grandmother."

"I never said that, I said I understood."

"Come on, think, where could she be?"

"She doesn't just leave places with no notes. Or clues." Clues!

I raced out to the front door. No scuffle, the door wasn't locked, (Prue forgets to lock her door more often than not), no note, she usually leaves a paper, hard copy, and scribbles a couple words using the stub of a pencil that still has some good left in it.

Maybe she and Carrie are just up the road. Maybe they decided to take a pleasant spring stroll to admire the daffodils. I didn't really believe she'd do that. Not during the cocktail hour.

A pessimist is never disappointed. Prue was not a friend of Lucky so why would his killer come after her? Then again, she said some trenchant comments about Lucky to Debbie and to

Penny and to poor Mattie. Could someone be after her because she knows too much? Prue has always known too much, why would today be any different?

"I don't know!"

"Then call this Tom Marten," Ben suggested.

I must have looked surprised. He nodded. I still wasn't sure I endorsed his friendship with the redoubtable and possibly deranged Penny Masters. But here he was encouraging a call to an old friend. Ben was a bigger person than I.

Tom gently informed me there was nothing he could officially do until 24 hours had passed.

"Could she be in a back alley poker game? Drinking illegally?" He didn't say what he really wanted to say, not over a cell phone. I let it pass.

"I did check the greenhouse," I said both to answer Tom and assure myself. "She's not there either."

"You need a GPS chip in her," Tom growled.

"I know; she won't do it."

"Where does she normally go on Tuesdays?" Tom acquiesced, which was pretty nice of him.

"Book club every other Tuesday, Brotherhood of Cornish Men every third Tuesday. Cocktails with Pat and Mike every afternoon, and she's not there," I recited.

"Where is the Brotherhood meeting nowadays?"

"They're still at the Library, Scott apparently hasn't found the balls to kick them out."

"They are a formidable group," Ben said sotto voice. "Give the kid a minute or two to brace up."

"Go there and call me when you find her," Tom instructed.

"If I find her."

"Allison," he warned.

"I'm going, we're going right now." I clicked off, snatched up my own purse and I headed out the kitchen door, Ben right behind me.

"Allison."

I stepped out the kitchen door, heading for his truck. "What?"

"Do you want to wear shoes to this event?"

I glanced at my bare feet and at the boots. Crap. I wasted valuable time finding a pair of shoes appropriate for hunting down my grandmother. I finally stepped into Ben's truck when the phone buzzed.

"I'm not there yet," I immediately protested.

"Allison," Tom's voice had completely changed. I stopped suspended between the truck seat and the ground and remained completely still and completely silent. His voice indicated the news was bad, I could feel it even over the dodgy reception. I held my breath for his next sentence, the one that will be about death, broken dreams and despair.

"Yes?" I tensed. I eased my leg back off the seat and stood in the driveway, phone pressed tightly to my ear.

"The hospital just called. Someone found Raul. He had no ID on him, and the hospital administration is anxious about payments. I would usually call Prue since I know Raul is staying with her, but since you can't get hold of her. . . " he trailed off.

"How is he?" Raul? Crazy Raul, hurt? "Was it a car accident? He doesn't pay attention like he should, especially when he's filming."

"No," Tom interrupted. "It wasn't a car accident." He paused again. "When he wakes up I hope he can identify his assailants."

I didn't know which way to turn. "Do you want me to go to the hospital right now?"

"Go to the library first, call me," he instructed.

Shaken, I slowly climbed into the cab.

"What?" Ben leaned over and looked at me quizzically. "Allison, talk to me, what happened? Did they find your grandmother?"

I closed my eyes. "No, not grandma and Carrie. Raul. Ben, someone beat up Raul!"

He threw the truck into drive and sped out the driveway. We drove down the street for exactly four seconds before I screamed. "Stop, stop, that's Carrie."

Ben twisted the steering wheel and the back the truck swung too far to the left, he righted it and we bounced up onto the sidewalk inches from my friend.

"Where were you!" I yelled out the window. "Where is my grandmother!"

Carrie didn't wait for a formal invitation. She yanked the back door of the cab and climbed in.

"Library. Ben, drive to the library."

Carrie dropped her head in her hands. "They called an emergency meeting before we left so we detoured over to the library. Prue went in and before I could follow, that Suzanne slammed the doors and locked them. Prue had the car keys, my phone, everything, in her bag."

Carrie snuffled, "don't yell at me I had no idea. All the senior citizens I know are tired, they are never up for this kind of strenuous activity."

"Welcome to Claim Jump home of the enterprising octogenarian," I felt churlish towards the whole lot of them. "So now we storm the Library. Why would they lock you out?"

Carrie rubbed her hands. It was a more a rhetorical question anyway.

A dozen cars were parked on the street in front of the library, some members parked in the theater parking across the street.

We found them all in the library with Miss Scarlet and a candlestick. Actually it was Sarah who stood guard at the front door. I banged my fist on the original wavy glass, threatening to break it. Sarah open the door, I pushed her aside like a cardboard paper doll. Scott stood at the librarian's desk, not wielding a candlestick, but rather punching numbers into his cell; he stopped when I crested the stairs.

"She's here," he confirmed.

"So I figured out."

"You're late," Prue was a little too cheerful for the circumstances. She limped from the right of the library where the chronicles of the Brotherhood were housed.

"We didn't mean any harm," Mary Beth, owlish in her black-rimmed glasses protested.

"We just asked her to attend an emergency meeting," Maria nodded, her grey curls shaking violently with the effort.

"Yes, a meeting," Suzanne favored Ben and me with a wide grin. One could even call it a shit-eating grin.

"Oh for God's sake." I put my hands on my not unformidable hips. "What the hell did you think you'd accomplish?"

"I don't know, Prue doesn't know anything," Suzanne's expression abruptly changed from satisfied to sour. Then just as quickly, as if she had delivered a pep talk to herself, she veered right back on track. "You must help us."

I was amazed at her temerity, did she not have children to temper her, maybe take her and put her into some safe rest home? There was an opening down in Auburn.

"And kidnapping my grandmother is suppose to make me feel more favorably disposed towards your project?"

"She was here for a emergency meeting, we needed to vote."

"You locked Carrie out."

"A secret vote." Suzanne quickly amended. "Members only."

I rubbed my eyes. Thank godness they weren't very good at this. Prue seemed okay. She was pale, she was tired and her foot probably hurt. But she was in one piece.

I flipped my phone open and scrolled down to the police office line.

"Who are you calling?" Suzanne lurched towards the phone, but I was too fast, I stepped aside and held the phone over my head as the number was dialed.

"Tom Marten, please."

"The cops? You called the cops? No one calls the cops." Marlene rolled her eyes as if calling the authorities was a sign of great weakness and lack of resourcefulness.

"I found her." I igored the protests from the criminal wanna bes.

"Good." It wasn't difficult to visualize him checking off at least one thing on his long to-do list. "In one piece?"

"Yes," I breathed out.

"Ask him if this will make the police blotter. Everyone reads that." Marlene suggested

"The Blotter only reports the 911 calls." Mary Beth pointed out. "Did you call 911?" She looked at my hopefully but I shook my head. Her face fell.

"But kidnapping is a crime right?" Suzanne Chatterhill immediately thought of an alternative. "That should make the paper. Allison, call the paper."

During this exchange, Ben happily wandered around the building. I forgot he hadn't visited the library before.

"And what is this room?" He pointed to one of the many tiny office spaces behind the main reception desk.

"The archive room." Suzanne abandoned me to give an interested outsider the tour. "Here is where we index newspaper articles and columns from the Gold Rush, so if you want to know what your great aunt Ethel was doing up here, you can look it up. Back then the paper actually reported the news."

I did not comment that the doings of Gold Hill Garden Club was only news because they were the only subscribers.

"We need a Cornish Day parade." Maria popped off.

"You have Cornish Christmas," I protested. I held my phone and kept my thumb hovering over Tom's name, just in case.

"Not good enough, that event is limited to choirs and pasties, we want more dignity than that!" Suzanne, abandoned her tour and Ben and instead dropped into a chair. The criminal life can be a hard one.

"I told you she wouldn't help," Prue said smugly.

"How about a commemorative bench?" Scott suggested. "I'll pay . . . donate the bench and the plaque."

"You people are impossible." I reached for Prue intending to hustle her out.

"Where are the quilts?" Scott asked suddenly.

Prue followed Scott's gaze. "Suzanne, where are the quilts?"

"Summer has three at the theater. Penny has many of course. I have one." Suzanne ticked off the numbers on her short fingers.

"I have one," Maria volunteered.

"I have one," Mary Beth chimed in. Great, Penny would take them all out. The question was, on purpose?

"Get rid of them," I instructed them tersely.

"We will not, those are works of art." Suzanne stood and smoothed her skirt. But she wasn't in a position to complain, what with possible accusations of kidnapping and extortion and all. I may file a police report. I may not. Hadn't yet made up my mind. And Suzanne knew it.

"Donate them?" Another member suggested.

"No." Immolate the homeless, Penny had already thought of that, no, let's keep everybody safe.

"The garbage," I instructed. "Keep them away from flames, send them to a landfill, any landfill."

I felt like I was speaking to a pre-school group and just announced the demise of the Tooth Fairy, not that I'd ever be that stupid. The kidnappers all looked at me, eyes round, expressions: suspicious.

"The quilts are filled with flammable material," I explained patiently.

"How flammable?" Suzanne demanded, determined not to part with her hard won prize.

"A burning cigarette would ignite it in under thirty seconds." It was cruel but I felt I needed to spell it out.

A collective gasp. They rose and took off as fast as budding octogenarians can move.

Prue limped to me, Ben caught her arm, and she leaned heavily on him.

"Who's going to get them from Summer?"

"I will," I volunteered. "Ben will take you to the hospital."

"But I'm fine," she immediately protested. "They didn't hurt me, just held me for a meeting."

Great, death by committee. Carrie rifled through Prue's purse and pulled out her phone. "I'm surprised they didn't have rubber hoses and cattle prods with them."

"Not for you. Raul is in the hospital and you apparently are as good as next to kin, plus the hospital would very much like to see your Visa to cover his expenses."

Prue's eyes were wide. It was a popular look this afternoon. "What happened?"

"He was beat up." Ben said succinctly.

Chapter Twenty-Three

Summer was easy to find. Her theater office overlooked most of Main Street, the church and Lucky's house. In fact, it seemed to loom over Summer's space, always there, reminding her of what she owed to the man. I admired my sale sign in front. The single flyer taped inside the otherwise empty flyer box seemed to work well. Apparently flyers were a waste of time up here, only kids and tourists like to take them, but people do want to know information about the house, if only to pass it along at the beauty shop. Worked for me. I had scheduled another open house this Sunday, I may hold a spontaneous open house tomorrow, Saturday, you never know, the tourists might be thawing.

What did Summer owe the man?

Summer's desk was covered with so many small scraps of paper it looked like a recycling bin had overturned. But she was probably one of those people who knew exactly where every unlikely piece of paper resided and what it said.

I stood in the office door until she noticed me.

"Why were Lucky and Penny such supporters of your theater?" I asked.

"Out of the goodness of his heart?" she offered hopefully.

"No, Lucky did nothing from the goodness of his heart, don't be naive." No matter how long a person lives in a small town, the reality of human nature always rears its ugly head and asserts itself.

"Nothing," she shrugged elaborately. "He just liked to support the arts." She nervously shuffled the files and papers around the surface of the desk.

"Summer, did you ever sleep with Lucky?"

"If that's what it would take, then yes I would have, but it never came up. I'm too close in age to Penny. He even commented about it."

"What about the quilts?" I leaned back and regarded the purple and yellow example hanging over the empty refreshment table. My eyes traveled up to the spotlights hanging dangerously close to the fabric. Did she know? Did she care?

"What about them?"

"Did Penny ever want to take them back?"

"No, I told her the winners of the quilts donated them back to the theater. It was a small fib, but better than telling her Lucky wouldn't allow the quilts out of the building."

"And that promise?"

"Was worth 10,000 dollars for the theater," she admitted.

"And with Lucky gone?"

She made a desperate gesture to the thick piles of paper. "Maybe I'll just sell them again. Double my money you know?"

"I know. But you may not want to sell them at all."

"Why?" Summer looked at me warily. So she didn't know, that was probably better for Summer.

"We are pretty sure the quilts are flammable."

"Like his houses?" Summer made the leap without much help from me.

I nodded.

"Then," she made a quick decision. "They are fine where they are, this is a brick building."

"You'd take that risk?"

"It won't be the first," she said with determination.

I arrived home just as the Marsh Avenue entourage brought Raul through the front door. The hospital had cheerfully released him in light of his lack of insurance and assurances that his wounds, for the most part, were superficial. Prue tucked him into a cozy bed on Carrie's floor and warmed him with a pile of non-threatening blankets. Brick followed every move she made until she couldn't stand it anymore and shooed him downstairs.

I found Brick pacing the floor examining the fragile chairs and rearranging every pillow as he passed.

"Who makes these things? Look at the workmanship. Honestly. Is this a real antique?" He flipped the chair over and studied the underside. "I thought not. How could Prue allow this in her house?"

I approached Brick cautiously.

"It seems like Raul will recover. Do you know why those men would beat him up?"

Brick glowered, as if I just flunked climbing the rope in gym, which I would have, had they had made girls do such a thing.

"It's like Laramie, Wyoming up here. I kept telling him we should move to the Castro but he likes it here, he likes your grandmother."

"Every gay man likes Prue," I replied.

Brick's expression changed as if it just dawned on him what he said. I didn't need to say much else. I just stood in the cold parlor. Wait for it.

Brick regarded me, his mouth opened in a good imitation of *The Scream*.

"What did I just say?" He demanded.

"You didn't say all that much and I'm not an expert, we've established that, but I think you just came out."

"It's about time." Prue bustled into the parlor. "He's awake and asking for you. You should move him to the city or LA where he can make films, he's just wasted here."

"You can visit us anytime," I reassured Brick.

Prue nodded, "and you can stay in the main house, I'm toying with the idea of getting paying tenants in the guest house."

"You aren't zoned . . ." I started, and then shut up, what real difference did that make?

It did not take long for Tom to ferret out the Neanderthals who hurt Raul. He stopped by to update us and to tell Raul in person.

"Two subcontractors, they are regulars at the Mine Shaft and were bragging about how they were paid to beat up a fag."

Tom shuddered in disgust and I liked him even better for it.

"It was a hate crime, can you arrest them for that?"

"Sure. And I did. They couldn't make bail because they spent it all on drinks for every patron at the Mine Shaft who was not a fag."

"Everyone."

"Every single one," he confirmed. "Since I am not interested in feeding those clowns on my dime, I sent them down to Sacramento. Besides, once word got out, a few people called the office and made it very clear that there are enough unhappy people in town to make it rather unsafe for those boys. Had to transfer them for their own good."

"Glad to hear it," I said.

"I thought you'd like that detail," he finally smiled.

"This last month has been pretty awful for you."

"My wife says I'm having nightmares again, although I don't remember them in the morning. The cleanup after that last fire wasn't pretty. I was the one who found Danny and Jimmy."

I groaned on his behalf.

He shook his head as if to clear the memory.

"Who did you marry anyway?" I asked apropos of nothing.

"Becky Fitzpatrick."

"Don't know her. She must not have hung out at the river."

"She did not," he confirmed with a smile. He scratched his head and started down the hall to leave. "Who knew that working in this town would be so crazy?"

"It wasn't crazy when I came up here as a teenager. Nothing happened here when I was young."

"Maybe we just weren't paying attention." He was right. There must have been controversy during Lucky's building, all that traffic, the bribes to the city council members that must have raised some eyebrows and some ire.

"Do you think it has anything to do with what's going on now?"

"Probably, everything has everything to do with something but I just don't know what."

There were no answers for that. We simply said good-bye and expressed our fervent wish to not have to speak again in the near future. I was tired of police, beatings, explosions, fire. My stay was supposed to be restful!

Speaking of aggravting, I encounted Ben in the front hall. "So, are you attracted to Police Chief Tom Marten?" He asked.

"Are you are attracted to Penny Masters?" I blurted it out because since we set the bed on fire, the heat between us had correspondingly dampened. I suppose that was normal, but it still worried me. Was he ready to drop me because I wasn't moving on the house?

"I'm not tired of you, but this has been distracting," he admitted. "And all this Claim Jump activity is far more stressful than I anticipated."

"That is part of the charm, always delivering more than you expect."

"So I'm learning," he said dryly.

I looked at him, "Tom Marten and I have history. But that's all, just history. I am only in love with you."

He regarded me thoughtfully. "You aren't looking for houses in River's Bend are you?"

"How can you tell?"

"Are you kidding? I use to get a barrage of suggestions, links, pages, web sites, then they dwindled, understandably enough, and now, nothing."

I took a breath; my heart started beating double time, as if I had one too many hazel nut cappuccinos with (now) skim milk.

"Al-I-Son," Raul's voice floated down from the second floor. In another book, it would be creepy, but I knew him and that he could call me was a good sign. I dashed up the stairs to see him.

Raul's face was swollen, his nose looked like it had been moved to the left, just a bit. He suffered from cracked ribs and was bruised all over. I turned down the opportunity to admire his bruises and stitches.

"You know Allison, I make lots of money keeping things off the Internet." And none of it paid in rent to Prue, I stopped myself from pointing that out; this was not the time.

"This time someone was not willing to pay," I concluded.

"Her father paid." Raul closed his eyes; deep purple bruises made him look vulnerable and fragile. "That poor girl, the ex-wife of that Danny, the boy who was calling you all the time last summer?"

"Mattie?"

"Ah, she has a name, she looks like a cowgirl?"

"That's the ex-wife."

"She was coming out of Penny's house as I as going in. Very mad that girl, I stayed off the path and out of her way."

"And you walked in with your extortion demands hot on the heels of Mattie's demands. That's great, it's a wonder the woman didn't shoot you right there."

He nodded. "But she's not a good shot, she didn't practice with Lucky at the gun range, hated it. Brick wants to move, I think that would be good, maybe this is enough Claim Jump for us."

"But I would miss the funny man with the indescribable accent.

"Allison!" Pat stood in the hall and bellowed my name. "You have to come now!"

Chapter Twenty-Four

I barreled down the stairs. Pat was red faced and goggled eyed. "You have to see this."

"You found Raul's video."

He just waved me to the kitchen.

This was another video, not posted on You Tube but from Raul's copious and badly labeled archives, it took this long for Pat, Mike and Brick to recover it. I immediately saw why Lucky would want this particular video repressed.

Lucky and Summer stood in the theater Lobby. Lucky leaned on his cane. Summer's hair color glowed red under the ceiling lights. There was no sound, but they both gestured to the quilts on the walls. Summer pleaded, Lucky was adamant.

"Selfish son of a bitch," Ben muttered. "Preventing his daughter's success, not letting her make her own living her own way."

"Can you play it again," I asked Pat. He punched the play button and ran the short video over again. Why was this suppressed? I scrutinized the video again.

"Preventing his daughter's success? Or keeping her buyers from self immolation?" I asked. "What if Lucky didn't want anyone hurt? What if he knew what Penny sewed into her quilts?"

"What if he knows it would be eventually traced back to him?" Ben countered.

We all huddled around Raul in the bedroom balancing plates of pasta.

"Did Penny tell you anything? Did she let anything slip?" I asked Ben.

Carrie patted Raul's hand absently.

"She talked about how all her life she had to hear about how great Lucky Masters was. How he built houses for the people, made the houses affordable. How wonderful. But you know, Penny thought her dad cared less about the finished houses and more about being able to mow down trees, clear away brush and forest. He liked the destruction of it all. She insisted on walking me through the house again. She loved the study the best, she showed me how the railing was low enough so the view wasn't obstructed, even when she sat at the desk."

"All 380 degrees."

Carrie and Brick smiled.

"Yes," Ben continued. "All 380 degrees. And Penny told me this was her dad's greatest achievement because he fought the council on the tree line restrictions and won, so he clear-cut the forest as far as he could to build as large a home as he could get away with. It was all about killing the trees. He even cut down the trees that interfered with the view."

"Some people would consider the trees the view."

"Poor thing, that kitten story," Carrie automatically wiped her eyes, but there were no real tears. "She's so lost. I think Prue should invite her to the next Brotherhood meeting. I mean really, what does it matter now?"

"I'll tell Suzanne to get right on that," Prue grinned.

I carefully twirled my angel hair pasta. Prue was safe, Raul would heal, Ben loved me. My little world was quite fine right now. Tom would find out who killed Lucky and who killed Mattie, that was his job. He would also need to ask Penny about the quilts, that too was his job. I would send him Raul's video of the quilt burning, that should at least help whomever would prosecute. I was out of the whole affair, it was none of my business. My work here was done.

I woke the next morning with two nagging thoughts. Carrie hadn't mentioned Patrick in the last 24 hours nor had she mentioned her parents. That was not good. And the Pest One inspection report for Penny's house had to be signed.

"Now it's my turn to visit the mysterious and misunderstood Penny Masters." I announced at breakfast.

"And what is your excuse?" Ben asked.

I tapped the thick folder of paper. "Paper work, anything I should look for?"

"Nothing," Carrie said.

"Everything," Ben said.

Prue rolled her eyes. "I am not inviting that woman to a Brotherhood meeting."

Carrie's phone rang and she snatched it up and disappeared down the hall, nice try, but we could still hear her.

"Are you sure?" Her voice kicked up a couple of tones, as if she were a Valley Girl instead of a Sonoma County native.

"Could I have more coffee please?" Prue seemed too complacent. What had she done? What had she told Patrick or worse, Carrie's parents?

Carrie returned after a very short phone call, but her expression was one of complete delight.

"He offered them jobs."

"He offered them jobs?" we all repeated like an obedient Greek Chorus.

Carrie nodded happily. "They accepted. They signed up, signed the paperwork, you know Cooper offers good benefits and salary and all that, and turned it all in. All in place, very proper. They were scheduled to start today."

I took another sip of coffee, and then another hoping it would help me understand what she was saying.

Ben thought about it for minute, then smiled.

"Go on, I'm a little dense this morning." I gestured with the coffee urn and poured more coffee for me. I brought the pot over to Prue and topped off her mug.

"Once you sign on to work for Cooper Milk, you're committed, there are a lot of forms and releases to sign. I guess over the years it developed that way. One of the forms states that if an employee fails the drug test, he or she cannot ever come within five hundred feet of any Cooper plant, office, or," she paused dramatically, "event for five years."

Oh, that wicked boy.

"They did not pass the drug screening," I guessed.

"They did not pass the drug screening!" Carrie cried.

"That is genius," Ben whistled appreciatively.

"Yes," Carrie favored us with a huge grin. "Yes he is."

Sarah spun around the open library floor.

"I used to come here every day after school," she pointed in the general direction of the elementary school. "I loved it here." She slid on the floor, something she could never do as a child, it wasn't proper and it wasn't quiet. "This was the children's section. I read every book on the shelves, except for westerns and science stuff. It was like paradise."

She stopped spinning. "Can you learn things just by reading books or do you need a class?"

Scott shoved his hands in his pockets. She was so beautiful it hurt to look at her. "It used to be that people educated themselves just by reading books."

She nodded. "Sure, I read about that. But to get a good job you have to have that degree. That's what Suzanne says."

"What if you don't need to work?"

She stopped spinning. "Everyone needs to work, that's what gives you purpose."

"Is that what your grandparents said?"

She turned away from him. "I took care of them my whole life. That was purpose wasn't it?"

He nodded and tentatively took a step closer. "Maybe the work doesn't have to pay?"

"Excuse me?" The couple both stopped and looked down at a very small person climbing up the stairs. For a moment Scott was completely flummoxed, he hadn't seen many people in such such tiny packages.

"Is this the library?" The little girl cleared the steps.

"It is, but we don't have many books here anymore, the new library is out across the highway," Sarah's voice was kind, but the girl was clearly disappointed.

"I know, but it's so far away. I can't walk there. I can walk here after school." The child pouted.

Scott looked at the child. "I do have some books."

Sarah glanced at him, surprised.

"Friends of the Library, they store their sale books here in the basement. Wait here."

He disappeared with a clatter of footsteps down to the lower level. Sarah watched him open-mouthed.

"Here," Scott rushed up, books sliding off his arms and crashing to the floor.

The little girl's face lit up at the sight.

He dumped the books on the only table left in the room. The girl pulled up on tiptoe to reach the books.

"We need a lower table." Scott pushed the books towards the girl.

"Can I borrow this?" She had pulled down a Bernstein Bears book and a copy of *Madeline*.

Sarah gently took the book and glanced inside. The old fashion card pocket and the stamp - Claim Jump Library - were still in good shape.

"Yes," Sarah said. "Bring them back when you're done. You can take more when you return these."

The girl nodded happily. "Is it okay to tell my friends?"

"Tell everyone. The Lewis Lending Library is open for business."

Scott stood stunned at what just transpired. Was it that simple?

Sarah turned to him, her face alight. "It's that simple!"

The dogwoods were finally able to fully express themselves in white and bright pink. The plum and cherry trees were covered in tentative pink, the snow was receding off the green grass. Spring in the mountains is precarious and fragile, likely to end with a sudden snowfall that breaks off tree branches and smothers new grass. Or spring can launch a surprise heat wave that just as effectively stunts new growth. I was prepared to appreciate the mild and uneventful weather. Today, Mother Nature was cooperating.

Pale sheets of snow in the shape of tree shadows hovered on the edges of Penny's front lawn, but the daffodils glowed with bright yellow promise. All was good. I just had to let go of all the possibilities and conjecture that surrounded poor Penny. She was my biggest client. Biggest clients are never easy nor without controversy. I pushed everything aside to concentrate on saving my career.

I pressed the doorbell.

"Exactly on time." Despite the early hour, Penny was dressed to kill in high dangerous heels and a Chanel red wool suit. In comparison, and don't think for a minute we didn't immediately compare, I was seriously frumpy in my now shabby chic funeral outfit. I hoped she had been so distracted by Ben she didn't remember my ensemble.

"Hi, good morning. I have some forms for you on the house."

"Oh," she looked behind me, as if Ben were hiding in the shadows ready to jump out and surprise her.

"I'm alone, Ben isn't here." I hoped she would let me in anyway.

"Come up to the office." She turned, assuming I'd follow and close the door behind me.

I walked two steps behind her through the living area with the soaring ceiling, down the hall lined with hanging quilts and up narrow stairs to her high tree house - like office. The stairs were covered with a thick shag carpet. I slipped off my own pumps before tackling the ascent. I tend to catch my heels on thick carpet and I didn't want to fall backwards down the stairs because of my shoes. It was bad enough I was clothed in the same outfit I wore to her house tour, tumbling backwards down the stairs would be the final indignity.

Before me, Penny's high heels dug efficiently into the carpet nap and she didn't even wobble. She managed her Jimmy Choos well.

"Paperwork?" She retreated behind a broad mahogany desk that was grand enough to emphasize our roles: she the boss, I the employee. I had seen it done many times. She wanted me to feel small and intimidated. I may be a Little, but I'm not easily intimidated.

"Yes, the Pest One and the general inspection. There's a lot of suggested work, you may want to consider reducing the price, unless you want to pay for the repairs."

"No, no, a price reduction may be fine, no buyers yet?"

"It's only been two weeks," I pointed out. Sellers in a hurry are not necessarily a good thing, they make mistakes, cut corners, lie.

"Are you doing everything you can?" she quizzed.

Instead of taking umbrage, I pulled out copies of the *Sacramento Bee* ads, the copy of the Craigslist ad, the printout of the MLS entry, a hard copy of the web site and glossy prints of the sale flyers. Sellers love to see as much paper as you can create.

She flipped through the piles in a desultory fashion. "I guess you're trying."

"Trying? I'm one of the best. A house like your father's is unique and unique properties don't sell in a week. Yell at me in six weeks, but not two."

She eyed me. I stood my ground. Do not insult my professional integrity.

She took a breath, then eased up a bit. "I apologize, I understand from Ben that you are the best. I just want all this," she glanced out the broad expanse of windows, "done, I want it all done."

"I can understand that."

"No, you can't, you don't know what it's like to lose what you love." Penny narrowed her eyes at me. It was difficult to hold my ground against that. The whole scenario, the surprise pregnancy, searching for a house for three, then, just as abruptly, losing everything, possibly even Ben in one bloody twenty-four hours. The hollowness in my chest was big enough to have a name. I knew loss. I wanted to sit down, but I held my ground.

Penny stepped back, reading my expression.

"Okay, you do know." We stood together in that silence, a shared moment. Maybe Carrie was right; Penny was just a lost soul.

" I lost my dad," she finally said into the quiet.

"I lost my baby," I said it out loud for the first time.

Penny did me a service and ignored my pain in favor of her own. It could have been my own admission, or not, but something broke in her and her story flowed out. I usually do get people to talk about themselves, ad nauseam, but this was different. She wasn't looking at me; she was looking through me to her memories. I realized I may just be in the way, but it was too late, she started to talk.

"He tried to burn it. After everything he knew, he still tried to stuff it into the fireplace." She studied the paneling in the study, what wasn't covered in glass, was lined in beautiful walnut. "I mean, look at all this wood. The house would have gone up in a second."

"It would have gone up pretty fast." Burn the quilt? Was he trying to get the quilts out of the house before her public tour? Was he trying to burn the place down? Have them both perish in the fire? That made no sense. Lucky was a survivor.

"I grabbed it. I'm stronger and younger of course. I won."

I envisioned a grim game of tug of war with a thick unwieldy quilt between them, dangerously close to a burning hearth. Penny was stronger, but maybe Lucky was more determined. Did he intend to create an accident? If the walls were filled with the same material, it would indeed have consumed more than the down town fire department could forestall.

"He fell," Penny voice was toneless. "Hit his head on the fireplace." She shrugged, "I thought he was already dead."

"No, you didn't." I looked her in the eye. She looked away first.

"Doesn't matter, it's done isn't it?" Her shoulders sagged in defeate. I did not know what to do, what to say. Did it matter? Was there enough money for Penny's defence?

"It's all done, Mattie is gone, Raul is gone, no one will know."

I shifted, clutching the long carpet nap with my bare toes.

"And you won't be telling tales either." From behind the papers she pulled out a handgun. A nice, shiny, new handgun.

I stepped quickly back. "But I just listed your house! Houses!"

Her mouth quirked to almost a smile. "I had a moment of weakness, you can always fix those moments of weakness, that's what Dad taught me."

It was a beautiful day, the clear blue sky arched from mountaintop to mountaintop. Fluffy clouds, dry air, the works.

"Beautiful view."

Her hand, unfortunately, did not waver.

"Yes, my dad loved this view, he created it just for my mother, but when she died, he left me here and moved to town. He said he wanted to be close to the action.

"He could have been lonely out here." I offered the idea to, you know, humanize the situation.

"No, he just wanted everyone to see his coming and going, he wanted the attention."

"We all want attention."

Penny turned the gun in her hands round and round, I couldn't tell if, (what is it called?) the safety was on or off. Does that mean the damn thing could accidentally go off? How would it feel to be accidentally shot? I swallowed and watched the gun move around, the metal flashing between her fingers.

"He drove my mother crazy, really crazy, for real. He was always looking for the advantage. Everything we owned was a fucking bargain, something he got for a song, or for nothing. And he didn't do anything that didn't directly benefit him, you know? All that crap about helping the community, nonsense, it was all about helping Lucky Masters do what he wanted."

"All those people died." The gun paused in her restless hands as she gazed out one of the windows: her unparalleled view. "She was right you know, that widow woman?"

"Mattie Timmons?" I supplied helpfully. I kept my eyes rigidly on Penny and on her twisting turning gun. She fondled it like worry beads.

"The spray foam was toxic and flammable. I suppose if the fire hadn't killed the residents, the long term exposure might." She shrugged.

"There was no proof of that."

"None, I remember when the manufacturer pulled the material. Dad was really mad since the next cheapest thing cost twice as much. You should have heard him, it was as if they stole money from him. It was all about the money. See this?" She gestured at her office with the gun. I couldn't keep my eyes off the weapon.

"This was to show off to the community that Lucky could build what he wanted, where he wanted, all it took was money."

I said carefully, "that is often right."

She shook her head. "There ought to be something to stand for besides money. I never found it," she said mournfully. "You people never liked me."

Well, she wasn't exactly likable. I suddenly remembered a story that circulated when I was still a teenager. Every Fourth of July, one of the teenage girls is voted Liberty Queen and rides in the Claim Jump parade. Penny was Liberty Queen three years in a row because Lucky bought hundreds of her raffle tickets and influenced the judeges. She didn't have to work for her win.

I would love the easy win, even just once. Except that today was not an easy win day, it was very likely a difficult lose day. I have faced guns before, but the last time I had, Ben had come charging in to save me. I didn't think that would be the case today. There was no reason for him to follow me. Everything was fine, and we were all happy and safe in our little bubble of goodwill. It suddenly occurred to me that routinely checking in with a loved one might not be the paranoid and subservient activity I had previously thought.

I had things to do, people to marry. I edged around the circumference of the room; it felt round because of the large windows and low built-in shelves. The expansive view pulled the eye out and you missed the corners and angles in the inside. I turned and turned again. Penny followed me with the gun like an awful carnival game: shoot the Realtor.

"So, you're a pretty good shot," my voice wavered, damn.

"I'm a terrible shot. My father tried to teach me. Bought me my own gun for Christmas, that was just a swell gift, I wanted a new sewing machine. He wanted me to be the son he never had. I wasn't good at it. I hated it. But it does the job, even if you aren't that accurate."

Oh good, I could just bleed to death from a stomach wound. Did that happen? I was behind on my television shows and mystery novels. I couldn't remember the salient details and of course, my brain wasn't exactly working at optimal levels. It was barely working at all.

I edged to the double French doors leading out to a small deck cantilevered over the valley below. It was quite a drop. How Lucky got THAT approved is mystery. No, I could solve at least that one, he probably just bribed the inspector. It's done all the time.

I opened the door and stepped out, making her follow. I couldn't reach the stairs and there wasn't anywhere else to go inside, except round and round, outside there were more distractions, some dodging room. In the back of my imagination I figured I might as well die beautifully and dramatically in the open air. I gripped the railing that seemed stable enough, but it was too low, I remembered Ben said Lucky didn't want to obstruct the view.

Penny followed me out. I miscalculated, there was less maneuvering room on the cantilevered deck than I imagined. The deck was not big enough for the two of us, the madwoman and her victim. She lunged at me, gun raised and aimed right at my stomach (the largest target on my body). I automatically deflected her hand and pushed her with my shoulder. I was barefoot and had better traction and grip on the damp deck wood. She teetered on her perfect high heel shoes. She wavered for a second, caught her balance and raised the gun again.

I dodged again, more from instinct than talent or training. The gun went off and the shot reverberated through the valley. Startled birds rushed from their perches and cried up to the sky. I imagined my soul was about to do the same.

I tried to grab the the gun, she shot again but the bullet just grazed me. The stab of pain cleared my head and banished the images conjured by my morbid imagination. I shot forward and grabbed the gun harder and tugged with all my might. She loosened her grip and I jerked the hot gun downward, desperately hoping I could avoid shooting myself in the foot.

She staggered and I pushed her again to gain more space between the two of us. Penny toppled back against the railing and it caught her just under her butt. She waved her hands to balance. I threw the gun behind me. It bounced on the wood deck once and then was silent. I was too distracted to care.

Her arms flailed, then pin wheeled, then suddenly stopped. She was over balanced, the edge of the railing that I had just found so comforting a few seconds ago, was, as I said, too low. I lunged forward and tried to grab her with my right hand and pull her back. But her hand missed mine. She overturned. The momentum from my push, her overbalanced height and those treacherous shoes did the trick. In a blink she disappeared over the railing. It was like a magic trick, one second she was there, then nothing, my hand grasped empty air.

I did not hear a sound after that. The whole world was still, holding its breath. A second later the birds began singing an odd, off key song.

The breeze was cold. My feet were cold. I huddled against the too low railing and tried to catch my breath. I had go inside to call Tom on the phone line. I knew not to call 911, we didn't want this in the paper. I could tell Tom any story I wanted, yet I would probably stick to the truth, it's easier to remember in the long run. I had already learned that regardless of what the truth was, the survivors get to write the story.

The day ended with a promise of summer. Ben and I walked downtown hand in hand, except when the sidewalk was so narrow we had to walk single file. I only limped a little, the gun graze was only worth two SpongeBob Band-Aids.

We walked past the coffee shop and up to Lucky's house. My sign waved cheerfully in the afternoon air.

"This won't sell for a while. I'll have to be up here a lot, and I'll probably list poor Penny's house as well. Do you mind? You can come with me, we can pretend we are away on an illicit getaway and stay in Prue's apartment, that seemed to work for us."

Ben stood at the fence and flicked a chip of paint off one of the fence staves.

"Except for the fire."

"You are pretty hot."

He smiled at me but his attention was on the house. "Do you think the house is tainted? You know, bad juju because of Lucky?"

I shook my head. "Buyers from Sacramento or the Bay Area don't even care about Lucky Masters. After a couple years, it won't matter."

And tomorrow I'd get rid of the baby doll heads. Poor Penny was unstable certainly, vengeful, definitely. Even as we spoke, Tom and his deputies were searching for the gun, failing that, he assured me the bullet lodged in the deck would most likely match the bullet in poor Mattie. That much was certain. What is not certain was if Penny intended for every resident of Claim Jump to die in an accidental fire.

Ben nodded "That's true, so you could reinterpret the situation, so to speak, if you wanted."

"I can do anything I want," I countered automatically.

"I like staying with your grandmother. She's great, but I think we'd be more happy with our own place."

"That's been the conversation for months now." I said it as gently as I could, I didn't want to startle him, but every once in a while I felt the need to state the obvious.

"I know. I like this house."

"What?" I didn't say it as loudly as it looks on paper. I said it very softly. Because, Mr. Ben Stone, Rock Solid Service had not uttered these words about any house, in any county.

"You do?" I pushed a bit just a bit. I liked this house too.

"Yes, I do."

"I thought you liked Penny's house."

"I do. But it's too far out of town and you want to be in town."

"I do, but are you sure?"

"I'll pay you 1.4 for it." I knew Ben was serious, he had the money, and he had the desire. He had me at "I like."

"It's listed for 1.8" I pointed out, muscle memory, I can't help it, negotiation is automatic. But Penny would have agreed to a lesser offer. She had said that.

"I have a feeling the estate will take the offer."

"You are probably right, especially since it needs a lot of work."

"Of course it does," Ben agreed pleasantly. "You'll have to divide your time between here and River's Bend until you sell your house."

"You mean you'd live here full time?" I gripped one of the fence staves it gave slightly, dry rot. Damn.

I looked up at the house. I loved the widow's walk, I loved the kitchen flooded with sunshine, I loved that it was walking distance to every restaurant and bar in town. Hell, we would be smack in the middle of everything.

"You like to be close to all the action," he commented.

"Nothing happens in Claim Jump," I insisted doggedly.

"No," he hugged me. "Of course not."

The End

Made in the USA
Charleston, SC
03 August 2011